Harlequin Presents...

Other titles by

LILIAN PEAKE
IN HARLEQUIN PRESENTS

Other titles by

LILIAN PEAKE
IN HARLEQUIN ROMANCES

Many of these titles, and other titles in the
Harlequin Romance series are available at your
local bookseller, or through the Harlequin Reader
Service. For a free catalogue listing all avail-
able Harlequin Presents titles and Harlequin
Romances, send your name and address to:

HARLEQUIN READER SERVICE,
M.P.O. Box 707
Niagara Falls, N.Y 14302

Canadian address:
Stratford, Ontario, Canada N5A 6W4
or use order coupon at back of books

LILIAN PEAKE

familiar stranger

Harlequin Books

TORONTO • LONDON • NEW YORK • AMSTERDAM • SYDNEY • WINNIPEG

Harlequin Presents edition published November 1976
ISBN 0-373-70666-9

Original hardcover edition published in 1973
by Mills & Boon Limited

CHAPTER ONE

THE afternoon was sultry and the sun, made hazy by the yellowing clouds which passed across its face, shone fitfully on the dark hair of the man sitting at the café window. He was gazing out at the floral attractions of the municipal park, the exotic colours intermingling in the rose garden, the subtly differing greens of the varied tree specimens and the lush foliage of the flowering bushes.

He was stirring his tea and continued to do so although the sugar he had added to it must have dissolved long ago. He looked as though he was turning over in his mind some tantalizing problem, the answer to which evaded him.

He would probably not have noticed the girl sitting across the room if it had not been for her dog. The animal, a wire-haired terrier, rose, stretched and shook himself. He stood panting, bored, waiting for the girl at whose feet he had been lying to rise and rejoin the life, the movement and the scent-trails outside.

He raised his nostrils and they twitched. Nose to the ground, he pattered across the floor. He snuffled round the dark-haired man's shoes, grew excited, wagged the lower half of his short lively body, flipped his tail madly from side to side and pushed his nose into the man's hand, which happened at the moment to be moving down to pat him.

Adrienne watched, frozen into immobility by the spectacle of her dog making up to a complete stranger. She couldn't understand it – it was almost as though he had found a friend.

'Flick,' she called agitatedly, 'Flick, come here!' But Flick was too overjoyed with his new acquaintance to obey her command.

She dived across the wooden floor and bent down to seize the dog's collar, but he evaded her and threw himself under the man's table. She went in after him, but her forehead came into hard and painful contact with the edge of the table. Dazed, she fell against the man's legs and his hands reached down to steady her.

He moved sideways off his chair and in doing so knocked against the table. His cup of tea spilled over, but he ignored it and gently extricated the girl from her rather embarrassing position. Her hand went to her forehead and she rubbed it ruefully, her eyes smarting as the pain momentarily took hold and mounted in intensity.

The man's eyes were anxious. 'Are you all right? That was quite a bump.' With the same gentleness, he removed her hand and examined the damage. 'Not quite as bad as I thought, but painful, I imagine?'

She nodded and stood up. 'I'm sorry about your tea,' she said, looking at the pool of brown liquid spreading over the table top. 'And the mess.' She remembered her dog and looked down. He was happily lapping the tea as it trickled to the floor. They both laughed. 'It's the sugar in it he can't resist,' she explained. 'I'll buy you some more.'

'You won't, you know. I'll buy you some, instead. Sit down.' He pulled out a chair opposite him and urged her into it. 'I'll get two more cups.'

The dog jumped up on to the chair beside her, put his paws on the table and started with his long pink tongue on the spilt tea. The man laughed again, but Adrienne lifted the dog to the floor. 'Stop it, Flick. Behave!'

The man returned with two more cups, and the woman from behind the counter came with him. She smiled sympathetically at Adrienne as she mopped the table top. 'I saw what happened. All right now?'

Adrienne nodded her thanks and the woman left them.

The man offered Adrienne the sugar. 'You know, that's the first time any woman has ever thrown herself at my feet. I'll have to record it in my diary.' Adrienne smiled and coloured slightly. The man was being very friendly and it embarrassed her. He looked at her forehead. 'You'll probably have quite a bruise there. But I suppose it could have been worse.' He stirred his tea, this time with a sense of purpose.

He looked at the girl, noting her fair hair, arched eyebrows, pale pink cheeks. She felt rather than saw him inspecting her, because she was determinedly studying her own tea. As she lifted out the spoon, the liquid swirled like a whirlpool, spinning the floating tea leaves and sucking them down into the centre. Her thoughts were spinning too. There was something about the man that puzzled her. Somewhere, she was sure, she had met him before, and yet she knew that until that afternoon she had never seen him in the whole of her life.

'What's your dog's name?' His voice, controlled, cultured, deep and just a little amused, broke into her thoughts. His eyes held a serenity and a calmness which hinted at a hidden source of power, a personality which radiated confidence and understanding and which he seemed to attempt to transmit to whoever was with him. This was a man who appeared to possess so much strength of character, so much ability to cope with any situation that arose, no matter how difficult, he would surely have no need to turn to any other human being for help.

Now he looked down at the black and white bundle lying contentedly at the side of the table, eyes closed, nose between paws, his breath rhythmically expanding and contracting his furry, well-fed body.

'His name,' Adrienne answered, still refusing to meet the stranger's eyes, 'is Flick.'

'And yours?' This forced her to raise hers to look at him and his smile seemed to imply that that had been his intention. His expression, as he searched her face, was quizzical and she coloured deeply. Such an encounter was quite outside her experience and she didn't quite know how to behave. Should she tell him her name? But there was no question about it – she had to. She simply didn't know how to refuse. She did not possess the easy, casual manner of other girls who would have known how to parry such a question.

'Adrienne,' she told him, 'Adrienne Garron.'

The spoon stirring his tea stopped for a fraction of a second while he absorbed the name. Then it continued with its rotary action until she thought it must surely go through the base of the cup. She longed to ask, 'What's your name?' as other girls would have dared to do. But her habitual shyness stapled her lips together and struggle though she might, she could not get the words out.

He did not allow the silence to last long. 'Why Flick?' The sudden question unbalanced her momentarily, like a see-saw with only one person on it. She was bumped out of her shyness to look at him again and this time he gazed his fill into the sea-blue eyes a foot or two away from his. But he was not allowed to do so for long.

7

'Because of the way he flicks his tail,' she answered, and looked down again. Why did he keep forcing her to look at him? What was he searching for when his eyes probed so deeply into hers? 'It was my mother's suggestion.'

'You live with your mother?'

She hesitated before answering. But again she told him the truth. 'Yes. She's a widow.' She hoped her attempt at curtness would silence him. It was no concern of his where or with whom she lived.

She began to wish the whole event had been a bad dream, that she was not sitting there discussing herself with a complete stranger – quietly-spoken and good-looking though he was. With an irritable foot she pushed gently at her dog's back, trying to stir him into activity. He was bored and restless before, why wasn't he bored now? He could get her out of this awkward situation which was getting beyond her control and which, she was shamefully aware, she had not the moral courage to bring to an end.

As she raised her eyes and looked at the man whose peace and solitude she had shattered, she knew that he had seen the agitated movement of her foot. She was also sure that he knew exactly what was going on in her mind. Something very near to dislike stirred within her for his apparent omniscience. He had no right to be so shrewd, so all-seeing. He was a stranger, and no stranger had the right to look at her like that.

He smiled, but she did not smile back. It was almost as though he knew he was irritating her and was delighting in it. She scraped back her chair and this awoke her dog. He roused himself, but instead of going to her, made straight for her companion.

The man played with him and roughed up his hair. 'Flick,' he said, 'so it's Flick, is it?'

Why did the animal have to be so uninhibited? Adrienne thought. Nuzzling up to the man as if he were a friend . . .

'Thank you for the tea,' she said frigidly. 'And I'm sorry about everything . . .'

The sooner she left the café, the sooner life would resume its normal tranquillity. She would say good-bye and never see the man again. But she could not get her dog to understand that the man was no concern of theirs. And he was egging Flick on, she could see that, probably to embarrass her even more.

8

'Flick,' she said sharply, *'Flick!'*

The dog paused, his head jerked round at the sharpness in her voice and, eyes alert, he watched her move to the door. She saw to her dismay that the man appeared to have every intention of leaving with them. In single file, with the dog in the middle, the trio emerged into the sunshine which had won its battle with the clouds and was shedding its warmth without interruption on to the earth below.

'Lovely day,' the man said blandly. Adrienne didn't answer. Was his skin so thick he couldn't see she was trying to give him the brush-off? He walked beside her, Flick jumping up at his hand and trying to catch the stick he had picked up from under a tree.

'Do you live far from here?' the man wanted to know, tantalizing Flick by holding the stick just out of reach.

'Not very.'

'May I walk with you?'

She glared at him. She wanted to say 'No, you can't,' but the words wouldn't come. Something prevented her from being unpleasant. It was not just her shyness. There was something about him that intimidated her slightly, some kind of innate power, an air of command which demanded and won respect.

And she was under an obligation to him, after all. Hadn't she caused him trouble, trespassed on his privacy by her stupid act?

'If you want to.' The words were grudging, but annoyingly her tone was not. Her sensitive ears picked up in her own voice a note of encouragement which had slipped in of its own accord and she chided herself for seeming to invite his friendly approaches.

He must have caught the invitation too, because the look he turned on her was warm, and touched, she was sure, with the slightest trace of familiarity. She coloured deeply and frowned.

They walked side by side as if they had known each other for years. Flick leapt and growled, rejoicing in having found a new playmate, and one at that who seemed to understand so well his canine needs. The stick was thrown, raced after, returned between eager white teeth, thrown again and once more returned.

There was not much conversation between his two

9

companions. Adrienne, normally a reluctant participant in small talk, was now more than ever determined not to converse with the man beside her. He had forced his company on her. But not only that, she was afraid that he might construe anything she said as giving him encouragement and letting him think she had invited his attentions. So she remained silent.

As they turned out of the park gates and walked along the pavement, leaving the shops behind, he said without preamble, 'You work for your living?'

The question startled her momentarily, partly because of the abrupt way in which it was delivered and partly because of his audacity in asking. She hoped her equally abrupt 'Yes' would dissuade him from pursuing the subject. But it didn't.

'Locally?'

'Yes.' She added, in anticipation of what she knew would inevitably come next, 'I'm secretary to an author.'

His head turned, his eyes assumed a look of intense interest. 'You are? Is he famous? Should I have heard of him? May I ask his name?'

She had expected these questions. Every time she mentioned the nature of her work, the first thing anyone asked was always, 'Is he well-known?' as if it conferred upon them some kind of reflected glory in speaking even to his secretary, if not the man himself.

'It's Clifford Denning.'

'Oh.' The man seemed disappointed, as so many others were as soon as they heard. 'Then I don't know of him. What sort of stuff does he write? Novels?'

'He – er – freelances,' she replied, refusing to be drawn any further.

'So he's not a novelist?'

'He – well, he—' She decided to tell him the partial truth, as she told all other questioners. 'He is, yes, he writes novels.'

Her tone implied that he would get no more information out of her on the subject. She wouldn't tell him, a perfect stranger, what she was forbidden to tell even the author's closest friends – that the man she worked for was indeed famous, that his pen name was Damon Dane, that he wrote detective novels and that his books, paperbacks mostly, provided him with a substantial income and a comfortable existence.

Before turning to writing such books, Clifford Denning had

struggled for years to produce what he termed 'real' novels, works of recognized literary merit. He had failed, but those years of effort he traded on. He had gathered around him friends and acquaintances, some of whom were renowned in the world of literature. On the strength of his conceived but as yet unborn masterpieces, he commanded and received their respect. So, for the sake of his reputation as a near literary genius, unmerited though it was, he had sworn his secretary to secrecy about the true nature of his writing. But for some reason, the man beside her would not be silenced.

'Are they obscure, these novels your employer writes? Or would ordinary mortals like me understand them?' He turned to her. 'Do you understand them?'

'I – er – yes, I understand them.'

'Ah, now we're getting somewhere.' When would the man stop his probing? 'If *you* can understand them, then no doubt I would. Are they, for instance, romantic? Historical? Political? Science-fiction?' She did not answer. 'Well?' he demanded, and there was an insistence in his tone which riled her.

She snapped, 'I'm not allowed to say,' then immediately wished the words unsaid. The statement implied intrigue and secrecy and the man, certainly no fool, was on to it at once.

'So there's some mystery about it?' The very word 'mystery' made her flinch. He was nearer the truth than he knew. Who was he, anyway? A journalist on the prowl, seeking perhaps some scandal he could blow up into banner headlines and large print?

She stopped where a narrow lane branched off the main road. Flick, knowing the way, raced along it into the distance. 'I live near here. Good-bye, Mr. – er . . .'

He did not supply the missing name, but put a hand on her arm instead. She stiffened, wishing Flick were not so far away. 'If you would forgive my saying so, Miss Garron,' was there no end to the man's impudence? 'I should very much like to see you again.'

'Oh, but I—' She moved an inch or two away. 'I don't—'

He broke in, giving her no chance to continue. 'Could we meet, go for a walk, perhaps, have tea in the park?'

She took a breath, started to shake her head, started to say, 'No, thank you—'

'This evening, perhaps? You see,' he went on as if in expla-

11

nation, 'I only arrived in the area today. I'm a comparative stranger to the district. It would be pleasant to have company,' he smiled and again there was the touch of familiarity which nettled her, 'feminine company, on my walks.'

She wanted to tell him, 'It's no good, Mr. Whatever your name is, I'm engaged. One day I'm going to marry my employer. I'm not just his secretary. Three weeks ago he proposed to me. We're keeping it a secret for the moment. I haven't even told my mother.'

She looked up at him – he was a great deal taller than she was – and noticed the way his thick dark hair, made a little unruly by the stiff breeze, fell foward over his forehead, saw the whiteness of his hand and the sensitivity of the long fingers as they ran through his hair, pushing it back into place. She wondered idly what his occupation could be that allowed his hands to remain so unspoiled. His quizzical brown eyes looked straight into hers, and his smile turned, chameleon-like to suit his mood, from familiarity into a subtle, almost urgent pleading.

She coloured and looked away. She must be resolute in her refusal, no matter how much his mute appeal, his touching desire for company found a spark of sympathy inside her. But she could not deny it – part of her was pleased by the message he seemed to be trying to convey – that she attracted him. She wouldn't be human, she argued, if she were not. But, flattered though she was by the compliments his eyes were paying her, she couldn't believe that he found her pleasing enough on so short an acquaintance to want to see her again. No man had ever shown such interest in her before, not even, she had to admit, her fiancé.

Yet, even as she hesitated, she knew what her answer must be. She was engaged, her loyalty and, of course, her love, were all for Clifford, whom she was going to marry. She looked at the man again, and enigmatic though his expression was, she was convinced he knew of her uncertainty and could sense the vacillation which deep down she was struggling to conquer. There was no doubt about it, this stranger was dangerously attractive.

At last he laughed and her heart bumped unevenly. 'You know, Miss Garron,' again that familiarity, as though, like a top business executive, he was accustomed to using people's names, 'if your thoughts over the last few minutes could have been recorded on a graph, they would have made an intriguing pattern with maximum and minimum points galore. I take it they have now flattened out into a straight line and the decision has been reached. Is the answer "yes"?'

Flick came bounding back and threw himself against Adrienne's legs, unbalancing her a little. The man's hand came out to steady her. 'Hey there, dog,' he cautioned, 'you've done enough damage to your mistress today without causing her any more!'

Flick's response was to turn his attention to the stranger and snuffle round his shoes again with uninhibited excitement.

'Well, Miss Garron,' the man asked, 'yes or no?'

'Well, I—'

'So it's yes. I always take hesitation for assent, especially in women and especially in the absence of a downright refusal. This evening, here at, say, seven-thirty?'

He bent down, lifted Flick with gentleness away from his feet and roughed up his fur. Then he straightened, smiled, raised his hand and walked away.

'Is that you, Adri-enne?' As she stepped into the hall, her mother's voice drifted down the stairs. She detected the faint emphasis on the last syllable of her name, the touch of affectation which always irritated her whenever her mother used it. 'I'm on the bed. I've drawn the curtains – I developed an awful headache. Could you cope, dear? Could you get the tea? I'd help if I could, but . . .'

Adrienne was used to her mother's headaches. 'It's because I'm so highly strung, dear,' she would say to her daughter. And she would succumb frequently, willingly almost, as though the possession of such an affliction gave her a certain status and set the seal on her superior brain-power over the rest of her acquaintances who were not intelligent enough to suffer from such an ailment. It also got her out of a great deal of work in the home, which had to be tackled instead by her daughter.

Adrienne called reassuringly that she could manage alone, sighed at the prospect of getting the tea instead of enjoying the luxury of being waited on for once and snapped at Flick for scurrying up to her mother's bedroom.

'Keep him away from me!' Lorna Garron's petulant voice

wafted down, almost submerged by the dog's pattering footsteps. He reached the hall and slipped and slithered along the stained and polished wood of the hall floor.

The cottage they all shared was not very large, but it was sufficient for their modest needs. Lorna Garron, who liked the picturesque, revelled in its age. The two bedrooms were small but comfortable, with sloping ceilings and casement windows. The lounge was long and narrow and provided a suitable backcloth against which Lorna could display her own personal touches of artistry. Her taste veered towards the unusual and oddments picked up at antique shops and Christmas bazaars were on show around the room, all of which had to be dusted individually and frequently, usually by her daughter.

The kitchen was small, too, and made even smaller by the modern equipment which had been packed into it, equipment which had been bought with the money left to Lorna by her late husband. His untimely death six years before had reduced her to a state of almost physical prostration and her daughter had been forced, by her mother's protracted helplessness, to take her father's place in the household, supporting her mother financially and taking all the major decisions affecting both their lives.

Adrienne prepared Flick's meal while he waited, sitting on his haunches, eyes wide and expectant, tongue out, watching every move she made. He dived as she lowered the dish to the floor and sank his teeth into the food as though he hadn't been fed for years.

As Adrienne cooked the meal for her mother and herself, she thought about the mysterious stranger. His face tormented her. She could not shake her own certainty that she had seen him somewhere before. But that was impossible. He had just arrived, he said, he was new to the district. She shrugged, trying to dismiss him from her mind. She had no intention of meeting him as he had suggested, none at all. She was not the sort of girl to go out with a man she had met so casually and whose name she did not even know. And if she hadn't been so tongue-tied, so stupidly slow, she would have told him so.

When the meal was almost ready, her mother called down that she couldn't eat a thing, and what was that awful smell of food that was making her headache worse? Again Adrienne sighed, but had to acknowledge that it was her own fault. If she hadn't been so preoccupied with thoughts of that irritating stranger, she would have remembered to ask her mother before she had started to get the meal.

Flick finished his food, sat back on his haunches and licked his mouth hugely. Adrienne rubbed him affectionately behind the ears and gave him his dish of water. He lapped it up, then barked to go out, racing down the garden after a cat.

Adrienne ate her tea alone. She wished she could get the man out of her mind. She cleared away and watched the hands of the clock move round to the time he had suggested they should meet. Now he would be waiting at the end of the lane. He would be staring along it, watching for her. She felt terrible at having to let him down.

She gazed out of the window, convinced now that her first impression of him was right, that he was really a nice man and meant no harm. Should she go and tell him, 'I'm sorry, but I've definitely made up my mind – I'm not coming for that walk with you?' She smiled at the ridiculous thought. If he saw her approaching he would assume she was going with him and would perhaps be even more disappointed when he heard her refusal than if she hadn't bothered to go.

The hands of the clock moved on. It was unforgivable, she chided herself, to let anyone down, even a complete stranger, especially one who seemed to want her company so much. She began to feel sorry for him.

Now it was an hour after the appointed time. He must have gone. With the suddenness of someone receiving a fatal blow, she crumpled into a chair. She had thrown away her chance. She would never see him again.

CHAPTER TWO

BEFORE leaving for work next morning Adrienne called in to see her mother. She was still in bed, having breakfasted from the tray her daughter had given her.

Lorna was sitting up, eyes closed, a pillow behind her head, hands folded on the bedcover, listening to the quiet music coming from the transistor radio at her side. Like her daughter she was fair, her skin pale and bloodless, but surprisingly young-looking in spite of her forty-six years. Her face was free of the lines and furrows which the normal strains and stresses of living usually engrave on the faces of those who have left their youth behind. There were no laughter-wrinkles, no marks of compassion or sympathy. It was more of an unblemished landscape, free of any signposts, or any manifestations of the passing of time. It was a face dedicated to selfishness, and when her eyes fluttered open, the expression in them gave confirmation of the woman's narrow, egotistical way of life.

'I'll get up in a little while,' Lorna said. 'I've got some of the fête committee coming to coffee,' she sighed, 'although I'd rather they weren't. Have you—?'

'Washed up? Yes. And I've tidied the lounge and set out the tray with cups and measured out the coffee and milk. All you've got to do is make it.'

Lorna's hand came out and touched her daughter's. 'What would I do without you?'

Adrienne shrugged and smiled back. 'Why think about it? I'll always be here, won't I?'

Well, it was true, wasn't it? she thought as she walked the few hundred yards along the road to Clifford Denning's residence. Even when she married Clifford and moved in with him, she would still be near her mother and able to give her all the help she needed.

Adrienne called to her dog. She always took him with her because her mother insisted on it, consistently refusing to look after him. She didn't want the responsibility, she said; he was worse than a baby.

As Adrienne passed the place where she had arranged to

meet the stranger, she averted her head as though some terrible crime had been committed there. Her conscience still troubled her, still nagged and grumbled like an irate parent because she had let the man down.

Flick was far ahead. He knew the way as well as she did. Clifford never made a fuss of the dog. He had no room in his life for animals. He had tolerated him up to now only for the sake of retaining the services of his secretary, and now she was his fiancée he had even less grounds for refusing to allow the dog into the house. So the arrangement continued.

Clifford's house was large and, if anything, even older than Lorna Garron's. It was certainly in a far better condition. The lounge was long and wide with oak beams overhead and a red brick fireplace. The windows at the back looked out on to cultivated gardens, roses, wooden seats and crazy paving. There was an attractive wilderness of trees at the end of the garden and in this miniature wood stood a small hut. This was Adrienne's office. Clifford could not stand the noise of a type writer, so he stationed his secretary and her clatter as far away from the house as possible.

Adrienne did not object. She loved the loneliness and the peace. In strong winds the trees swayed and hissed. In summer their leaves sheltered her from the sun and cast lacy shadow patterns across the windows of the hut. In winter the trees were gaunt and stark, but she saw them as friends, an army protecting her from the snow and the bitter cold.

And always her dog was with her. On fine days she would leave the door open so that he could come and go as he pleased. In cold weather he would lift a paw and scratch at the door and she would stop typing and let him out.

Clifford never came to the hut. She took dictation from him upstairs, waiting patiently while he thought out phrases, spoke them, corrected them and thought again.

She had no definite office hours. Sometimes he would ask her not to come in the morning, and work instead in the afternoon and evening. Now she was engaged to him, she saw no more of him than when she was merely his secretary. His question, 'Will you marry me, Adrienne? Will you be my wife?' had made little difference to their relationship, except that now and then he would remember to kiss her when she left him or arrived for work.

When she lifted the latch of the ancient front door and went upstairs, he was as usual in his bedroom. She found him as she had left her mother – in bed. But that was not unusual. He often did not get up until mid-morning. His thoughts flowed better, he would say, when he was completely relaxed, and he could only do that successfully in bed. His heart, he said, was not as sound as other people's. He had to take care, to rest his body as much as possible, to cosset himself a little.

Flick rushed around the bedroom, taking Clifford's slipper in his teeth and shaking it until he was reprimanded by his mistress. He skidded round the room on the sheepskin rugs which were scattered over the polished wooden floor and sent the wastepaper basket flying. Then he worried the crumpled bits of paper which were strewn across the rugs.

Adrienne, still a little shy of her fiancé, did not know whether to kiss him good morning, but he was so irritated by the exuberance of the dog that he did not notice the absence of her embrace.

'Get him out of here,' he said petulantly, so Adrienne pushed Flick out of the room. He raced along the landing, peered through the banisters and sniffed at all the closed doors. One door in particular intrigued him and he snuffled at it for some time.

Adrienne heard Clifford call impatiently, so she closed the door and left Flick to it. She knew he would eventually make his way to the kitchen where Mrs. Masters, Clifford's house-keeper, would make a fuss of him.

She took her notebook from a drawer and prepared to take dictation. She studied her fiancé as she waited for him to collect his thoughts. He was forty-three, only three years younger than her mother, and his face, like her mother's, bore few lines, but whereas Lorna was usually pale, Clifford's colour was high. Adrienne supposed, with a little twinge of worry born of her new responsibility as his wife-to-be, it was his heart complaint which caused it.

His cheeks were full, whereas her mother's were thin. His light brown hair was touched with grey, his neck filling out in tune with the rest of his body which was growing weighty with self-indulgence – heart or no heart, he would not cut down on his food intake. In a moment of unpleasant truth, Adrienne acknowledged that he was beginning to look his age. But she was eighteen years younger than he was. In the years to come she could give him all the strength, both moral and physical, that he needed.

Dictation was interrupted by morning coffee, brought in by Mrs. Masters, a tall, thin woman whose gaunt physique belied her warm nature. She exchanged a few cheerful words with Adrienne and left them.

They drank their coffee in silence. Adrienne did not dare to talk. She knew Clifford was deep in thought, working out the next few paragraphs, or planning a whole episode. She acknowledged with a rueful smile that as his secretary she had been well trained. She should, she told herself, make him an ideal wife, never speaking out of turn, never interrupting the flow of his thoughts. But the prospect did not worry her. His books were his life, and a woman never stopped her man from doing anything that was dear to him.

They worked until lunch-time. When she left Clifford to go home, she bent down and waited for his kiss. He raised his mouth absently and touched her cheek, not her lips. She quelled her disappointment by telling herself she must not be selfish; his thoughts were on his work. She really had to learn not to mix the business part of their lives with the more personal side of it.

Her mother was up when she arrived home. The coffee morning had gone off well and now the washing-up awaited her. Without resentment – she had been well trained at home, too – Adrienne washed the coffee cups before getting lunch. Her mother set the table and subsided into a chair with a sigh. She had had a busy morning, she said.

When Adrienne returned to work, she took with her all the notes Clifford had dictated and went straight to the hut at the end of the garden. She unlocked the door and Flick pushed past her, sniffing at all the familiar corners, then ran outside again amongst the trees.

She typed for some time, completely absorbed in the work she was doing. She heard Flick bark excitedly and decided he had found a stray cat up a tree. The hut door opened.

A voice asked, 'How's the bruise?'

She swung round, her eyes almost starting from her head. She could not believe it – there he stood, that stranger, so tall he had to bend his head to avoid touching the top of the doorway, relaxed, smiling, enjoying her bewilderment and confusion. She could not answer, she could not get a single word out. Her heart was pounding like half a dozen kettledrums until the sound of it almost deafened her.

He wandered across the hut and touched the bump on her forehead, but she jerked away. 'Blue, as I expected, as blue as your eyes.'

Flick charged in, growling and snapping at his shoe laces. 'Hallo, dog,' the stranger said, 'we meet again.' He picked him up and Flick stayed panting in his arms. 'We had a fine time together this morning, didn't we?'

'What – what do you mean?'

'Ah, so your mistress can speak. I began to wonder.' He put the dog down. 'He sniffed at my bedroom door, obviously recognizing my scent. I let him in.'

'You're staying here?' The stranger nodded. 'So that was why Flick seemed to know you yesterday – he recognized the smell of the house on your shoes.'

'An excellent piece of detective work. Worthy of your fiancé, I should say. He should record it in one of his books.'

'What do you know about Clifford's books?'

'A lot, a hell of a lot. I am, after all, his brother.' He smiled. 'Yes, I thought that would stun you. Has he never mentioned me? No, I suppose not. He doesn't like me very much. Never has.'

'So that was why—'

'Why what?'

'Why somehow you seemed so familiar yesterday. I was convinced I'd seen you somewhere before, yet I knew I hadn't really.'

'My God, don't tell me I resemble my beloved brother. I couldn't bear it!'

'But – you questioned me yesterday about his books. If you knew about them why—?' She drew in her breath. 'You were testing me! To see how much I would give away?'

He smiled his assent.

'And you arranged to meet me, knowing all the time I was engaged!'

'You didn't turn me down, did you?'

'I – I—' But she could not defend herself. 'I didn't say I would meet you.'

20

'You didn't say "no" either, as any good little engaged girl should have done. Why didn't you come clean? Suppose I'd been any other man and had pursued the matter? What would you have done then? You *must* love my brother.'

'So you were testing me in that as well?'

'As soon as I heard of my brother's engagement, I was intrigued to know what sort of girl would tie herself to *him* for life. I knew it couldn't be for love—' She gasped at his arrogance. 'So I reckoned it must be for his money. I was right, wasn't I?'

'No, you were not!'

'Forgive me if I say I don't believe you. Unless,' he looked at her keenly, 'it's out of pity.'

'Of course it's not. It's – it's for—' She stopped. Somehow she just could not get the word over the obstacles of her lips.

'Don't tell me you love him?'

'Don't let your brotherly prejudice blind you to his good points.'

'Has he got any? That's news to me, and I've known him long enough.'

She allowed her eyes to linger momentarily on his face 'You're younger than he is.'

'Now that is a statement I could not refute if I tried. I am, indeed. I'm his junior by seven years.'

'That makes you – er – thirty-six.'

'Good heavens, dog,' he addressed Flick who was lying at his feet, 'she can do arithmetic!'

Adrienne turned impatiently to her work, but before she could resume her typing, there was something she had to say. She said, a little sheepishly, 'I'm – sorry I had to let you down last night. Did you wait long?'

He threw back his head and laughed. 'I didn't wait at all. I didn't turn up. I never intended to. Did you?'

She flushed scarlet. 'No, of *course* I didn't.' She cursed herself for being caught out. She hoped her back, which she deliberately turned towards him, would make him go. She just did not like her fiancé's brother.

'I've been asked by Mrs. Masters to tell you that your cup of tea is awaiting you.'

'I usually have it here, while I'm working.'

'Ah, but this time we're having it in style, in the lounge, in

21

my honour.'

Reluctantly she walked with him through the trees, along the curving path, through the rose garden to the house. All the time Flick jumped up at him, ran round him and made dives at his feet. He did not seem to mind.

'At least your dog likes me.' He smiled down at her. 'Even if his mistress doesn't.'

Clifford greeted them, sitting on the couch, legs crossed, his mood touchy. 'You've been long enough.' He looked at them both with something like suspicion. 'You seem to know each other.'

'Very astute of you, brother. But of course, with your probing detective sort of mind, one should expect it.' He showed Adrienne to an armchair with mock courtesy. 'We met yesterday, in the park.' He sat down and watched her pour out the tea, keeping his brother waiting for an explanation. As she handed him a cup, he said, looking at her, but addressing Clifford, 'To be perfectly honest with you, I picked her up.'

She went crimson and slopped his tea in the saucer, but she didn't apologize for her clumsiness. She was too angry.

Clifford said, 'What the blazes do you mean?'

'It's not true, Clifford,' Adrienne protested, her voice rising in an effort to clear herself. 'It was the dog—'

'I'm sorry, my dear Adrienne,' she resented the stranger's easy use of her first name, 'but it's perfectly true.' He turned to his brother, grinning. 'It was simple. I've never found it so easy to pick up a woman in my life.' With malicious satisfaction he watched Adrienne's anger increase, then turned his malice on his brother. They seemed to have returned to boyhood and were fighting each other with words instead of fists. 'Your fiancée even consented to meet me last night to go for – er – a walk.'

His twisting of the truth, the way he smeared the two inno-cent words with a deeper, more sordid meaning, made her almost violent.

'*I did not!*' she cried. 'I *never* agreed to meet you!'

'Ah, but you did. You agreed tacitly. You didn't say "no", and the use of that short but effective two-letter word is usually good enough to let any man know where he stands with a girl. If she doesn't say "no", in effect she says "yes".'

Clifford looked bewildered. 'Did you know who she was?'

'Yes, because she told me her name. That was something else

she did willingly. But she didn't ask mine. I'm still puzzled about that.' He smiled at her baitingly. 'Don't you bother to ask a man's name before you agree to go out with him? Are all your affairs so short you feel it's not worth knowing? One-night stands and all that?' He smiled at her wrath and said to his brother, 'Your fiancée looks as though she would like to throttle me.' To her he said, 'It's not advisable to maltreat your future brother-in-law. It introduces such an unpleasant atmosphere into the family.' He turned to his brother again. 'Talking of introductions,' he grinned, 'you'd better do the honours. We haven't – officially – met.'

With some reluctance and considerable embarrassment, Clifford said, 'Adrienne, this is Murray, my younger brother. Murray, my fiancée, Adrienne Garron. This is quite ridiculous.' He rose. 'I don't believe a word you've said, Murray. Adrienne of all people would not be a party to a casual pickup.' He turned to her with a gesture of appeal. 'Would you, my dear?'

She walked across to him and put her hand on his arm. 'You know I wouldn't, Clifford.'

He patted her hand and went out. With a tight, sardonic smile Murray watched them. 'Exit leading man, after passionate show of love. Leading lady runs after him, eager for more.' He made a noise of disgust. 'This is like watching some puerile stage play with a cast of ham actors. When will the two main characters come to life?'

Flick awoke from his doze as his mistress moved to the door. He started to follow.

'Hey, Flick!' The dog turned at the sound of his name. 'Come for a walk with me? Walk?' Flick went mad, responding to the familiar word and the promise in the voice. To Adrienne, Murray said, 'Got a lead for him?'

'Yes, it's in the hall. Why?'

'He wants to come for a walk. And I want to take him.'

'You might ask me. He's *my* dog.'

'The dog's asking. Can't you see?' Flick was running round Murray's legs in ever-decreasing circles. He bent down to fondle the dog. 'At the present moment,' he looked up at her, 'Flick's the only friend I've got in the world.' He added as an afterthought, 'May I take him?'

'If you like,' she answered grudgingly. As they went out of

the door her eyes moistened with something like jealousy. She could not believe that her dog could transfer his love and allegiance so quickly and so ardently from her to the man she had come to dislike so much.

Adrienne was at her typewriter when Murray returned. The door of the hut opened and Flick pushed his way in. He flopped down near the desk, tired and panting.

'One animal safely returned to owner.' Murray walked over to a filing cabinet and rested his back against it, folding his arms and making no apology for disturbing her. 'He didn't miss you. I threw sticks for him and he loved it. Do you throw sticks when you're out with him?'

'Of course I do.'

He smiled arrogantly. 'We share something then – a stick-throwing tendency. A small but definite step towards establishing better relations between us. After all, we are soon going to be members of the same family, united by marriage, so to speak, in a roundabout way.'

'There's no need to keep reminding me of the fact,' she said sourly.

He laughed loudly. 'I can see we're really going to hit it off as in-laws, the important word being "hit".' He wandered to her side and read some of the words she had typed. 'What's this one? *Laser's Luck*, by Damon Dane.' He inspected the bookshelves above her head and read out some titles. '*Gamma Two* by Damon Dane, *Quasar Fantastic* by Damon Dane. How he does churn them out! Has he turned to science-fiction?'

'No, they're all mystery stories. He just chose up-to-the-minute titles.'

Murray read a few sentences of the books she was typing. 'This is all the most arrant nonsense. No wonder he's so ashamed of the stuff he writes he wants to keep it a secret. I suppose you know who – and what – you're marrying? His intellect always was less than a sparrow's. And that's probably being unkind to sparrows!'

'He's doing very well on it,' she blurted out defensively.

'Yes, he is, isn't he? Which no doubt pleases you. After all, before many months have passed, you'll be sharing his fortune.'

Sulkily, she said, 'It sounds as though you're jealous.'

He gave a short disclaiming laugh. 'What of – his girl or his fortune?'

'His fortune, as you call it. Your earning potential is no doubt a lot less than his.'

'Big words,' he sneered, 'for such an *ignorant* young secretarial assistant. You know nothing about my earning potential, or my bank balance. Or me. You don't even know what my job is.'

'But I do know,' she said, the words spilling out despite herself, 'that you hate your brother and because I'm going to marry him you therefore hate me.'

' "Hate" is hardly the right word. I'm indifferent to my brother. And to whoever is stupid enough to consent to marry him.'

There was a painful silence. She stared at the words she had typed. They did not seem to make sense.

He bent down and caught at her chin. His eyes were only a few inches from hers and there was an odd compassion in them. 'Why do you make me say things to hurt you? Because I know I do. I can see it by your eyes. I've only known you – what? – a few hours, but for some reason, although you're so damned young and innocent, I seem to *want* to hurt you. No woman has ever had that effect on me before. The opposite, yes – to heal, but not to hurt.'

'I told you,' she answered bitterly, 'you already regard me as an extension of your brother and you're really getting at him through me. Remember that before very long I'm going to become part of him.'

He released her chin abruptly. 'Quite the little psychologist, aren't you?' He was back to hurting her again. 'You'll be having me on the analyst's couch next, if I don't watch out.' He returned to the house. Flick started to follow, but Adrienne ordered him back.

She tried to put the man out of her mind, but even in his absence his presence dominated the room. His face still filled her eyes, his voice her ears, his words her thoughts. And she was afraid.

CHAPTER THREE

WHEN Adrienne arrived for work next morning, Clifford appeared to be asleep, but he struggled into a sitting position when she stood at his bedside. He was unshaven, which was unusual, and he looked a little pale, but his voice, when he spoke, was normal. She saw the remains of his breakfast on a tray beside his bed.

'Not too good today, my dear. I have to be careful, you realize that?' He found her hand, pulled her down and pecked her on the cheek.

Adrienne was surprised and a little worried. He was not usually so demonstrative towards her, despite their new relationship.

'You do understand,' he went on, 'that when we're married, our life together will not be quite the same as other couples'? With my heart complaint, I have to take care. You do understand?' he repeated. His eyes, childlike as they sought reassurance, demanded an answer, the right answer.

She gave it. 'Of course I do, Clifford.'

He nodded, satisfied and indicated a drawer across the room. 'In there you'll find a chapter in longhand. I wrote it yesterday evening after you'd gone home. I felt the urge and had to get it down.'

'I would have come if you'd rung me, Clifford. I wouldn't have minded.'

He patted her hand. 'I knew that, my dear, but I wouldn't dream of taking advantage of your good nature to such an extent.'

She found the papers and he said, as she prepared to leave him,

'When you've finished the chapter, you might as well go home. Have the afternoon off and call in this evening, I might feel better by then.'

Murray appeared in the hall and watched her walk down the stairs. 'You look subdued. Anything wrong?'

'It's Clifford. He's not too well.'

'What's the matter with him?' He spoke abruptly.

'It's his heart. Don't you know he suffers from heart trouble?'

'Did he tell you that?'

She nodded. 'Don't you believe it?' She was exasperated. Was the man quite inhuman? 'How can you let your prejudice blind you to the truth? Why are you so hard where he's concerned, even when he's ill?'

'Spoken like a typical engaged woman, full of anxious dread about her beloved.' He spoke cynically. 'My dear girl, as you're his wife-to-be, let me reassure you. He is *not* ill. He does *not* suffer from heart trouble. He imagines it. It suits his purposes to do so.'

His scepticism angered her. 'Go up and see him yourself. Then you'll see how poorly he is.'

'I will.' He was up the stairs before she had finished speaking. On the landing he turned and called down, 'Is he off his food?'

'He's had his breakfast. I saw the tray.'

'As I thought. The day my dear brother is off his food I'll know he's really ill.'

Adrienne spent the afternoon walking with her dog. She had cleared away the lunch and washed up with reluctant help from her mother. When Adrienne told her she was not going to work because her employer did not feel well, her mother seemed anxious – not about the man – she had after all never met him and had no idea of her future connection with him, but because she thought she would have her daughter at home all the afternoon.

'I'd like to rest for a couple of hours, dear, to ward off my headache. I've got a committee meeting this evening at Mrs. Manley's and I must be fit enough to attend.'

'It's all right, Mother, I'm going out. I'll take Flick.'

Her mother looked relieved. 'Don't think I want to turn you out of your own home, darling,' she patted her daughter's hand, 'but I can only fully relax when the house is empty.'

So Adrienne went for a long walk across the fields while Flick raced in all directions. Afterwards, they went to the café in the park. As she entered, Adrienne looked round a little fearfully, but there was no tall, dark-haired man, no familiar stranger waiting there to torment her.

That evening, Clifford seemed a little better but was not, he said, in the mood to work. 'Come in the morning, Adrienne. I shall be back to normal by then, I hope.'

Flick was waiting in the hall. 'Come on,' she said to him, 'we'll go for another walk.' She fixed the lead to his collar.

'May I join you?' Murray was at the lounge door.

Adrienne frowned and hesitated, but he didn't wait for an answer. He followed her out. 'Where to?'

'I usually go across the fields.'

'The fields it is.' He took the dog's lead from her hand. She resented his action, but said nothing. Why couldn't she say to him, as other girls would have done, 'The dog's mine, not yours. You're just an interfering stranger and I prefer my own company to yours'?

'How did you spend the afternoon? You weren't in the hut, I looked in.' So he had gone looking for her – to annoy her again, probably.

'I did what I'm doing now. I went for a walk.'

'On your own?'

'With Flick.'

'Is that how you always spend your spare time? No hobbies?'

'Walking is my hobby. Anyway, it gets me out of the house.'

'Is that essential? Does your mother work at home?'

'My mother doesn't work. She just likes the house to herself sometimes. She – she likes to rest a lot.'

'Why, is she ill?'

The man was asking too many questions. 'She's a bit like Clifford. Sometimes she's ill, sometimes she's all right. She has a lot of headaches.'

'Has she seen a doctor?'

'Yes. He gives her tablets. But she still gets headaches.' She looked up at him, caught his thoughtful expression, felt suddenly the need to confide. 'It's almost as though she *wants* them, she almost – enjoys them.' She went on slowly, 'If she weren't my mother, and if it didn't sound cruel, I would say that she – well, uses them to get herself out of things.'

Something flashed across his eyes as he looked down at her. He asked with a smile, 'Acting the tame psychologist again? You really have missed your vocation.'

She flushed and turned away. They had reached the fields

28

and he bent down to release Flick from the lead. The dog bounded away, delighting in his sudden freedom.

Murray said, his voice quiet, 'What sort of things do these headaches get your mother out of?'

Adrienne shrugged. 'The housework, the cooking and so on. I do it all myself now.'

'Don't you have any domestic help?'

'Good heavens, no! We couldn't afford it. I fit in the work at home with my work for Clifford.'

'So you divide your time between waiting on your mother and waiting on your fiancé? You run from one so-called invalid to another?'

'I don't look at it like that. I just accept it as my way of life.'

'Don't you ever go out? Is your only relaxation going for walks?'

'What's wrong with that?'

'All right,' he patted her shoulder. 'Don't take umbrage so easily.'

The path ran parallel to the hedge and grew narrow as it ran alongside the wheat that was growing in abundance on the rich, cultivated farm land. He let her walk in front of him and they went in silence in single file for some time. Flick was far ahead and out of sight.

When the path grew wider again, they walked side by side. She looked up at him and asked, a little shyly, 'Murray?' He smiled down at her, his expression oddly kind. 'What is your job?'

He laughed. 'I wondered when that question was coming. Take a guess.'

'Well, when I met you the other day, I did think you might be a journalist. Or even a detective.' When he laughed again she said defensively, 'You ask so many questions.'

'You're way out. I'm taking part in a research project at a university.'

'Oh?' She was full of interest. 'What is your subject?'

His hesitation did not last more than a few seconds. 'Let me try to frame it in simple words.' He smiled. 'No disrespect to your intelligence, of course. The project in question is researching into the effects of diet on certain parts of the human body.' She waited for more, but it did not come.

'Are you a university lecturer?'

Again the hesitation, so slight it passed unnoticed. 'Of a sort, yes.' With that she had to be content.

'You're not – married?'

'No.' He laughed again. 'Are you taking an interest in me because you're my future sister-in-law and therefore feel a certain responsibility for my welfare? Or is it because, for reasons best known to yourself, you simply want to know?'

The question confused her, but she compromised by answering, 'Both.'

They came to a stile. Flick had already squeezed underneath it. Murray climbed over first and helped Adrienne across it. He put his hands on her waist and lifted her down. For the merest second he held her where she was, between his hands. 'Light as a feather,' he commented. She coloured and he smiled. 'Such timidity in one of a generation that is alleged to be so permissive, so free with its favours! Talking of generations, how old are you, Adrienne?'

She did not mind telling him. 'Twenty-five.'

'And my brother is forty-three, which makes him – let me see – eighteen years older than you. You know that, I suppose?' She nodded. 'Doesn't it worry you?'

'Why should it?' She was bristling again. 'When you love someone—'

'Do you, Adrienne?'

She fenced. 'Would I have agreed to marry Clifford if I didn't?'

'You might.' Flick came bounding up with a stick in his mouth. Murray took it from him and with a sweep of his arm flung it as far as he could. The dog raced after it.

Adrienne changed the subject quickly. 'I expect you've got a girl-friend?'

He grined provocatively. 'Since that's a rhetorical question, it doesn't require an answer.'

She frowned at the grass beneath her feet. 'You're telling me to mind my own business?'

'Another rhetorical question, but this time I'll answer it. Yes.'

The rebuff quietened her for a while, as no doubt he had meant it to do. Then, 'How long has your mother been a widow?'

'Six years. My father was more than twenty years older than she was.'

'Ah, now I get it. It runs in the family.' At her query he elaborated, 'Marrying someone years older than yourself. Like mother, like daughter, as they say.' He became thoughtful. 'What would it be like, I wonder, if I were to marry a girl eighteen years my junior? She would be – er – eighteen.'

He shook his head. 'It doesn't appeal. It would be like marrying a child. I should want someone more mature.' He looked around. 'It's getting dark. We'd better go back.' He whistled to the dog.

'Anyone would think,' Adrienne thought resentfully, 'that Flick was his dog, not mine!'

Flick came racing back, pushed his way between them and raced on.

'Will your mother be alone?'

'Yes. She'll be back from her committee meeting by now. But she won't mind. She watches television a lot.'

'You must lead a lonely life. No wonder you have a dog to keep you company.'

She answered quietly, seriously, 'I don't know what I'd do without him.' The searching, almost pitiful look he turned upon her seemed to penetrate to the depths of her mind, revealing to him the path of her thoughts as clearly as if he had taken an X-ray photograph. She found herself wishing that he were not so perceptive, so knowledgeable. It was not right that he knew so much about her without being told. But what it was he knew, she could not tell.

Adrienne felt that there was permanently about Clifford's bedroom the atmosphere of a sickroom. What was worse – and try as she might to stifle the thought, it would not be suppressed – he seemed to glory in it. His manner, his habits were already geared to a premature old age, and even to an unquestioning acceptance of it.

Sometimes Adrienne wondered why Clifford had ever brought himself to propose to her. He did not seem ready to admit another person into his private world. He was not, Adrienne was sure, mentally adjusted to marriage. In his life, his mental processes and his mind were paramount, not his body. Fear stung her, like the prick of a needle. A woman

31

couldn't marry a mind. There was another side to marriage besides the sharing of thoughts. There was the physical side, the merging into one person, the interchange of love.

But, she reminded herself, he had warned her. 'Our life together,' he had said, 'will not be quite the same as other couples'.' She felt an odd desire to talk to Murray. There was something about him that invited confidences, that inspired others to pour out their hearts to him and receive an answer, a reasoned, balanced answer to their problems.

But she remembered the other side of his nature – his cynicism and his taunts which every mention of his brother provoked, and she recoiled at the thought of confiding in him. He wouldn't understand. He would laugh at her and tell her what a child she was, how immature and ignorant. No, she couldn't talk to Murray.

She spent the morning taking dictation from Clifford. He seemed brighter and was back on form. Words and ideas came pouring out of him. As she left his bedroom at lunch-time, Murray came out of his. By the provocative look in his eyes, she could see that relations between them were back on the old footing. Yesterday evening's walk, the truce, the understanding and sympathy they had shared might never have been.

'Hallo,' he said, his tone challenging. 'Been – er – working hard?' Her frown was intended as a reprimand, but it failed. He grinned. 'It's just that, being a man, my mind – er – wandered. And wondered. After all, you are engaged to him.'

She glowered. 'We worked, and I mean worked.'

'It's all right.' He lifted a placatory hand. 'Knowing my brother only too well, I'm sure you did. He can't help it, it's just how he's made. Now if I'd had a woman working in *my* bedroom for the entire morning . . .'

The sentence hung tauntingly in the air. She swept down the stairs and he watched her all the way.

That afternoon Adrienne typed the work Clifford had dictated earlier. She was halfway through when Murray came in. Flick began to demonstrate all over again his affection for his new friend. Murray crouched down and played with him, using a sort of gentle roughness the dog had come to understand and love.

Adrienne sat, tense and waiting, her hands clasped. Whenever this man walked in, his personality seemed to fill the hut until it overflowed with him. He rose, brushed his hands together to free them of dog's hairs and looked at her rigid back.

'I see I'm receiving my usual welcome from my future sister-in-law.'

'I wish you would stop calling me that.'

'Why?' He sat sideways on the desk and put his hands in his pockets. 'Changed your mind about marrying my brother? I wouldn't blame you if you had.'

'No.' She glared at him. 'Nothing would make me do that. It's just that the term "sister-in-law" keeps reminding me of my future relationship to you.'

He threw back his head and laughed. 'Your repartee is improving. At least it's sharpening your wits having me here. When I leave, we mustn't lose contact, otherwise they'll fall into disuse again.'

She was shot through with apprehension. 'Are you going away?'

'Not yet. Why, do you want me to?'

'No.' She turned pink and mumbled, 'I mean, you've only just come, haven't you?'

He looked at her reflectively. 'If you want to know, I'm spending most of my long vacation here.'

She did not respond. She was afraid to, in case she gave herself away again. He picked up her left hand.

'Why hasn't my brother given you a ring?'

'He wants to keep our engagement a secret for the moment.'

'Why? Is he ashamed of you?'

'Of course not. He simply doesn't want the publicity. He said it would be bad for his heart. And also, the press might discover his pen-name.'

'So what?' He flung her hand down. 'I've never heard such feeble excuses. Well,' he rose, 'there's one way of making him buy you a ring. I'll tell him that if he doesn't I'll give you one myself!' Before she could reply, he had walked out, calling over his shoulder, 'I was told to tell you your tea is waiting for you in the lounge.'

When she entered, the atmosphere was strained. The two men seemed to have been having an argument. They both watched her. Murray was sitting on a stool next to an armchair. He patted it.

'Come and sit here, Adrienne.' The invitation was delivered in the tones of an order. She bristled. Nevertheless, she complied.

Clifford watched as his brother handed her some tea and offered her a biscuit, which she refused.

As she drank, Clifford said, 'Shall I buy you an engagement ring, Adrienne? Would you like that?'

Now she knew what the two men had been discussing.

'For heaven's sake,' came from Murray, 'don't *ask* the girl. *Tell* her. Of course she wants a ring.' He took her left hand in his. 'Look at it, naked and unadorned. She's yours, man, you ought to want to tell the world.'

But Clifford persisted as if his brother had not spoken. '*Do* you want a ring, Adrienne?'

She pulled her hand sharply away from Murray's fingers which were beginning in a subtle, almost imperceptible way to caress hers. Their eyes met. Confused, she glanced away. All the time Clifford was watching, distrustful, uneasy. Murray knew it, and seemed deliberately to be playing on his brother's apprehension. Again they were back in the past in the welter of childish torments and adolescent rivalries. But now the battle was more poignant, the weapon more sophisticated, the thrust deeper. Murray was, for reasons of his own, provoking his brother to jealousy.

She sensed the mounting tension and hated Murray for the pain he was inflicting on Clifford who, she knew possessed by far the weaker of the two personalities and therefore had no means of retaliating effectively against his brother's provocation. Adrienne gave her fiancé the answer he wanted. 'If I wore a ring, we'd have to announce it officially, then everyone would know. And you'd hate the publicity, Clifford. You told me that yourself.'

Her tone indicated that as far as she was concerned, the matter was closed, but Murray would not be quiet. He broke in, addressing his brother. 'If you made no announcement, just bought her a ring, who would know you were the man involved? That terrible thing called "publicity" you're so frightened of need not come into it.'

'But of course it would,' she said sharply to Murray. 'I'd have to tell my mother, and really,' she smiled affectionately to soften the implied criticism, 'she's the world's worst gossip.'

Murray exclaimed, his eyes wide, 'You haven't told her yet? I thought a girl's mother was always the first to know!'

Adrienne stood up. She had to bring the discussion to an end. It was her businesss and Clifford's, not Murray's. 'I must get back to my work.'

Murray stood, too. His arm went round her shoulders and he jerked her against him, holding her resisting body close. He looked at his brother, challenging him.

Clifford's colour rose. It crept up his neck, over his face to the line of his hair. He drew in his lips like a small boy watching a favourite toy being given away to a visitor's child. With a resolution foreign to his nature, he walked across the room, linked his arm in his fiancée's and pulled her away from Murray.

Murray grinned like a man who had achieved his purpose and was satisfied.

Clifford escorted his fiancée to the door. 'Soon,' he promised, 'I shall buy you a ring.' It was a positive statement, but even so he could not resist asking, 'Would you like that?'

She looked defiantly at Murray before she answered, 'Yes, I would.'

A few mornings later, Adrienne was typing in the hut when Murray appeared with two cups of coffee. 'One for you,' he said, putting it on her desk, 'and one for me.' He took the biscuit from his saucer and tossed it to Flick, who opened his mouth, caught it with a snap and devoured it with a satisfying crunch.

'Sorry to interrupt the perfect secretary,' Murray said, looking not in the least sorry, 'but I'm bored stiff.' He looked round for somewhere to sit and found a folding chair leaning against the wall. He opened the chair with one hand, holding his coffee with the other, and sat down. 'Mrs. Masters dropped heavy hints to get me out of the kitchen, although I did my best to get down to her level by listening dutifully to her list of ailments. When she ran out of aches and pains we discussed the weather, then she started baking and told me in unmistakable terms to go.'

'So having nothing better to do,' Adrienne smiled and sipped her coffee, 'you were reduced to seeking me out. I suppose even your future sister-in-law was better than nothing?'

'You suppose right.'

'You can't stay long. I'm busy.'

'As usual, I'm very welcome.'

If she could tell him how welcome he really was, she thought, she would fill a book. He drank his coffee to the last drop and put the cup down with a thump. Then he stood up and Adrienne had to hide her disappointment. He said, 'I only came to ask a question, which is – are you going for your usual walk this evening?'

'Weather permitting. Why?'

He shrugged. 'Just thought I might go with you. I've got nothing better to do. My brother's poor company. He broods so much about his damned books.'

'So once again I'm better than nothing?' He didn't answer. 'You can come if you like.'

'That's exceedingly gracious of you. May I call for you?'

Now Adrienne had to hide her pleasure. 'If you want to. About seven o'clock?'

He took out his diary with a flourish. 'I'll even make a note of it. Seven p.m.,' he wrote, 'date with my future sister-in-law. And dog.' He put his diary away and went out, looking pleased with himself.

Adrienne was ready and waiting when he arrived. She had put on trousers and a sleeveless blouse and carried her cardigan. She would not admit to being excited, but it bubbled up inside her like champagne frothing out of a bottle. It would not be denied. She had told her mother about Murray, that he was her employer's brother – she had to be careful not to call him Clifford – that he was staying there for a holiday and that he liked walking.

Lorna Garron reclined on the couch – her usual pose – but she had used a little more make-up and a trace more perfume behind the ears. Adrienne wondered why she had bothered.

Murray saw Adrienne looking out for him and as she opened the door, he asked provocatively, 'Nice to see I'm welcome for a change. Were you counting the hours until I came?'

'Not just the hours, the minutes and seconds as well,' she wanted to tell him.

'Where's your mother?'

'What a nice young man,' came gushingly from the lounge. 'He's asking to meet me.'

Murray raised his eyebrows. 'May I go in?' Without waiting for an answer, he did so. Adrienne could not understand why he appeared so anxious to meet her mother. Since he was not her fiancé, he should not behave as though he was.

'Good evening, Mrs. Garron.' He stood looking down at her, hands in pockets, a smile on his face, his eyes searching, analysing and summing up.

Adrienne was astonished at his self-possession. It was almost as if he were used to inviting himself into people's living-rooms, as though it was expected of him and was his right.

Lorna commanded, 'Introduce me to this charming young man, Adri-enne.' The affectation was there and Adrienne knew her mother was aiming to impress.

'Mother,' she said stiffly, 'this is Murray. Murray, my mother.'

'Mr. Murray?' The plucked eyebrows fluttered upwards as the smooth, white hand extended towards him and was taken in a brief, firm grip.

Murray looked at Adrienne and there was a warning in his eyes. Confused, Adrienne corrected herself. 'No, I mean Mr. Denning.'

He came to her rescue. 'I told her to call me Murray. It's more friendly. After all, I'm not her employer, just his brother.'

'Then,' the flutter came again, 'may I call you Murray, too?'

'Why not?'

'I'm Lorna, Murray.' With studied grace, she lowered her feet to the floor and patted the cushion beside her. 'Do sit down, Murray, and talk to me. I lead such a lonely life. I have my dear daughter, of course, but I see so few new faces. Especially handsome young men.' She looked at her daughter with a trace of condescension. 'You're the first young man she has ever brought here. She doesn't seem to attract them somehow.'

Colouring deeply, Adrienne said, 'But Mother, he isn't—'

'You know,' Murray cut in, 'you astonish me.' He examined Adrienne in excruciating detail. 'She has everything a man could possibly want in a woman. There's no doubt about it, some lucky man will whisk her away from you one day.'

He was smiling, but his eyes were watchful and he saw a

37

frown plough a furrow between Lorna's eyes. But she banished it immediately in case it left a mark. The doubt was in her voice, though, when she spoke. 'You think so? Oh, I do hope not. What should I do without her?'

Murray's eyes met Adrienne's. They sent a message, 'Take warning from that.'

Lorna said, 'Adrienne darling, get me another cushion so that I can rest my head on it. I shall have a headache soon, I can feel it in my bones.'

Immediately concerned, Adrienne searched for a suitable cushion. Her mother rejected the first two, but the third was found to meet the necessary requirements. Adrienne placed it at precisely the right angle between her mother's head and the back of the couch. Murray rose and with great delicacy lifted Lorna's feet so that she was lying horizontally again.

'Comfortable now?' he asked with a smile.

'How absolutely marvellous,' cooed Lorna, 'to have two people waiting on me! You know,' she looked up at Murray, 'it would be wonderful to have a strong man about the house again. It makes one feel so secure, so – so cherished!'

Murray laughed and Adrienne searched his face for mockery, but found none. He seemed accustomed to dealing with fluttery, demanding women who imagined they were ill. In a situation such as this, full of pretence and affectation, she would have expected the cynic in him to take command, but instead he was the essence of charm and consideration. She was bewildered by the change in his manner.

Flick whined at the back door. He had been prowling round the garden and had heard Murray's voice. Adrienne let him into the kitchen and he scurried along the hall and flung himself at Murray's legs. Murray made a fuss of him and said, 'Time we were off, Flick.' To Lorna, 'Your daughter's taking me for a walk. I'm a comparative stranger here and she's introducing me to all her favourite haunts.'

'My daughter's always going off on her own,' Lorna said. 'She's a solitary person. Even as a child she preferred her own company.'

'Oh dear,' said Murray, pretending to be concerned, 'perhaps I'm intruding on her solitude and she's too polite to tell me she doesn't want me.'

'Of course I want you,' Adrienne snapped, and it was only

when she saw his mocking smile that she realized what she had said. She had fallen into his trap and was annoyed and embarrassed as he had no doubt meant her to be.

'Do come again, Murray,' the voice from the couch rippled after them. He promised that he would.

Flick went ahead and Murray lifted the cardigan from Adrienne's arm. Surprised by his solicitude, she thanked him.

'I'm always the perfect gentleman,' he smiled irritatingly, 'except in certain – er – circumstances. A lot depends on the woman I'm with.' The change in his mood grated on her. But she knew that he would never treat her with the kindness and consideration he had shown to her mother.

She would not, however, be provoked. Instead she asked, 'What did you think of my mother?'

'She was as I expected.' He seemed unwilling to say more and she did not like to press him.

They walked in silence along the lane and reached the road. There were no pavements and now and then, when cars passed, Murray would call a warning to the dog.

'There's no need,' Adrienne told him, ingratitude giving an edge to her voice. 'He's sensible, he's been properly trained.'

'I'm sure he has.' Murray smiled down at her, 'with you as his owner. All the same,' he became serious, 'it's always better to avoid accidents, rather than have to deal with their unfortunate consequences. You see,' he smiled again, 'I believe in preventive medicine.'

After a pause she asked, 'Did you tell Clifford you were coming out with me?'

'I did. He objected, but I told him if he didn't like the idea, he should go with you himself. Has he ever taken you out?'

She didn't answer his question directly. 'We've only been engaged a short time.'

'What difference does that make? Let's face it, engaged couples do a lot more these days than go out with each other. Anyway, we two aren't even courting, yet this is the second time I've been out with you.'

'But he told me he can't go for walks. Because of his heart complaint.'

'For heaven's sake, girl,' he said angrily, 'he hasn't *got* one!'

'How can you be so positive? You know nothing about it. You're not a doctor. I know what it is, of course. It's simply that you're so prejudiced against him it's warped your judgment.'

He laughed as though he found what she had said really amusing. 'Say what you like,' he commented good-humouredly, 'I understand my brother better than you do. The time may come when that situation is reversed, but you're not married to him yet.' He threw a stick for Flick. 'Tell me, does Clifford tolerate your dog?'

'No.' She frowned. 'He can't bear Flick near him.'

His head turned swiftly. 'And you're intending to marry the man? You must be out of your mind.'

'That is a problem,' she said weakly. 'I shall face when it arises.'

'You can face it now, because I can tell you what will happen. On your wedding day, you'll have to say good-bye to Flick.' His eyes were cruel. 'Let me know, won't you? I'll take him over. I'll even buy him from you, if you like.'

She paled and said tightly, 'Thanks for the kind offer, but it won't be necessary.'

'Won't it?' His voice was hard. 'Wait and see. The time will come when I shall be forced to say "I told you so".'

They were silent for a long time. They reached the stile and climbed over it – this time he did not help her – and they walked on side by side until they came to an open space.

'Let's sit down,' he said. 'I want to talk to you.'

Her heart jolted at the authority in his tone. He removed his jacket. 'I'll be gallant and give you something to sit on.'

'Won't you feel chilly?'

'If I do you'll have to cuddle me, won't you?' He smiled, sat down and patted the space beside him. She lowered herself into it. Their shoulders were touching. For some reason the contact troubled her, but he did not seem to notice and pulled idly at tufts of grass. She hugged her legs, rocking a little like a child. Flick settled down beside them.

The sun was slipping towards the horizon out of a turquoise sky into a bed of orange-red and gold. The west was radiant with colour, and Adrienne stared at it fascinated.

He said suddenly, his words shattering her reverie like a brick smashing through a pane of glass, 'Couldn't your mother get a job?'

Her mind was bounced back to earth like an apple falling

from a tree before it was ready. 'My mother – *work*?' She laughed without amusement. 'It would be beneath her dignity! Her life consists of drifting from one coffee morning and one so-called committee meeting to another.'

He said decisively, like a doctor making a diagnosis, 'I've come to the conclusion that her only ailment is boredom. Work would be her salvation.' She turned her head and looked at him, surprised by his confident summing-up of her mother's problems. 'Voluntary work is the answer. Helping in a hospital, old people, sick visiting. It would be therapy both for her and for those she assists.' He took a handful of grass and examined it as though it were under a microscope. 'When your father died, how did she take it?'

She answered, wondering at the depth of his interest, 'She went to pieces. She relied on him utterly. His death was sudden – his heart gave out. He was in his sixties – much older than my mother, as I told you. He wanted to retire earlier, but my mother said she would miss the money too much, so he kept on working just to please her. She sat back and let him get on with it.'

He raised his eyebrows, but did not comment. After a moment he said, 'This evening she extolled the virtues of having a "strong man" in the house. With your father no longer there, you no doubt were forced by circumstances into taking his place. Therefore you are now the "strong" factor in her life. No wonder she shied away from the idea of your ever leaving her.'

'But,' she pointed out, trying to convince herself of the correctness of her statement, 'when I marry Clifford I won't have to leave her. I shall be living near enough to see her and help her every day.'

He leaned back on his elbow and his eyes narrowed. 'My God, is *that* the role you've mapped out for yourself – the part of housemaid, servant, unpaid companion-help? You're prepared to spend the rest of your life, passively and unresistingly splitting yourself in two, dividing your love and loyalties between an "ailing" husband and an equally "ailing" mother?'

She shrugged, hoping he would not see through her carefully assumed indifference. 'I accept it. I'm going into it with my eyes open. I'm not fighting against it.'

'No, of course you're not. It would be out of character if you did. Now I've met your mother, all the pieces are fitting together like a simple jigsaw puzzle. And you fit very neatly into the picture.'

She was on the defensive at once. 'What do you mean?'

'I mean this. Without even realizing it, you've been conditioned over the years by your mother's querulous and incessant demands into accepting blindly and unthinkingly the similar ways of your fiancé. You regard my brother's peevishness, his fussing about his health, his constant desire to be waited on, as nothing out of the ordinary because they are your mother's ways, too. Which is why you can accept him without question as your future marriage partner and don't shrink from the idea of waiting on him for the rest of your life.' He went on savagely, 'Loving doesn't enter into it. It's habit, the old Pavlovian business of conditioned reflex.'

She moved impatiently. She was frightened by the picture he was painting. It was too realistic, too minutely detailed. It was more like a photograph than the product of an artist's imagination.

He asked softly, probing like a surgeon at an operation, 'Don't you want children?'

'Of course I do.'

'Well, that's too bad for you. Clifford vowed once never to have them. Couldn't stand their noise, he said. Hasn't he told you? Not all men are born with the paternal instinct, you know.'

She clasped her arms round her legs again, pressing her chin against the hard bone of her knees. She was taut and uneasy, straining to escape from what he was saying like a dog at the end of a leash. His words were tormenting her like a wasp buzzing round a locked room threatening to sting. She knew now why she had instinctively felt afraid when he had said he wanted to talk to her.

'Do you have to go on?'

He said gently, 'I want you to face the truth, Adrienne. My brother is weak. He wants you as his wife because you're young and active and he can watch you doing the things he's never allowed himself to do. He will live through you. Mentally, Clifford is a decade or so older than his years.' He touched her shoulder. 'Are you listening, Adrienne?'

She did not reply, because she couldn't trust herself to

speak.

'If you ever had a baby,' Murray persisted, 'he might, to be blunt, "father" it – notice I said "might" – but he won't be a father to it.' He lay back, resting his head on his hands. He closed his eyes, but he still had not finished with her. 'Anyway, this I can tell you – you won't only have separate beds, you'll have separate rooms. It won't be a true marriage.'

'Will you be quiet?' she cried, unable to restrain her anger now. 'Why are you talking to me like this? To get your own back yet again on your brother? To hurt me, as you said the other day? To make me unhappy even before I marry him?'

'Better to tell you before than after, sweetie,' he said evenly.

Her head shot round and she stared at his recumbent body. The word he had used, the intensely personal way he was talking, the nearness of him, aroused her beyond words.

'*Don't call me that!*' she almost shouted.

He rolled on to his side and eyed her lazily. 'Why not? Does it excite you, disturb you, bring out in you a feeling of sensuality which is perfectly normal but which shocks you because of what it does to you? A feeling which my brother, with his ignorance of the needs of women, has never coaxed into life? A feeling which dismays you because once it's awakened you might not be able to control it and goodness knows where it might lead?' He edged nearer and softened his voice. 'Because it "reduced" you, as you in your self-conscious, prudish way would call it, to the level of a woman, a real, living woman, with desires and passions?'

He had not touched her, yet she felt as though he were making ardent love to her.

'You know,' he went on, 'you won't be able to spend all your married life suppressing those desires. They'll up and out when you least expect them to. You're young. You'll find the frustration impossible to bear. It will be hell.'

'How can you speak with such authority,' she asked desperately, 'on a subject you know nothing about? You're not a married man.'

He paused before replying and seemed to be trying to find the right words. He pulled at a strand of grass and proceeded to tear it to pieces. 'In the course of my work I've seen the results, I've witnessed the stresses and strains, the physical disorders which such – suffering, there's no other word for it – can give rise to in women, and men, too.' He took her hand – her left hand – between his. She did not attempt to withdraw it.

'Listen to me, Adrienne. Marriage isn't only a sharing of worldly goods. It's a giving of yourself entirely to the man you love, it's an intimate act. . . .'

She dragged her hand from his and clapped her palms over her ears. 'Stop it! Do you think I don't know that?'

He lay back again, reverting to cynicism. 'So you know all about the birds and bees? I began to wonder. But rest assured, it's a knowledge any woman married to my brother will scarcely need. Sex and all its attractions have always played a very insignificant part in Clifford's life. You'll find out. If at any time in the future you wish to annul the marriage, it won't be difficult. You'll still be as you are now, virginal, pure, un-violated. Any doctor would testify . . .'

'I refuse to listen any longer!' She pulled on her cardigan, got up and walked away. Flick who had been wandering round them in circles, followed her, and after a while, Murray caught them up. She felt his arm come round her shoulders and al-though she jerked petulantly at his touch, he did not remove it.

'Sorry I had to hurt you again, Adrienne, but I couldn't leave it unsaid. I couldn't let you go into this marriage blindly, without being aware of the truth.'

'I don't believe it is the truth. I think you hate Clifford so much you're doing your utmost to poison me against him.'

He was silent for so long she looked at him. He was frowning deeply. 'I'm sorry if you think that,' he said at last. 'It isn't true. I wish I could convince you that I'm speaking impartially.'

They were nearly home when he said, 'Well, has our con-versation made any difference to you? Has it made you change your mind?'

They were standing at the end of the lane and Flick was half-way along it, visiting his favourite haunts before the last remnants of daylight disappeared.

'That's what you want me to do, isn't it?' she flung at him. 'Then you'd be able to crow over Clifford and claim another victory against him.' It was dusk now, but even so she could see his eyes harden. 'Well, the answer's "no". I'm more determined than ever.'

His lips tightened. 'Just like a woman! Sympathy for the underdog, no matter how ill-advised that sympathy might be. I should have known better.' He turned from her and strode away, anger in every step.

When he had gone, her bravado disintegrated like a piece of china splintering on a tiled floor. He had gone, but all he had said lingered in her mind. His words ate at her confidence, at her certainty about her own future, like the sea slowly and imperceptibly eroding the rocks it had hurled itself against for centuries past.

CHAPTER FOUR

CLIFFORD had not breakfasted when Adrienne arrived for work next morning. He was, as usual, still in bed.

'Mrs. Masters has a cold, my dear. I wouldn't let her get near me. In my state of health it would be too much of a risk.'

'I'll get your breakfast, Clifford,' Adrienne offered at once. 'Just tell me what you want—'

He listed the food he usually had brought up to him on a tray. 'Look round the kitchen, you'll soon find everything. But whatever you do, keep away from Mrs. Masters.' Adrienne was touched by his concern for her, but was quickly disillusioned by his next remark. 'I don't want the cold germs brought to me by you!'

Clifford was very particular about his menu. Half a grape-fruit was to be cut into sections and all the pips removed. The bacon had to be cooked in a special way, the egg to be firm but not overdone. The instructions were so long and detailed Adrienne almost reached for her shorthand notebook.

Murray came down while she was cooking the food. 'What the devil—?' he exclaimed. 'You're not acting the dutiful wife already?'

She muttered, hoping to silence him, 'Mrs. Masters has a cold.'

'I know. I've seen her. But she's not so bad that she can't do her work.'

'Clifford says he won't have her near him in case he catches it.'

He folded his arms and hunched a shoulder against the doorway. 'So the obliging servant, the faithful fiancée rushes to obey her lord and master's orders and gives him what he wants.' He grinned. 'Don't misunderstand me, will you? In everything except in one respect, I mean.'

She ignored his provocation. 'Someone's got to feed him.'

'He – er – couldn't feed himself, could he? He couldn't get out of that bed he clings to like a baby to its mother's bosom and do a bit of real work for a change?'

'Look, I *offered* to do this . . .'

46

'I'm sure you did. Getting into practice for after the wedding ceremony. Note that I omitted to say honeymoon. Knowing my brother, there won't be one. It'll be straight back to work and no nonsense.' This time she reacted violently to his baiting and he grinned derisively, 'Flick!' The dog rose immediately and went to him. 'Save me, boy, protect me! She's about to fling herself at me in a self-righteous rage.' He bent down and whispered to the dog, 'I wish she would. I'd catch her and wouldn't let her go.'

'Excuse me,' Adrienne said frigidly, waiting for him to move from the doorway and let her pass.

'Good heavens,' he eyed the contents of the tray, 'Clifford isn't going to eat all that! My word, he may not have heart trouble now, but if his appetite for food doesn't diminish over the years, he'll get so obese he really will develop a heart complaint. Tell him that from me, will you? And if you continue to overfeed him after you're married you'll find yourself a widow, young but not very merry.'

'I wish you wouldn't joke about such matters.'

'My dear girl I assure you I'm not joking. I'm perfectly serious. Believe me, I know what I'm talking about.' He put out his hands to take the tray. 'Allow me.' Under protest she let him take it and followed him up the stairs.

Clifford fussed about the position of his pillows, asking Adrienne repeatedly to change them until they were comfortable. He told her to clear his bedside table and swing it round so that it extended across the bed and he could rest the trayful of food on it.

With a sardonic smile, Murray leaned against the chest of drawers and watched. Clifford asked her to close the window as there was a draught. 'I simply must not catch cold. It might do irreparable damage.' He looked defiantly at his brother as he spoke, but Murray merely smiled.

At last Clifford was settled and ready to begin his meal.

'Shall I leave you now?' Adrienne asked.

'If you please, my dear. While I eat I like to think and I can't do that when there is someone else in the room.'

'Good God!' she heard Murray mutter disgustedly as he followed her out. 'With no disrespect, he's your mother all over again.' He was behind her as she went downstairs. 'How at home you must feel in his company! Conditioned, I said, and I was right.'

Adrienne swept into the kitchen, but he followed her there. 'He sends you – his future wife – out of his bedroom so that he can think. *Think!* With you around no man should want to think, he should want to act – like this.' He caught her arms and swung her round to face him. She struggled and he let her go.

'What's the matter, afraid of me?'

'No,' she said icily, 'I have work to do, things to wash up.'

'Domesticated little piece, aren't you?'

'Don't insult me.'

'That isn't an insult. In a man's language that's a compliment. But then you're not engaged to a man, so you wouldn't know. You're engaged to a dictating machine.'

Flushed with anger and an emotion which was swiftly becoming unmanageable, she faced him. In spite of herself, her voice became appealing. '*Please*, Murray, will you leave me alone? Will you stop arou—' she caught back the word, 'stop annoying me?'

'All right,' his eyes gleamed, 'I'll stop *arousing* you – for the moment.' He left her and Flick followed him up to his bedroom.

She spent the morning typing. Before she left Clifford's house she washed up his breakfast dishes to save Mrs. Masters the trouble. She offered to cook the lunch, but the housekeeper would not hear of it.

'I've only got a cold, dear,' Mrs. Masters said. 'As long as I keep away from Mr. Denning, it will be all right. Mr. Denning's brother will take him his food, I'm sure.'

Adrienne put her head round Clifford's door and he told her he was about to get up. She said, 'I'm running short of typing paper, Clifford. Before I come back this afternoon, I'll take a bus into town and buy some, shall I?'

'No need to go by bus. Murray will give you a lift. He's got nothing else to do.'

'No, thank you. I'd rather go on my own. I should hate to trouble him.'

'He won't mind,' Clifford insisted. 'He'll be in his room, I expect.'

Reluctantly she tapped on Murray's door and Flick came rushing out. Murray seemed preoccupied and his mood was distant. 'Yes?'

Taken aback by his manner, Adrienne murmured, 'I'm sorry if I disturbed you. I didn't realize you might be busy.'

He did not invite her in. 'I was working. What do you want, besides your dog?'

'Clifford said you would take me into the town this afternoon to buy some more paper, but it doesn't matter. I'll go by bus.' She looked at him defiantly. 'I would rather go by bus.'

'Oh, would you? In that case, I'll take a leaf out of your book – I'll be perverse. I'll give you the lift you require. Come here at,' he consulted his watch, 'two-fifteen precisely. Don't be late.' He closed the door.

She was not late. At two-fifteen exactly she and Flick presented themselves at Clifford's house. Murray came into the hall. 'Good. You're on time. Punctuality is a fetish of mine,' he grinned baitingly, 'especially in my women.'

She said uncomfortably, 'I didn't know you had any. And even if you have, I'm not one of them.'

'You're certainly not. You've got "Danger keep out" written all over you. Handling you is like handling radioactive material. You have to do it by remote control.'

He bent down and hooked his finger under Flick's collar and led him into the kitchen, closing the door before the dog could attempt to follow.

Traffic built up as they approached the town and Murray was none too pleased when Adrienne told him the stores she wanted – a firm of wholesale stationers – was at the other end of the town. They were caught behind a bus and as there were so many cars coming towards them they had to wait patiently while the passengers stepped off the bus one by one.

A mother carrying a push-chair struggled down to the pavement with a small child clasped awkwardly in her arms. She unfolded the push-chair and put the child, aged about nine months, into it. Someone spoke to her as the bus pulled away and before she could strap the baby into the seat, he had pitched forward on to the pavement. As his head struck the paving stones he screamed.

Murray manoeuvred the car to the kerb. 'Stay there,' he told Adrienne curtly, and was out of the car and picking up the baby before she was aware that he had moved from the driving seat. He talked to the mother, gave her back the child, felt his head with exploring fingers and seemed to be reassuring the distraught mother. He urged her away from the kerb and continued talking to her, apparently trying to calm her. After a while she smiled and nodded and seemed to be thanking him profusely.

Murray returned to the car, looked over his shoulder before driving away and said, 'All's well. I told her the baby had suffered no damage, but offered to take them both to the nearest hospital if she wanted to make sure. But she took my word for it.'

'How do you know the baby was all right?' Adrienne challenged. 'You're not a doctor.'

'As you keep saying,' he commented mildly. 'But years ago,' he flicked her a smile, 'I took first aid lessons. I knew they'd come in useful some time. One of these days I might even have to patch you up – for instance, after your first fight with your husband. But that's as unlikely as man landing on the sun. Clifford never fights. He argues and goes on and on interminably until you give in if only to shut him up.' He glanced at her. 'That's another side of him you know nothing about, isn't it?'

He put the car into the correct position for turning right and when he had completed the manoeuvre, she said sourly, 'According to you he has no good qualities. That's why I don't take seriously what you say about him. You're so prejudiced.'

'There's none so deaf . . .' he taunted softly. 'All right, incredible though it may seem, you're in love with him. And love is blind, they say. At first, perhaps it is, but in time the blindness wears off and you're left facing the stark truth. Then, when it's too late for you to do anything about it, you'll come to me and say, "you were right." '

Adrienne bought the typing paper she needed then went shopping for her mother. Murray followed her round the store carrying the wire basket uncomplainingly. 'Anyone would think,' he commented as they left the supermarket, 'that you were training me to be your husband. Have you ever been shopping with Clifford?' She shook her head. 'Never?' They passed a café. 'Have you ever had a cup of tea with him? No? Well, you're going to have one with me now.'

They sat at a table in the window and watched the people passing by. When the waitress appeared, Murray ordered a pot of tea for two.

'Cream cakes?' he asked Adrienne. 'No? Sensible girl. They're not only bad for your health, they're bad for your figure.' This, as they were served with their tea and left alone, he studied in detail, to Adrienne's embarrassment. 'Time enough later on for you to start putting on weight through over-eating as a form of compensation for your frustrations.' He smiled blandly at the look she gave him. 'You don't believe me, do you? You're so immature and unawakened, you simply don't understand what I'm talking about.' He leaned back, hooking his arm over the back of the chair, and contemplated her.

'After you're married,' he persisted, 'and have discovered what a cold fish my brother is, some man will come along and awaken in you all those longings you're battening down so se-curely now. And my word,' his eyes grew brooding, 'I can just imagine what it would be like to be on the receiving end of that awakening!'

She went for her usual evening walk with her dog. Lorna said as she was leaving, 'Joan Smithers said at coffee this morning there's a rumour going round that a suspicious-looking man's hanging about the village. He's been seen loitering near the school and wandering across the fields.'

'It's all right, Mother,' Adrienne assured her, 'I've got Flick with me.'

'Oh, it's not you I'm worried about. I know you can take care of yourself. I'm the one who's scared, here on my own. Don't be out too long, Adrienne, will you?'

Adrienne smiled as she walked along the lane. She should have known better than to assume that her mother was worried about her. In Lorna Garron's life Lorna and Lorna's material well-being came first. It was a lesson Adrienne had learned at an early age. As Murray had said, it had conditioned her think-ing to such an extent that she accepted unquestioningly that she also came second in Clifford's scheme of things.

As she walked across the fields, she thought about Murray. She would have given a great deal to have him beside her, talking, making her laugh or annoyed. She would even have welcomed his provocation and his taunts. But, she had to remind herself severely, he was not for her. His world, what-ever it might be, was as different from hers as the atmosphere on the moon differed from that of the earth. When he went away, as he must before long, he would take with him so much more than just himself. He would take his humour, his energy and his vitality. A whisper like the ripple of a stream over stones told her that he would take part of her with him, too. But she pushed the thought away like a child rejecting food it didn't want.

She did not see Murray again for a few days. She knew he was still there because she heard him talking to Mrs. Masters and playing with Flick in the kitchen. She wondered if he was keeping out of her way, but decided that even that was too optimistic a thought. He was plainly indifferent to her and felt it was not worth his while to seek her out.

One morning she took Flick into the kitchen, then climbed the stairs to Clifford's bedroom. She heard voices inside. As she raised her hand to knock she heard Murray say,

'For heaven's sake, man, touch her sometimes, make love to her. She's going to be your wife. You can't go on treating her like an employee, sending her home when the day's work is done. This I will tell you. She's as unawakened as you are, so don't expect any "help", as you call it, from her. If you want that sort of "help", marry a widow.'

She retreated along the landing and did not catch Clifford's reply, but Murray, his voice raised, went on, '*What?* She's *cold?* I'd give a lot to prove to you she's not. Try kissing her – and I don't mean her cheek. See what response you get, from yourself as well as from her.'

It sounded as if Clifford was asking his brother's advice, and getting more than he had bargained for. Murray's voice came again, scathing, hard, 'If you think that, brother . . . My God, if you suspect *that* you've no right to be marrying any woman, let alone an attractive, desirable . . .'

She ran away, down the stairs to the kitchen. She fondled Flick, lifted him up and pressed him against her burning cheek. 'Mr. Denning's talking to his brother,' she explained to Mrs. Masters.

A door opened upstairs. 'There,' the housekeeper said, 'they've finished now, dear, you can go up.'

Slowly Adrienne mounted the stairs, hoping Murray would have gone into his room, but he was standing on the landing watching her. He did not greet her with a smile.

'Have you been here long?'

She shook her head, avoiding his eyes. 'Not long.' She asked dully, 'May I go in?'

'Why ask me? I'm not my brother's keeper.'

The bitterness in his voice made her look at him and she saw the anger in his eyes.

Clifford's hand came out and he pulled her down. His lips made for her cheek as usual but their direction changed and found her mouth. Their lips came into contact and his kiss was like that of a hesitant youth. She felt no response at all.

He seemed pleased with himself. He patted the bed. 'Sit down, my dear. I'm feeling fitter this morning. I think I shall get up soon.'

His hand was still holding hers and she let it remain there. 'That's good, Clifford. Do you want to dictate some notes to me first?'

'Yes, I think I will. My mind is particularly lucid today.' He smiled. 'It must be the effect you have on me.'

She smiled weakly and felt a little sick inside. 'It's not me,' she wanted to say, 'it's your brother's influence, your brother who has boosted your confidence, given you a false kind of boldness and instructed you in how to handle me.' But it won't last, she told herself. In a day or two he will have forgotten the advice and will need to go back to Murray for help again, for an injection of courage, for another lesson in the management of women.

She spent the day working. As she was leaving at tea-time, Clifford asked her, 'Will you be busy this evening?'

'No, just going for my usual walk.'

'Will you spend the evening here with me instead, my dear?' He caught her arm and his eyes pleaded. He didn't say, as Murray would have done, 'May I come with you on your walk?'

For some reason she could not explain, she felt troubled, but replied at once, 'Of course I will. I should like to.'

Later, when she arrived, Murray was in the lounge. He rose as she entered. When she took her place beside Clifford, Murray leaned back with his elbows on the mantelshelf and eyed them sardonically. Clifford, with a gesture resembling one who had been dared to do something, put his arm round her. Obligingly she shifted along the couch towards him. Murray's smile grew broader.

'Plainly I'm in the way,' he murmured. 'Never let it be said that I intruded on a courting couple. Where's Flick?' he asked Adrienne sharply.

'With Mrs. Masters. Why?'

'I'm taking him for a walk.' It was not a question, it was a statement and it could not be refuted. He went out, calling to the dog.

Adrienne was forced to sit quiescent beside her fiancé, listening to her dog going mad with joy at the prospect of being taken out by someone who was little more than a stranger, and yet who seemed to have pushed her into second place even in her dog's affections. Not even with Flick, she thought sulkily, did she come first any more.

Her annoyance with the man who seemed to be pulling her life to pieces like someone tearing petals off a flower grew too intense to tolerate. When he returned, she would tell him in unmistakable terms to leave her – and her fiancé – alone and let them run their own lives as they wished without interference from him.

But she did not see him again that evening. He must have come in the back way, left Flick with Mrs. Masters and gone up to his room.

The time passed slowly. Clifford turned on the television and they watched for a while. When he turned it off, he began to talk, and it was all about his work. Adrienne tried to introduce other subjects, but he plainly was not interested. She became reconciled in the end, acknowledging that nothing else mattered to him. His work, his writing was all-important, and he was not only unwilling but apparently unable to talk about anything else.

When the daylight had almost gone, he put his arms round her and kissed her. He was awkward and constrained, but she forced herself to respond to him within the bounds of her limited experience. She tried, in her unskilled, innocent way to help him show his feelings for her. After a while, he stopped and turned on the light.

Blinking, as brightness took the place of the gloom, she saw that he looked satisfied and even a little smug. He would probably tell his brother in the morning that he had tried the experiment and it had worked.

But as she took her leave of him and walked home in the

darkness with Flick at her heels, she knew he had failed lamentably to stir her in any way. But there was a feeling for him growing within her which she could not define, and she began to realize that he had a very real need of her. His proposal of marriage had been no sudden passing whim. He wanted her as his life partner — provided, she told herself with a flash of insight, she played the part, the strictly subordinate and undemanding part which, writer that he was, he had written for her in the story that was his life.

She did not see Murray next day. As she worked in the hut she kept stopping to listen, fingers poised to type the next words, imagining she could hear his footsteps. But he didn't come. Mrs. Masters brought her cup of morning coffee and her afternoon tea. She began to long for the sight of him. Even that would be enough, without hearing his voice or feeling his touch. She chided herself that she was being a fool. It wasn't Murray she was engaged to. She should feel like that about Clifford, not his brother.

She went for a walk that evening, swinging Flick's lead from her fingers, and strolling past the wild flowers growing in the hedgerows. She breathed in the fragrant summer smells, potent as wine, and drifted into a dream to the accompaniment of birdsong. As she turned the corner, she saw a man waiting at the end of the lane. She stopped in her tracks. She thought it was part of her dream. She couldn't believe he was really there, waiting for her.

Flick picked up his scent and scampered towards him, scattering earth and stones as his paws skidded backwards and his body thrust forward.

Murray bent down and fondled the dog. 'Ball of fire, that's what you are,' he muttered as he played with him. He straightened. 'Hallo,' he said. No explanation. He took the lead from Adrienne's fingers.

'How did you know,' she asked, masking her pleasure with irritation, 'I would come?'

'I felt it in my bones, as your mother would say.' He smiled, he seemed happy, relations between them were, for a while, on an even keel.

'Instead of the fields,' he said, 'we'll go to the park. The café, I assume, will still be open?'

She nodded 'At this time of the year they don't close until it's nearly dark. But,' she objected, on principle and simply to show him that he couldn't dictate to her at will, 'I always go across the fields. Why should I change tonight? Suppose I don't want to go to the park?'

But he overrode her feeble objections with his usual arrogance. 'Too bad if you don't. We're going. Come on.' He took her hand and although she tried, she could not twist her fingers from his.

'Why have you come out with me?'

He smiled mockingly. 'I'm on holiday. I felt the need of a woman's company, even if it is only my future sister-in-law's. Anyway, I want to get to know her a little better.'

She wondered what he meant by that. In the café, they found a corner table and Flick settled under it while they drank their tea. Adrienne remarked, after a while, 'If you dislike your brother as much as you say you do, why do you spend your holidays with him?'

He laughed. '*Touché!* But I don't, usually. I go abroad, or to the lonely stretches of coast in the north of England or the west of Scotland. This time,' he smiled, 'I came for a purpose – to meet the woman my brother suddenly announced he was going to marry.'

'To vet me, you mean?'

'Well, I'm not a veterinary surgeon, nor are you an animal, in the accepted sense of the word! Perhaps a more appropriate way of putting it would have been to say that I wanted to "examine" you.'

'And have I passed the test?'

He smiled enigmatically. 'I never divulge the results of any examination. It's against professional etiquette. Any – er – vet would tell you. But,' his hand covered hers across the table, 'I can say this. I had decided in advance that if I didn't approve of my brother's choice, I would tell him so in no uncertain terms and take a hurried leave. The fact that I'm still here should give you a clue to my observations and conclusions where you're concerned.'

'In other words, you like me?'

He eyed her lingeringly. 'If I didn't know it would be out of character, I'd assume you were fishing for compliments. But,' he removed his hand from hers, 'let's put it this way. I don't dislike you.'

She flushed with chagrin at his uncomplimentary turn of phrase, and he regarded her with a lazy smile. They were silent for a while, watching people wander into the café and take their places in the queue at the self-service counter. Many of them were young couples, hand in hand, or with their arms about each other. Adrienne looked at them with unconscious envy and coloured when she discovered Murray was watching her.

He turned his head and stared across the room, through the window to the park outside. His thoughts seemed to have drifted away and when he spoke again, his expression was serious. 'You may wonder at the lack of brotherly affection between Clifford and myself.' He did not wait for her response. 'He was seven when I was born and until I made my appearance, the darling of our parents' hearts. Then, all those years later, I came along, and in the way that parents have, the direction of their affection changed and I became their pride and joy.'

When he paused she said softly, 'And I suppose Clifford grew jealous?'

'He did.' He frowned and pain clouded his eyes. 'He grew to hate me as the years went by. He told stories about me, got me into trouble with lies and false accusations. I was too young to know that he was only doing it to regain our parents' attention, and I hated him for it. He started to be "ill", and the more concerned my mother and father grew about him, the "worse" he got.' He came back to the present. 'Am I boring you?'

She shook her head, willing him to go on.

'He developed "pains" all over him, and apparently decided that his chest was the best place to concentrate on, as that was more or less where his heart was. They took him to specialists galore, and Clifford enjoyed every minute of it. He didn't believe the doctors when they said he wasn't ill, nor, after a while, did my parents. In the end, Clifford convinced himself he had heart trouble and convinced them, too. They forgot about me in their concern for him. He had won the "battle".'

He looked straight at her. 'Now do you understand when I tell you his heart is as sound as yours and mine? That it's all a figment of his imagination? That he's "using" it still to gain attention and "love"?' He saw her doubt and said bitterly, 'I can see you're still unconvinced.' He added, in a curious tone,

'It's history repeating itself.' He took her hand between both of his. 'Look, if I tell you I know what I'm talking about, that I'm—' He stopped and pushed her hand away. 'What damned use is it talking to you? You wouldn't believe me, whatever I said.'

She played with the salt and pepper containers which were still standing on the table, twisting them round agitatedly and moving them as though they were pieces on a chessboard. 'It's no good, Murray, you can say what you like, but you won't make me change my mind.'

He removed the salt and pepper from her restless fingers and put them out of her reach as though she were a naughty child. 'Won't I? I haven't finished with you yet.'

After a while he asked, 'Would you like another cup of tea?'

She shook her head and said, 'Where do you live, Murray?'

'In a flat near my place of work. You must come and see it some time.' Her heart leapt at the invitation, although it was so carelessly given. 'It's two or three hours' train journey from here.'

'Have you many – friends?' she ventured.

'A few. Why?' He smiled. 'Are you fishing again, trying to discover if any of those friends are women?'

She shook her head vigorously. He smiled unbelievingly and said, 'Time to be getting back.' He bent down. 'We're off, dog.'

Flick stretched and made for the open door, trotting in front of them all the way. It was dark when they reached the end of the lane. Flick wandered round, waiting for them.

Murray rested his hands on her shoulders and moved her towards him. She stiffened, wishing she could see his expression, but there was no light, not even the moon to cast a shadow. She could feel his face close to hers, his breath brushing against her skin.

'I'm going to kiss you good night, Adrienne.' He said it quietly, without emotion. It was a statement of fact. 'I'm going to kiss you as my brother will never kiss you in the whole of his life, not even after you're married to him.' His hands slid down her arms. 'Unclench your fingers.' But he had to prise them open. His voice softened. 'Put your arms round my neck,

58

sweetie.' She did not resent the endearment now. She lifted her arms and did as he had told her. 'Relax,' he whispered, 'let yourself go slack against me.'

As if under hypnosis, she complied. Then he pulled her body against his and kissed her with an ardour which saturated her senses and crushed out of existence any desire she might have had to resist.

By the time he had finished, her will-power had gone beyond recall and all she could do was to lie limp and quiet in his arms. Her mouth was upturned towards his and although she was not aware of it, she might even have been asking for more.

His second kiss was different. It was persuasive and compelling and she found herself answering his passion with a fervour which matched his and which, by his actions, he had seemed determined to arouse in her.

He stopped at last and said with unmistakable triumph, 'I knew it, I knew it was there!'

As she lay against his chest, inert and emptied of emotion, his words, his strange elation at his success, pushed their way into the tumult of her thoughts and reality entered with them. Her joy was trampled underfoot and died a painful death. With an agonized jerk she pulled away from him. What was it he had said to Clifford? 'I'd give a lot to prove she's not cold.'

She choked, her voice thick with tears, 'So it was an experiment! You did it to prove to yourself and consequently to your brother that you were right. Now you know I'm not a frigid, passionless creature devoid of feeling. I can be aroused by a man, a man who's as expert at lovemaking as you are. You can go back and tell Clifford you were right about me.'

'So you overheard us yesterday?' His voice was harsh.

'Yes, unintentionally. And tonight you set out to see what response you could get from me, didn't you, as you advised your brother to do? Now you've tested it and measured it, you can return to him in triumph, and boast to him you've succeeded in doing what he's never been able to do – move me to passion. You've done your research. Your experiment's worked.'

'Will you be quiet!' He caught her against him, but she managed to struggle away.

She cried bitterly, 'What were you intending to do – teach me how to kiss and make love so that I could become "experienced" enough to give my fiancé the "help" you say he needs?'

He put his hand over her mouth to stop her talking, but she twisted her head away like an enraged animal. 'Or were you perhaps trying to make me fall in love with you, and thus chalk up another victory against him? At one stroke depriving him of his fiancée and having your own back on him for all those years of unhappiness you allege he caused you in childhood?'

She was crying now because even as she spoke, she knew the damage had been done. She loved this man, loved him as she knew she would never love the man she was going to marry. Her voice wavered as she whispered, 'You've done your worst, but you haven't won. You've lost this particular battle because I'm still going to marry Clifford. He needs me, I know he does. I can't let him down.' She turned to go.

'Adrienne!' His hand came out to stop her, but she wrenched herself away and ran from him, along the lane towards her home, with Flick racing at her heels.

CHAPTER FIVE

ADRIENNE dreaded meeting Murray next morning, but because of the situation which awaited her, it was unavoidable.

When she took Flick into the kitchen, Mrs. Masters said, 'Mr. Denning's not too good, dear.'

Now what? Adrienne wondered as she went upstairs. Was it really his heart this time?

When she knocked and opened Clifford's bedroom door, Murray was there. He was holding Clifford's wrist, but dropped it as soon as he saw her. She thought abstractedly that it was a surprisingly affectionate gesture for a man to make who disliked his brother as much as Murray alleged he did. In his other hand he was holding a thermometer and he was shaking it to make the mercury in it contract. His eyes, which met hers momentarily, were cold. 'Your fiancé insisted that I took his temperature. He's only got to sneeze and he reaches for his thermometer.'

'It's just as well this time,' Clifford murmured, resting his head against the pillows.

'It's up a bit,' Murray said noncommittally. 'It's a feverish cold. You've obviously caught it from Mrs. Masters, despite your precautions which I knew were futile anyway. Colds usualy go round the household.'

'Can't you give me anything for it?' Clifford moaned, turning his cheek to the pillow.

'Are you sure it's only a cold?' Adrienne asked Murray. 'How do you know? You're not a doctor. It could be the start of something worse.'

'Good God,' he eyed her contemptuously, 'I should hate to be *your* doctor when – *if* – you have offspring, and they start getting childish ailments. I'd have to prescribe for you as well as your kids, you'd be in such a nervous state.'

She ignored him and turned to her fiancé. 'Would you like me to call the doctor, Clifford? Tell me his phone number—'

'No, you will *not* call the doctor.' Murray's words came through his teeth. 'He has a cold, nothing else. And stop fussing, for God's sake. Your loved one won't die on you, not of a common cold.'

Again she ignored him. 'Can I get you anything, Clifford? Anything to drink—?'

He reached out and took her hand. 'Thank you for being so considerate, my dear.' She bent down to kiss his cheek, but he held her off. 'No, no, I don't want you to catch it.'

'Of course he doesn't,' a derisive voice murmured behind her. 'If you got it he'd have no one to wait on him and fuss over him, and that would be calamitous.'

She swung round, her eyes blazing. 'Would you mind your own business?'

He shrugged and leaned against the chest of drawers, folding his arms. He smiled, but his eyes were narrow. 'I'll forgive you for your unpardonable rudeness under the stress of the appalling circumstances.'

She hated his sarcasm, but could not retaliate because although he was smiling, his eyes flashed a warning and she realized there were limits beyond which he would not allow her to go.

'Have the day off, my dear. There's no need for you to work today.'

'I certainly won't go home, Clifford. I'll sit downstairs in case you want anything. Just call and I'll come.'

He nodded and she left him. Murray followed. On the landing he said, baitingly softly, 'If I called, would you come to me?'

'I certainly wouldn't!' she bluffed, turning away, head in the air.

His hand came out and he swung her round. 'After your performance last night, I've only got to do that,' he clicked his fingers, 'and you'd come without scruple, without hesitation.'

'Oh, leave me alone!' she breathed, and ran down the stairs.

She returned that afternoon and sat in the lounge reading through the work she had typed the previous day. Murray was in his room. Clifford was sleeping.

The telephone rang. She ran to answer it, afraid that it would awaken Clifford. A woman's voice asked, 'Can I speak to Professor Denning, please?'

Adrienne took a deep breath. 'Do you mean Mr. Clifford Denning or—'

'No, I mean Professor Denning, Dr. Murray Denning. I believe he's staying at that address?'

Adrienne nearly dropped the receiver, but she controlled her voice and asked, in her most precise secretarial tones, 'Who is speaking, please?'

'Tell him this is Gretel Steel, will you?'

Adrienne climbed the stairs, her feet oddly heavy, and tapped on Murray's bedroom room. He opened it. 'Yes?'

'Professor Denning?' she asked.

He raised his eyebrows. 'I am.'

'There's a phone call for you. A lady called Gretel Steel.'

His eyes came alive. 'Thanks.' He was down the stairs before she had time to take breath.

'Murray here,' he said to the caller. 'Gretel, my dear, how nice to hear from you. When did you get back?'

Adrienne crept past him into the lounge and shut out his voice. So this was his secret lady friend, the woman he was so reluctant to talk about. She had been away and now she was back. She sounded pleasant and young and there was no doubt at all that he had a high regard for her. Adrienne leaned back in the armchair and closed her eyes. She was crying inside and they were tears of despair.

So he was a professor, a highly-placed academic, outside her sphere, living in a totally different world, and sharing it with friends on his own intellectual level. How he must be laughing at his brother's fiancée for her ignorance and her lack of education!

She heard him say, 'When can I see you? Can we meet halfway? Book in somewhere, stay the night, perhaps . . .'

He rang off at last and came into the lounge, dropping into the chair on the other side of the fireplace. 'Well?' He was challenging her. 'Aren't the questions going to start?'

She said accusingly, 'You told me you were a lecturer, doing research . . .'

'In essence that was correct. I *lecture* – note the difference in the word. I'm also involved in research.'

'But you're of professorial status?' He nodded. She asked, 'How long ago did you get your doctorate?'

He frowned. 'My—?'

'Your Ph.D. Your doctorate.'

'Oh, sorry to be so obtuse. Some years ago now.'

'And is Miss Steel your – your girl-friend?'

'You're incredibly curious about the women in my life. I wonder why? For your information, she's *Mrs*. Steel. She's a widow, wife of the late Professor David Steel, who died tragically just over a year ago in a flying accident.' He paused. 'David was my best friend.'

'I'm sorry.'

'She's just returned from a year's leave of absence researching at an Australian university. Her sister lives there, so she stayed with her, hoping it would help her get over the loss of her husband.'

'Is she a – a colleague of yours?'

'She is. She works under me, in my department. So I shall be seeing a lot of her from now on.' He smiled. 'Finished? If you ask any more questions about her, I shall begin to think you're jealous.'

She flushed deeply and tried to give her attention to the typed words in front of her.'

He leaned forward. 'Are you, Adrienne?'

She answered, her voice surprisingly cool, 'I'm engaged, remember.'

He gazed at her left hand. 'And he still hasn't bought you a ring? Isn't he so pleased and proud you've agreed to marry him he wants to let all other men know "this flower is not for you to pick"?'

She asked, looking at the papers on her lap, 'Would it have stopped you last night, if I'd been wearing a ring?'

'No,' came the unequivocal answer, 'nothing would have stopped me last night.'

Clifford called and she was out of the room and up the stairs to him as fast as Murray had been in getting to the telephone.

He was sitting up and asking for water. She gave him a glass and he drank deeply. He looked so flushed she grew worried.

'How do you feel?' she asked with a smile, trying to keep the anxiety from her voice.

'About the same. Where's Murray?'

'Downstairs,' she answered, surprised again at his apparent reliance on his younger brother. 'Shall I ask him to come up?'

He nodded. She called to Murray and he sprinted up the stairs. 'Well?' He seemed as unsympathetic as ever.

'He's terribly hot. Do you think I should send for the doctor?'

Murray did not reply. He went into the bedroom, put his hand on Clifford's forehead, then rested his fingers on his brother's wrist as though he was taking his pulse. Adrienne watched the action with amazement. He stood for a few moments as if counting the pulse rate. As he did so, he smiled at Adrienne. When he had finished he said to her, 'My first aid lessons coming in useful again.'

'Am I all right?' Clifford asked, his voice hoarse.

'As right as anyone can be with a feverish cold.' He left them and went into his room. Adrienne heard him call her. He was holding out two tablets. 'I keep a supply of these in case of emergencies. Give them to him with water.' He added, with a glint in his eye, 'Nurse.'

She did as he had told her without question. It seemed natural in the circumstances to be taking orders from him Clifford swallowed the tablets almost, it appeared to Adrienne, with childish pleasure, as if they contained some magic ingredient which would make him better.

Adrienne stayed with Clifford for the rest of the afternoon. He improved as the time passed and brightened a little, although they did not talk much.

At tea-time she left him, saying she would return later to see how he was. She told her mother that her employer was ill with a cold but she was going back that evening to catch up on her work. Her mother accepted the fact, having grown accustomed to her daughter's uneven hours of work.

'But don't be back late,' Lorna urged, 'not as late as you were last night. I don't like to be left alone too long, darling.'

Adrienne remembered with a mixture of pain and pleasure the reason for her delayed return the night before. She assured her mother that she would not be away too long this time.

Clifford had had a reasonable meal, judging by the emptiness of the tray at his side. She remembered with a smile Murray's words, 'When my brother is off his food, then I'll know he's really ill.'

Mrs. Masters collected the tray then Clifford produced some notes he had written after she had left him. 'Only a few, my dear, very roughly written, but I wonder if you would mind typing them this evening?'

She took them down to the hut, and Flick followed, taking up his usual position at her feet. It was growing dark, so she turned on the light. Some time later, when it was black outside and the moths danced agitatedly against the windowpanes in a futile attempt to break through the invisible barrier, she happened to look up. There was a noise outside and her heart leapt, thinking it was Murray.

Her eyes were drawn to the window. A face was staring in. She opened her mouth to shriek, but nothing came out. Flick started up, growling and snarling, his barks filling the hut. The staring eyes in the ugly face shifted to the dog, who was making short sharp dives towards the window. The man moved away and disappeared. Adrienne froze with terror, thinking he was coming in.

Flick ran to the door and jumped up at it repeatedly, bouncing up and down and making enough noise to frighten a horde of intruders. But no one came. After about ten minutes, during which she could scarcely breathe for fright, she ventured to the door.

Somehow she would have to find the courage to get to the house. 'C-come on, Flick,' she whispered, 'stay with me, boy.'

The dog seemed to understand. As she dived out of the hut and ran between the trees, he stayed by her side and they raced together to the house. She flung open the kitchen door. It was in darkness. Mrs. Masters had gone upstairs. She groped her way across the room and burst into the lounge. Murray was there. He stood as she entered and she almost fell into his arms.

She was white with terror, her body was shaking and she could not speak for chattering teeth.

'Good God, what happened?' Murray asked, but she couldn't answer. Flick, still excited, ran round in circles, snarling.

She clung to Murray and his arms tightened. 'What is it, Adrienne? Tell me.'

Haltingly, she explained. 'It m-must have b-been the man my mother told me about, the one who's been s-seen wandering round the village.'

Gently Murray lowered her into an armchair. 'I'm going out to have a look.'

'No,' she fastened on to his hand, 'don't! He might still be there. He might hurt you.'

He extricated his hand from hers and smiled. 'Don't worry about me. I can take care of myself.'

He was out for what seemed to Adrienne to be an interminable length of time. 'No sign of him,' he said, returning at last, 'but the fence at the end has been broken down. He must have come across the fields and climbed over into the garden. We'd better give the police a ring.'

'Murray,' she pleaded, 'don't tell Clifford. It might worry him.'

'I wouldn't dream of telling Clifford. "Worry him" is an understatement. He'd go frantic – not about you, don't fool yourself – but about all his precious books which he keeps in that hut.'

When he came back he told her, 'They said they would alert all the police in the area and we're to let them know if the man makes his appearance again.' He smiled down at her. 'Calmer now?'

She nodded. 'I'm sorry for – for throwing myself at you. I was so scared. I didn't know what I was doing.'

'I was aware of that,' he commented dryly. 'I knew it wasn't because you loved me!' He frowned. 'I don't think you'd better work down there any more at this time of night until they've caught up with that prowler. If Flick hadn't been there. . . .'

He crouched down and fondled the dog. 'You look after your mistress, boy. Take good care of her.' He straightened. 'I think you'd better forgo your evening walks for the present, Adrienne. With a character like that around, it's hardly safe.'

'I'd better not tell my mother, either. She would worry – not about me, but about being left alone.'

'It's extraordinary,' Murray mused, sitting down, 'how alike they are – your fiancé and your mother. Do they both put themselves first – always?'

She took some time in answering, then said dully, 'Yes.' She leaned her head back and closed her eyes. She still had not recovered fully from the shock. He did not speak, but she knew he was watching her.

'So,' he said after a long silence, 'you come first in no one's life, not even your own.'

She opened her eyes and stared at him.

'You regard yourself not as a person in your own right, but as someone whose sole reason for living is to serve others, to wait

67

on them, carry out their orders and anticipate their demands, however trivial. Even to yourself your own wishes come second.' She shrugged.

He persisted, and his voice held a note of warning, 'If you don't consciously alter the course of your life, Adrienne, you'll spend the rest of your days torn between your husband and your mother, making yourself the prop they both lean on, until the weight becomes so great you'll crack under the strain. You'll become a physical and nervous wreck.'

She remained silent. She knew in her heart that what he was saying was true, but it seemed beyond her powers to do anything about it. Events were carrying her with them. It was like being in a rowing boat without oars. She was deprived by circumstances of the means of determining her own course and she had to go where the current took her.

He came to sit on the arm of her chair. His fingers closed over her wrist. She knew he could feel her racing pulse.

'Shall I give you something to calm you down?'

She wanted to tell him that nothing would calm her down while he was so near. She looked up at him. 'You mean a drink? No, thanks.'

'No, not a drink. That would stimulate you. I mean a sedative.'

'No, thanks, I'll be all right soon.' He did not move away. His fingers shifted until they found her hand and rested there. Her pulse rate increased and she wondered if he knew.

She said, her eyes closed, 'I've got to go down to the hut to clear up. I can't go home and leave it in a mess.'

'I'll come with you, then I'll take you home.'

In her gratitude for his thoughtfulness her fingers pressed his. She realized what she had done and tried to remove them, but he held them fast. She stood up and freed her hand. She said, a little wildly, 'I'll go down to the hut now.'

He followed her into the garden, Flick leading the way. She shivered. 'Cold?' he asked, putting his arm round her shoulders.

'I left my cardigan on my chair. I was in such a hurry to get back to the house, I forgot it.'

He helped her on with it and while she put the typed pages into order, he played with the dog. She locked the hut behind her.

In the hall she said, 'I must say good night to Clifford. Flick,' the dog turned at the sound of his name, 'stay here, boy.'

'It's all right,' Murray said, 'I'll look after your hound while you give your beloved a passionate kiss.'

The return of his sarcasm grated. It was as though the harmony between them had never been.

'Did you finish typing the notes I made?' Clifford wanted to know as she went in.

'Er – not quite. But it won't take me long in the morning.'

He held out his hand for what she had done. 'Thank you, my dear, for working so late. I hope,' he said abstractedly, already examining the pages, 'you're not too tired.'

His mind was not on her at all, so she didn't feel it was necessary to answer. 'Are you feeling better, Clifford?'

He looked up immediately, his attention caught by the subject nearest to his heart. 'A little, thank you,' he replied guardedly, as if unwilling to part with his illness too soon.

'By the morning,' she said cheerfully, 'you'll probably be back to normal.'

'I doubt it, my dear, I doubt it. These things tend to hang on. And I have to take care, you know. I'm never one hundred per cent fit.'

'I know you aren't, Clifford,' she said placatingly, 'I was only trying to cheer you up.'

He smiled. 'I realize that, but I faced the fact long ago that I can never be quite the same physically as other men.' He took her hand. 'You are aware of that, Adrienne, aren't you?'

She nodded, and forced a smile. What was he trying to tell her? Something she already knew – that their married life together would be 'different'? That she could only ever hope to be a wife in name, nothing else? As if she didn't already know, she thought with unaccustomed cynicism, and it was a sensation which frightened her. Did it mean that deep down, she was already rejecting the idea? That Murray's kiss had revealed to her as well as to him the depths to which she could be stirred by a man's lovemaking? That now she knew herself better, she would be dissatisfied with a loveless marriage and that before many months had passed, she would long for the physical love she would forever be denied?

What was the matter with her? She was tired, that was the

trouble. She had had a bad shock. Those moments of terror had shaken her more than she realized. She bent down to kiss him, but he pushed her away. 'No, no, my cold – you mustn't catch it.'

It was almost as though he was relieved that a barrier existed, one which removed the necessity for any physical contact between them.

Murray walked with her to the cottage. He refused her invitation to go in. They stood outside, looking at each other in the darkness. He had not touched her and his conversation had been as impersonal as that of a stranger.

He said, 'I'm going away tomorrow.'

Her heart seemed to miss a beat. 'For long?' she asked, afraid of the answer.

'A couple of days. I'm meeting Gretel. It's over a year since I last saw her.' He must love her, she thought, to have waited so long and so patiently.

He went on, 'Don't worry about Clifford. Where his health's concerned he's a bit unbalanced. He suffers from an excess of imagination. Most of it he pours into his books, but what's left he expends on imaginary ailments and afflictions. He weaves ill-health around him like a web, and now he's caught in it and can't get out. Take it away from him and he's nothing left to live for! Ironic, isn't it? He loves you because you bolster his illusions, you don't laugh at them, you take them seriously. As long as you realize that, and are content with what will be your lot in your life with him, all will be well. But once you start questioning it. . . .'

He did not finish the sentence. He bent down and stroked Flick, who responded joyfully to Murray's playful affection.

In the light from the uncurtained window, Adrienne caught the look on Murray's face. It belied the cheerfulness of his voice. It had a resigned sadness about it that made her want to wrap her arms about him and hold him until the sadness went away. He straightened but still he did not touch her.

'I hope you enjoy yourself,' she said, keeping her voice steady. 'I expect Gretel will be so happy to see you again after all this time.'

'The happiness will be mutual. Good night, Adrienne.'

'Good-bye, Murray.' He walked away. He did not seem to notice the finality of the word.

CHAPTER SIX

MURRAY failed to return when he was expected. There had been no word from him and a week went by. Life went on as usual. Adrienne took dictation in the mornings, typed in the afternoons.

One day she asked Clifford, 'Will your brother be coming back?'

Clifford shrugged. 'Probably not, now Gretel's home.'

'But what about his things?'

'He'll ask us to send them on. He's done it before. He probably took a lot of stuff with him. There won't be much left here.'

'Will they – will they marry?'

Clifford shrugged again. His brother's affairs plainly did not interest him. 'There's nothing to stop them now. Years ago, before Gretel met and married her husband, Murray was in love with her. But she chose the other man.'

'Is that why he's never married?'

Clifford, anxious to get on with his work, answered briefly, 'I've never asked him. Now let me see, where were we?'

Even Flick seemed to miss Murray. At Clifford's house he would wander up the stairs and snuffle at the bottom of Murray's bedroom door as if trying to find out whether he was hiding in there.

'We're two of a kind,' Adrienne thought ruefully. 'We both love him.'

Ten days went by. Adrienne gave up all hope of his ever returning. She had been right to say good-bye. She would probably never see him again. But perhaps it was best that way. She was committed to marrying Clifford. He needed her, he loved her – even Murray had acknowledged that.

One afternoon Clifford said, 'I think it's time I invited some of my friends here for a literary evening. Since it's my turn – we hold them in rotation at our various residences – I mustn't let them down. As soon as I've recovered completely from this cold, I'll look out a list of addresses and dictate a letter for you to type. There will be at least a dozen people, perhaps more, all

71

of them writers.' He looked at her. 'I don't think I've held a literary evening since you came to work for me?'

She said no, he hadn't.

'You must come along, my dear. I'm sure you'll enjoy it. You do – er – understand that nothing must be said about my work, that my pen-name is a closely-guarded secret? Amongst such distinguished and accomplished people, it would hardly be appropriate to divulge it.'

'Of course I understand, Clifford. Like our engagement, I'll say nothing whatever about it.'

He moved to sit beside her. For the first time for days, he put his arm round her and pulled her close.

'You understand about that too, Adrienne? I'm proud of you, my dear, extremely fond of you, in fact,' he obviously could not bring himself to use the word 'love', 'but it's the publicity I'm so afraid of. Not only would my work suffer, but my health, I'm sure, would not stand it.'

She assured him soothingly that of course she understood. Hadn't they agreed that she would not wear a ring in order to avoid the publicity he so dreaded? He was so delighted by her reasonable attitude that he kissed her – on the lips. This time she kissed him back – Murray's tuition was already taking effect – but Clifford seemed a little startled by her ardour, subdued though it was. He drew away, seemed overcome, and uncertain as to how to proceed.

She flushed deeply, her heart pounding with humiliation, thinking herself in the wrong. She must not let it happen again. Physical love certainly did not seem to come into Clifford's life story. The plot was too sombre, too serious, too blameless to leave room for the pleasures of love.

It was high summer now and the trees which encircled and dominated the hut were in full leaf. Adrienne was typing and the door was open. Birds were twittering and squabbling in the branches overhead. Insects buzzed. A bee lost its way and flew round the hut bumping against the filing cabinets, rising to the shelves and vainly seeking nectar amongst the bright covers of Clifford's books. Flick snapped at it idly, but Adrienne spoke to him sharply and at last it flew out.

There was a noise outside. Alert at once, terrified that it was the staring man come back to get her, she sat rigid, immobilized by fear. Then Flick made a mad rush for the figure filling the doorway and stumbled over his own short legs in his pleasure at seeing the familiar stranger who stood there, smiling.

'*Murray!*' Joy supplanted the fear in Adrienne's eyes. 'You're back!'

'By heaven,' he said, wandering in, 'it was worth going away to receive such a welcome from my future sister-in-law, not to mention her faithful animal.'

'But you gave me such a fright! I thought it was—'

'That horror of a man come back. Don't spoil it. You wouldn't have looked at him with the delight with which you greeted me, young woman.'

She tried to explain it away. 'It's just that I didn't expect you back. Clifford said—' She stopped. If she put it into words it might come true.

'And what did Clifford say?'

'About you and Gretel.' She turned away. 'I almost expected you to be married to her by now.'

He walked round the desk so that he could see her face. 'Did you? And what would your reaction have been if I had?'

She forced herself to smile brightly. 'To wish you both every happiness.'

'Well, I'm not married – yet, so you can keep your good wishes to yourself for a bit longer. I'm still single, if not exactly heartwhole and fancy-free.'

So he was still in love with her. Perhaps she didn't return his love at present, perhaps it was too soon after her husband's death. But Adrienne was sure no woman could resist Murray for long, so his marriage to Gretel was inevitable. He might even suggest a double wedding. She shrank from the thought.

He sat in the other chair. 'We had a series of long, long talks. We discussed the past and the future. Her year in Australia seems to have done her a lot of good. She's a great deal more serene now than when she went away. And eager to start work again.'

'Like me,' she said, with a grin. She was drunk with the pleasure of seeing him again and did not care that she might be provoking him.

He looked at her keenly, saying with some surprise, 'You've

73

acquired some impudence while I've been away. It suits you. What's been happening — has my brother — er — liberated you?'

Her face clouded. 'No.' But she managed to smile again. 'I've got a number of letters to type inviting people to a literary evening which Clifford is giving.'

He put his hand to his head. 'Oh no!' he groaned. 'Why didn't I stay away a bit longer?'

She looked through the list of addresses and grinned again. 'Your name isn't here. You haven't been invited.'

He leaned towards her threateningly. 'Oh, haven't I?'

'No, but I have.'

'In that case,' he said dryly, 'I'll definitely stay away.' Before she could reply, he clicked his fingers and Flick came bounding up. 'Missed me, dog? More than your mistress has done. She's being rude to me, boy. What should I do to her? Spank her? She's asking for it!'

He looked up and their eyes met and she coloured at the expression in his. He put the dog aside and rose, stretching lazily. 'Long journey that, by car. When is this accursed literary party?'

'Next weekend.'

'I've a feeling,' he remarked, walking to the door, 'I'm going to be otherwise engaged that evening.' He went out.

The night before Clifford's 'literary gathering', as he was disposed to call it, Adrienne told her mother about it. 'I'll be home later than usual, so don't wait up for me. It may go on for quite a while.'

'But, darling. I shall be alone the whole evening. You'll have to leave before the end.' She tried another approach. 'Must you go? You're only Mr. Denning's secretary. He's probably only asking out of courtesy.'

She could not put her mother right on that subject. Once Lorna knew about the engagement, it would go all round the village. But she was relieved her mother had accepted her attendance at the party so tranquilly, having anticipated an argument and even tears. But she should have known her mother better.

When Adrienne arrived home from work the following evening, it became clear that her mother was not as reconciled as she

74

had thought to her evening's absence. She had obviously been brooding about it all day and had decided to be awkward in the way that only Lorna could be.

She greeted her daughter, 'Why can't I go with you? I never go out anywhere.' She invoked the wheedling tone that Adrienne hated. 'Just pop back, dear, and ask that nice Mr. Denning – I'm sure he must be nice, though I've never met him – if you can bring me. It would be absolutely wonderful to meet so many charming and intelligent people.'

Adrienne felt her muscles contract. How could she ask such a favour of Clifford? He was, after all, still her employer. 'No, Mother, it can't be done. It would be taking advantage of his good nature.'

But would it? she wondered. Her mother was his future mother-in-law. He had to meet her some time. Lorna detected her daughter's vacillation, and deciding it was her own mixture of persuasiveness and whining which was once again yielding results, she put on the pressure.

'I shall be alone, darling, and I don't like being alone so late at night, especially with that nasty man still around the village. If only the police would catch him. Why, darling, when you come home, you never know what you may find. *Anything* could have happened to me!'

'Her imagination,' Adrienne thought wryly, 'is at times almost the equal of Clifford's!'

But it was not her mother's persuasiveness which decided her in the end. It was the thought that it would offer an excellent opportunity for them both to become acquainted. It would be a casual meeting with no particular meaning attached to it. Surely Clifford would not object?

'Just pop over, darling,' her mother urged again, 'and ask your nice Mr. Denning.'

'All right, I will.'

Lorna sat down, stupefied by her daughter's sudden tractibility, and congratulated herself on her expert handling of her offspring.

Flick tried to follow as Adrienne dashed out of the door, and barked indignantly when she shut him in. She couldn't risk putting Clifford in a bad mood by taking her dog.

Murray met her on the doorstep. 'What's wrong?'

'It's my mother.'

75

Immediately came the question, 'Is she ill?'

'Good heavens, no. She just wants to be invited to the party.'

He laughed loudly. 'You must hand it to her. Not many people would have the nerve to invite themselves to a gathering of such distinguished, conceited and self-opinionated pseudo-intellectuals.'

She asked uncertainly, 'Do you think Clifford will object? He's never met her.'

'Then it's high time he did.'

'She doesn't know I'm engaged to him.'

'Then likewise it's high time she was told. I simply cannot understand his desire to keep it a secret.'

'Murray,' her hand rested on his arm, 'you won't tell my mother, will you?'

He turned away. 'What exactly do you take me for?' Apparently she had genuinely hurt him.

She said she was sorry and went to find Clifford. He was a little dubious on hearing her request, but he made no objection. He seemed, if anything, more scared than affronted. Adrienne told herself he should have been delighted at the opportunity of meeting her mother, then chided herself for her disloyalty to her fiancé.

So she was able to carry the glad news to her mother that Mr. Denning said she could go to the party. Lorna was as delighted as a small girl. Adrienne felt a stab of pity. It was true that her mother rarely went out. She lived a dull, lonely life and if it weren't for the interminable coffee mornings and occasional trips to town by bus, she would hardly go out at all.

'Will that charming young man called Murray be there?' Lorna wanted to know.

Adrienne told her he might be. 'By the way, Mother, he's a university professor. He's a Ph.D. His name is really Dr. Murray Denning.'

Lorna glowed. 'Oh, if I'd know that when he came . . .' She didn't say what difference it would have made to her behaviour towards him if she had. 'Dr. Murray Denning.' She practised the name like a child enjoying an ice cream.

Lorna dressed elaborately and made up her youthful-looking face with meticulous care. She looked even younger than usual, and a feeling of latent pride welled up in Adrienne. Her mother really was remarkably good-looking for her age.

Adrienne wore a dress she had bought when she had first become engaged to Clifford, thinking that he might suggest an engagement party. But the dress had hung, unworn, in the wardrobe ever since. As it seemed there was to be no engagement party, she thought she might as well wear it now. It was pale blue and sleeveless and cunningly cut so as to reveal the attractions of her figure. She fluffed out her fair hair and fixed blue star-shaped earrings to her ears. She clipped a matching bracelet round her wrist.

Mrs. Masters opened the door. Flick rushed past and dived up the stairs, making for Murray's room. While Mrs. Masters took her mother's coat, Adrienne raced up after him. Flick was sniffing and yapping at Murray's door and she bent down to tug him away by the collar when the door opened. Murray's jacket was off and he was adjusting his tie.

Adrienne straightened, her face flushed, and apologized for the behaviour of her dog, who had now made his way between Murray's legs into the room. Murray's eyes appraised her in detail and he smiled mockingly.

'If Flick's owner showed the affection for me that her dog does, I should be flattered beyond words, especially when she looks as attractive as she does now. She should make a highly decorative sister-in-law, and a pleasing addition to the Denning family.'

'Will you be quiet!' Adrienne muttered, her eyes flashing a warning. She pointed downstairs. 'My mother.'

'Oh. Sorry.' He shrugged into his jacket. 'Nearly ready.'

Adrienne's eyes opened wide. 'Are you coming? I thought you were going to be otherwise engaged.'

'Changed my mind.' He ran a comb through his thick dark hair and said to Flick, 'Out, dog.' Flick ran down the stairs and Mrs. Masters shooed him into the kitchen.

Lorna was waiting uncertainly in the hall. Murray followed Adrienne down the stairs and held out his hand to Lorna. 'Nice to see you,' he said as if he meant it.

Lorna responded at once. 'Good evening, Professor Denning.' She rolled the words round her tongue. 'Dr. Murray Denning.'

Murray's eyebrows lifted.

'Adrienne told me,' Lorna explained, and Murray laughed.

'Oh, I see, just practising. Your formality really had me worried for a moment.'

'I've been wondering,' Lorna commented, eyeing her daughter askance, 'when I would be seeing Adrienne's nice young man again.'

Adrienne coloured furiously. 'He's not my young man, Mother. You don't understand. He's—'

'You see, Lorna,' Murray said, with a sly look at Adrienne, 'she's disowning me already. She doesn't love me any more.'

'Oh, but she does.' Now Lorna looked anxiously at her daughter. 'She couldn't help but love you. You're so nice!'

Murray threw back his head and laughed. Adrienne scowled at him – he really was enjoying the joke, and the more she frowned the more he laughed.

Clifford appeared at the lounge door, uncertain, self-effacing. But his eyes fixed on to his future mother-in-law as a baby's hand fastens on to an adult's finger. To have said he was astonished, Adrienne thought, would be an understatement. He appeared to be suffering acutely from shock.

It was Murray who performed the introduction and it was obvious that Lorna was as charmed with the older brother as she was with the younger.

'So nice to meet you at last, Mr. Denning. My daughter has told me so much about you—'

Clifford's eyes met Adrienne's in an anxious question. She gave an almost imperceptible 'no' with a shake of the head. He relaxed, plainly relieved that his future mother-in-law had not yet been informed of the part she was destined to play in the story of his life.

It was not really a party, Clifford was at pains to point out as he escorted Lorna into the lounge. It was going to be a literary evening, a 'gathering' of enlightened, artistic minds. Murray smiled sardonically at Adrienne as he walked by her side into the room. A number of the guests lived locally, Clifford explained, while others had come from some miles distant.

Introductions were made – Adrienne noticed that Clifford referred to her as his secretary. She also noticed that some of the faces she smiled at smiled back at her with their noses slightly uplifted, condescending and patronizing to one of such inferior intellect. How would they react, she wondered, if she were to tell them that she was engaged to their host?

Her mother, by her practised charm and her own slightly condescending manner, established herself at once as one of the assembled company. She sat herself at her host's side and cleverly wormed her way into the conversation he was having with another man. Adrienne wondered at her mother's ability to adapt herself so well to such company, to appear to be able to talk their language when she led such a sheltered, vacuous life at home.

She herself possessed no such self-assurance and adaptability and stood uncertainly looking round, trying to decide where to sit. No one took the slightest notice of her.

Murray's arm stretched out and pulled her down on to the couch. 'Stop looking like a frightened rabbit,' he whispered. 'They're no better than you are, sweetie. They only think they are.'

She turned grateful eyes towards him and when he smiled into hers her heart lurched as though it had been caught in a trip wire. He elaborated on his theme, which saved her the trouble of having to recover her balance and find something intelligent to say in reply.

'You'll have to do better than this when you're married to Clifford. You'll need much more self-confidence, otherwise this lot,' his hand indicated with derision the assembled company, 'will trample on you, literally, if they could get away with it. Have you noticed,' his arm went round her waist and Clifford's eyes settled on his brother reprovingly, but the arm stayed where it was, 'how they gather together in tight little circles? You could almost label them. Some are what is termed euphemistically "unpublished writers" – the ever-hopefuls. Others are freelance – they sell their stuff to whoever is willing to pay for it. After that there are degrees of success and you come to the ones at the top – those taken there partly by ability but largely by luck.'

'Where,' she whispered in Murray's ear, feeling her fiancée's eyes upon her now, 'does Clifford come in the hierarchy?'

He laughed. 'Well, speaking purely as a brother and not as a literary critic, if you judge by ability, near the bottom, but if you go by success, at the top. You take your choice.'

The door was flung open and every male eye brightened. The girl who entered was young in years but in experience probably twice her age. In looks she was entrancing; her trouser suit, embroidered with silver thread, clung to her figure drawing attention in the minutest detail to its desirability.

'Clifford darling!' Hands outstretched, she advanced on him. He turned his cheek and tolerated the kiss she gave him. 'Delightful to see you again.' She flung her eyes round the room like a cowboy lassoing a stallion. By now all the men were standing. She considered them. The noose hovered. 'Where's this marvellous brother of yours you've told us about?'

Relieved to rid himself of the limelight, Clifford motioned the girl towards Murray who, by now, was looking with appreciative yet slightly sardonic eyes at the girl who was advancing towards him.

The noose fell and tightened. Murray was caught. He moved to take her outstretched hand. Someone promptly took his place beside Adrienne, but even if he hadn't Murray would not have returned. The newcomer, who was still holding his hand, saw to that.

'How wonderful to meet you, Mr. Denning.' Even she did not appear to be aware of his proper title, which oddly enough semed to be something of a secret.

He bowed mockingly. 'And I,' he said, 'would have missed the experience of a lifetime if I had not met you.'

She laughed charmingly, taking him seriously. He sat in an armchair and his attention seemed entirely taken up with the girl who by now had drawn up a stool at his feet.

She gazed up into his face. 'You know,' she was saying, loudly enough for Adrienne to hear, despite the buzz of conversation which was rising to the level it had reached before the girl made her appearance, 'I'm not one of these clever writers. I'm an artist.'

Your name?' Murray asked, eyebrows raised.

'Désirée, Désirée Charters. And yours is Murray. Clifford has told us. May I call you that?'

'Why not?' was the amused answer.

'And do you write?' the girl asked, her long-lashed eyes searching his.

'Only letters,' he answered, and her laugh rang out.

'Then what is your job?' she persisted. 'Are you terribly clever?'

'I do my best,' he answered with mock-modesty. 'I'm in research.' He added as an afterthought, 'Dietetic research.' He looked as if he was thinking, 'That will fool her', and apparently it did. It silenced her for the moment, but she spoke to him with her eyes instead of her lips which were pouting a little as her chin rested on her hand.

Rigid with jealousy, Adrienne turned away, only to encounter a man's face a few inches from hers. 'Hallo,' the mouth said. 'I'm Augustus Charles. Who are you?'

She drew back a little, but immediately wished she hadn't. The man's face was even less attractive at a distance than in close-up. His eyes were puffed, his cheeks appeared to have a day's growth of beard on them, his hair was grey and too long for his years. She inched along the couch away from him, but he edged towards her again. She looked appealingly at Clifford, who seemed for some reason to be frowning at her instead of the man who was pursuing her. But he clearly had no intention of helping.

She turned back to Augustus Charles. 'I'm Adrienne Garron.'

'And do you write?'

'No,' she answered simply, 'I type.'

He shook with laughter at what he took to be a joke. 'No, seriously,' he persisted, 'what stuff do you turn out?'

'I type,' she repeated, 'Mr. Denning's books. I'm his secretary.'

She thought the man's interest would diminish, but it appeared to increase. 'Now that is a breed I love,' he commented with a leer, 'the secretary bird. They have such possibilities.' He leaned nearer.

Adrienne retreated. She turned appealing eyes to Murray. He was looking at her but, like his brother, had no intention of coming to her rescue. He seemed actually to be enjoying himself watching her futile attempts to escape from the man at her side.

Someone brought in drinks. The man called Augustus seized two from the tray which was thrust under his nose. One he gave to Adrienne, the other he drank himself, in one gulp. Before the tray had moved on, his hand had fastened on to another.

Murray's new admirer was sticking to him like syrup to a spoon. She took two drinks, one for each hand. She said something to Murray and he laughed. Sick with envy at the girl's technique – why couldn't *she* make Murray respond like that? –

Adrienne reconciled herself to having to tolerate her companion a little longer. The tray came past again and Augustus stretched out and captured another drink, which disappeared down his throat as rapidly as the others. It was beginning to have a marked effect on his behaviour.

His smile turned into a lopside lecherous grin. 'There's only one thing to do with a secretary bird,' he said in a voice loud enough for the entire company to hear, 'and that's this.' He swivelled his head round, reconnoitred her profile and placed a strategic kiss on her cheek. Then he raised his hand to turn her head and kiss the other cheek. This time she was ready for him, but as she jerked her head sideways, his hand knocked against her glass and the liquid in it ran in a golden-brown stream down her dress. The material sucked it up greedily and she felt it soaking through to her skin.

Augustus mumbled his apologies. Clifford said, in scolding tones 'Adrienne!' as though it had been her fault.

'Oh, darling!' came from her mother.

Murray tried to rise to help her, but his new-found lady-friend put out a hand to prevent his doing so.

Adrienne, scarlet with humiliation and anger, ran out to the kitchen followed by commiserating laughter from the assembled company.

Mrs. Masters said, 'Oh, poor Miss Garron,' and seized a cloth, soaked it in water and sponged the dress with a sympathetic hand. After a while most of the stain, having been treated quickly, had gone, leaving behind a damp patch.

Flick fussed round her for a few minutes, then flopped down and went back to sleep.

'That should be all right now, dear,' Mrs. Masters said. 'It'll dry with the warmth in the air.'

Adrienne thanked her and opened the kitchen door to find Murray on the other side of it.

'Can I help?' he asked.

'You're too late,' she snapped, disregarding the rather pained expression on his face.

'All I did was offer—' he began, but she cut in acidly,

'How could you bear to leave your lady-friend? How could you tear yourself away?' She knew her feelings were showing and that he would not miss the fact.

'Don't pour out your ire on me, young woman,' he retaliated.

'I had nothing to do with it. If you will make a spectacle of yourself and allow a licentious male famed for his debauchery to make love to you . . .'

She knew she had asked for his censure, but it brought her to the edge of tears. It was one thing to have to tolerate the humiliation which followed the accident. It was quite another to have insults flung at her by her fiancé's brother whose own behaviour could not escape criticism.

'It was no such thing, and you know it! Anyhow, you can talk! What about that girl who's fastened her claws into you like a bird of prey? You're not exactly discouraging her . . .'

'But, my sweet,' his fingers imprisoned her chin and his hard eyes bore into her moist ones, 'I'm not an engaged man. I can encourage women as much as I like. With or without your approval.' He released her chin and she rubbed it. 'Of course I'm encouraging her. I'm only human. She won't let me go, she's one big green light. And I love women who know what they want – and go all out to get it.' The anger in his eyes frightened her. He continued, his tone suggestive, 'I'm slowly getting her drunk. And why? Because she told me that she's more willing in that condition, it breaks down her inhibitions. And who am I to close my ears to the promise contained in those words?'

He was hurting her now, and he knew it because she could not hide her anguish. He went on harshly, 'Later, I shall take her home, in my car.' With almost clinical detachment he watched her reaction, saw her eyes fill, her lip tremble. 'Why, I do believe you're jealous. Well, I always did enjoy handing out consolation prizes, especially to pretty girls. Perhaps this will keep you happy.' He tipped back her head and kissed her.

The lounge door opened and she pushed Murray away, but she could not escape Clifford's reproachful eyes. 'Adrienne!' His tone admonished her.

'It's all right, brother,' Murray drawled, 'don't blame her, I'm the one doing the kissing. I'm only following the example of your much-respected associates whose morals aren't exactly of the highest order. Male or female, it makes no difference, they're all the same. If I were you, I should let the assembled guests know that this girl is yours. Announce your engagement. That should keep the males at bay, even me. But until then . . .' He pulled Adrienne towards him and kissed her again. His brother looked on, limp and flaccid, a few feet away. Then, still unprotesting, he turned and went back into the lounge.

'My God!' muttered Murray, pushing her from him, 'you see what you're marrying. He's only half a man. He should have punched me – his own brother – on the nose for that. Instead he just stood there and let me do it!'

He strode up the stairs and slammed his bedroom door. Adrienne sought the peace of the dining-room to compose herself. When she felt calm enough to return to the lounge, Clifford had resumed his seat beside her mother again, as if nothing had happened. Augustus was in the chair Murray had vacated. Désirée was still on the stool, but her eyes were not gazing with dog-like devotion at him. They were searching the room for the man who had temporarily escaped her clutches.

Mrs. Masters wheeled in the food and Adrienne helped her distribute it. Clifford, aided and abetted by Lorna, piled his plate high with savouries. Most of the other guests helped themselves, but Adrienne could not eat a mouthful. She wondered if Murray would come back.

A young man sauntered across the room and offered her one of his cheese straws. She took it, thanking him. He asked her name and told her his was Martin Stevens.

'Are you a novelist?' she asked, making polite conversation.

'No. I write terribly intellectual articles for exclusive literary magazines. I also review books – only the best, of course! Those which are beyond the understanding of ordinary folk, like Augustus's over there,' he pointed with a cheese straw, 'which are so unfathomable even the critics can't work them out, but we pretend we can because we don't want to be made to look fools!'

She laughed and his interest in her became more personal. 'I haven't seen you at our gatherings before. What's your particular line?'

'Charming men, obviously,' said a dry voice beside them.

'Go away, there's a good fellow,' Martin said good-humouredly to Murray. 'I was working round to the point when I could ask her for a date.'

Murray's arm came round her shoulders. 'Sorry, old chap, you're trespassing. This girl's private property.'

Martin gazed from one to the other, then looked pointedly at

Adrienne's left hand.

'No,' said Murray, pulling her closer, 'I know there's no material evidence of it yet, but that will be remedied.'

To drive home his point, he kissed her on the forehead. Martin shrugged and left them. Murray dropped his arm and wandered back to sit in the chair now left empty by Augustus. Désirée, still on the footstool, looked like a contented tigress which had just been fed. She stretched out a hand, her fingers scarlet-tipped, and rested it on Murray's knee. He smiled down at her and Adrienne could have sworn she purred.

She was standing alone again in the centre of the room, but this time Murray was too preoccupied to come to her rescue. Afraid that Augustus would pounce if she did not find sanctuary, she went across to her mother, who made room for her on the couch. Clifford, on Lorna's other side, still looked at her with reproach. She felt conscience-stricken, as though she had really wronged him. On impulse she walked round to his other side. Affectionately she put her hand on his shoulder and urged him along the couch, forcing her mother to move also, and sat down beside him.

Clifford smiled and his smile held forgiveness. He was still eating and Adrienne noticed that her mother was replenishing his plate whenever it threatened to become empty.

Murray levered himself out of his chair while Désirée's attention was elsewhere, and walked across to sit on the arm of the couch. He bent down and whispered in Adrienne's ear,

'If you want your husband-to-be to avoid contracting genuine instead of imaginary heart trouble, you won't do what your mother is doing to him – overfeed him. He's putting on weight as it is. You may not have noticed it, but as I haven't seen him for some time before this visit, I find his increase in weight noticeable. Take warning, after you're married satisfy his appetite in other ways.' With this parting shot he left her and returned to Désirée.

When it was time to go, Murray escorted Désirée to the door, turned, raised a nonchalant hand to Adrienne, called 'good night' to her mother, and went out. Adrienne heard his car revving up outside and her mind crept out after it into the darkness. He had kept his promise – he was taking Désirée home.

While Lorna found her coat, Clifford caught Adrienne in the hall.

'Tomorrow we shall buy the ring, my dear.' The inevitable question followed the unusually positive statement. 'Shall we?'

'But, Clifford, are you sure—?'

'Of course I'm sure. I'll do as Murray suggested. I'll give you a ring.'

So Murray's kiss had had the effect he desired – it had forced Clifford's hand. He was going to commit himself quickly to the engagement at last.

Clifford kissed her. He put his arms round her as he had seen Murray do earlier that evening, but unlike his brother's his lips were gentle and undemanding. Murray was right, Adrienne thought as Clifford let her go, he needed someone to help him. If only she knew more . . .

She walked home with her mother, Flick bounding ahead.

'Lovely party, Adri-enne,' Lorna said affectedly, the aura of privilege still clinging to her at having been allowed to share the evening with such distinguished people. 'Do you know, daring, that lovely man Augustus Charles has agreed to open our fête? Such a famous writer, too. He asked me if there was a licensed hotel near the grounds because he didn't fancy doing a thing like opening a fête 'dry'. I don't really know what he meant.'

'He meant, Mother,' Adrienne smiled at her mother's ingenuousness, 'that he wanted a few drinks inside him to warm him up first.'

Lorna laughed gaily and changed the subject. 'Darling, how could you let that nasty young woman Désirée take your young man away from you like that?'

They had reached home now and Adrienne opened the front door and let her mother and Flick into the house. She frowned, feeling suddenly chilled. 'What young man?'

'You know very well, dear. Murray,' she couldn't resist adding, 'Dr. Murray Denning.'

'But, Mother, you don't understand, *he's* not my young man.' She placed undue emphasis on the most important word and her mother caught the inflection. They were standing beneath the hall light. A moth had come in with them and was fluttering round it above their heads. It dived low and Flick snapped at it.

'Then, darling,' her mother asked, bewildered, 'who is?'

86

'Come into the sitting-room, Mother,' Adrienne said wearily. 'I hadn't meant to tell you. Clifford wanted to keep it quiet, but—'

'*Clifford*? *He's* your young man? But how can he be? He's your employer!' Her voice rose to an impossibly high note.

'I'm engaged to him, Mother. A few weeks ago he asked me to marry him and I agreed. He just didn't want anyone to know yet.'

'But, darling,' her mother said weakly, 'he's only a little younger than I am.'

Adrienne nodded. 'Three years. He's forty-three.'

Lorna was speechless. 'But,' she got out, 'Murray. What about Murray?'

'He,' her daughter answered heavily, 'is going to be my brother-in-law.'

There was a long, uncomprehending silence then Lorna murmured, 'Clifford, my son-in-law!' She shook her head.

'Mother,' Adrienne was near to tears now, 'you should really be congratulating me, shouldn't you?'

'Darling, I'm so sorry. Of course I'm happy for you. I just can't get used to the idea of your getting married.' Then, plaintively, 'What will happen to me?'

Adrienne answered, pushing her own problems to the back of her mind, 'I'll be near you, Mother. I'll see you every day.'

But Lorna was staring blankly at the opposite wall. 'I'll be alone, quite alone. I never thought you'd marry. I never thought you'd ever leave me.'

Adrienne put her hand to her head. This was a reaction she had not bargained for. She said, as though her mother was ill, 'You're tired, Mother. You'll feel better about it in the morning.'

But, she thought, as she saw her mother up to bed, will I?

CHAPTER SEVEN

BY morning Adrienne's doubts had resolved themselves into a positive plan. She would choose her moment and ask Clifford if, after they were married, he would consent to her mother going to live with them. He need not see much of her. There were a number of spare rooms in his house, so her mother would be able to have a bed-sitting room of her own.

But for the moment and for two good reasons, she would keep her plan to herself. First, the engagement had not been officially announced. And second, although it would undoubtedly solve the problem of her mother's future, the thought of having her with them for the greater part of their married life somehow depressed her. The more she thought about it, the more she felt incarcerated, like a potholer hopelessly trapped by a fall of rock blocking the way to the surface. Nevertheless, she had to face it, it was the only answer.

Clifford took her to the most expensive jewellers in town to buy the ring. The setting was a cluster of diamonds fashioned into a scintillating star. It cost a great deal of money.

They were sitting on the couch when he slipped it on her finger. He put his arms round her awkwardly and kissed her, his lips compressed and innocuous.

He said, entreating her to understand, 'Adrienne, you probably realize that I find it impossible to put my feelings for you into words. I'm made in such a way that I can't even put them into actions. But—' he took a breath and battled against his incoherence, 'I'm very fond of you, Adrienne. I need you, my dear, more than I can say. I appreciate all you've done for me and the pleasure you've already brought me. even before we're married.' He finished, hesitant now, having expressed himself more emotionally and more fluently than she had ever thought possible, 'I look forward every morning to your arrival.' He stopped, took a breath and brought his speech to an end. 'Just having you here is enough to bring me happiness.'

She was moved beyond words. She leaned forward and kissed him. He did not kiss her back but smiled in response. She asked trying to lighten the atmosphere, 'Shall we drink to our engagement?'

He nodded and went to the sideboard. Murray came in, looked from one to the other, sensing strain. Adrienne showed him her left hand, her smile challenging, her eyes as hard and bright as the diamonds on her finger.

Murray looked at the ring, then at her. His eyes were unfathomable. 'So my brother has committed himself at last! That little object must have cost him a small fortune.'

'We're – we're drinking to it.' Her voice wavered. She could not understand his tone or his expression. It was, after all, something he had been urging his brother to do for a long time. 'Will you join us, Murray?'

He answered coldly, 'Count me out. It's not my engagement.' He left, snapping the door shut.

Lorna, when she saw the ring, gave a little shriek. 'It's perfect darling. Let me try it on. I wonder if it fits.' It was a little large on her slim finger. 'I absolutely envy you, darling, having a ring like that. What a perfect setting, and what a lot of money it must have cost!'

The possession of an engagement ring made no difference to Adrienne's relationship with Clifford. Life went on as before. She worked for him, went home at the usual times, returned occasionally to spend an evening with him. Murray's manner towards her was more distant, more restrained. He joked with her less, but his affection for Flick seemed, if anything, to increase.

While Adrienne was working, he took the dog for long walks. She would watch them go, longing to accompany them, wanting to return to the old easy relationship with Murray. All that seemed to have gone now and she wished she knew why. Ever since Clifford had given her that ring . . . Sitting in the hut, she stared at the cluster of diamonds and as her eyes filled with tears, the stones sparkled and almost blinded her. If the ring formed such a barrier between her and Murray, she didn't want it.

Then she pulled herself up. Murray was going to be her brother-in-law. He loved Gretel. She, Adrienne, had Clifford, who needed her. He had said so, and that was something she must never forget.

The day of the fête dawned windy and sunless, but as the time moved on towards the opening, the clouds dispersed and the sun shone. During the morning Adrienne typed for a while, finishing some work left over from the previous evening. She called in to see Clifford before she left for home and Murray was with him.

'Clifford,' Murray said in decisive tones, 'I'm borrowing your fiancée this afternoon. I'm going to the village fête and I want company. Any objections?'

'But I—' Adrienne began.

Murray cut in, 'You were intending to go, weren't you?' She nodded. 'Right. Then you can come with me.'

She looked at her fiancé. 'Do you mind, Clifford?'

He frowned, wanting to refuse but not daring to do so. Murray knew it. 'Don't worry,' he said, 'I have no intention of eloping with her. Or of violating her chastity.'

Clifford blushed. 'I don't mind,' he said uncomfortably.

'I knew you wouldn't,' Murray said blandly. He looked at Adrienne. 'We want to be there for the opening. I wouldn't miss Augustus Charles's performance for the world. I'll call for you, two-thirty prompt. Is your mother going?'

'Yes, but she's helping, so she'll be leaving early.'

'Shall we walk, or go by car?'

'I'd prefer to walk. It's not far down to the village.'

'Then walk we will. Flick, at least, will be delighted.'

Flick was. He bounded ahead along the narrow road which wound its way down to the village.

Adrienne said, staring at a blackbird which was standing on the grass verge preparing to take flight as Flick approached,

'So you took Désirée home after Clifford's party.'

'Yes.' He looked down at her with a half-smile as if waiting for the next question.

'Did you—?'

Flick approached the blackbird cautiously.

'Yes, I did.' After an agonizing pause he added with a wicked grin, 'Kiss her good night.' He waited again and went on, 'She's an expert at kissing – unlike you. Her lips held an irresistible invitation.'

Adrienne responded, her lips tight, 'Oh.'

The blackbird flew away with a agitated swish of its wings.

Murray caught her hand. 'Just what are you thinking? That I was unable to resist her charms? Well, you're wrong. I'm more fastidious than you appear to think in my choice of women.

90

Satisfied now?' She nodded, smiling with relief. 'I needn't have told you at all, need I? I could have kept you guessing. After all, it was no business of yours. You're only going to be my sister-in-law, not my wife.'

She blurted out, 'Clifford told me you were once in love with Gretel.'

'I was, once.' He did not go on and she didn't dare to probe any further.

The taped music, amplified by loudspeakers, told them they were approaching the fête. Murray called to Flick and put him on the lead.

Adrienne spotted her mother at the cakes stall and pulled Murray after her. Lorna saw them and waved. Murray surveyed the produce on display. 'Makes my mouth water,' he said. 'Which of these tantalizing exhibits do you recommend?'

Lorna pointed to a cream gâteau. 'Definitely that one, Murray.'

He asked he price and handed over the money. She wrapped it carefully and he took it, then with a bow handed it back. 'For you, a gift to my brother's future mother-in-law.'

Lorna's eyes shone. 'You really mean it? But it was so expensive.' Murray waved away her thanks.

He looked round. 'Where's Augustus Charles? Ah, there he is.'

Augustus was walking, a little unsteadily, up the steps of the rostrum from which he was going to make his speech of welcome. His face was flushed, his eyes slightly glazed. He had obviously found a suitable hotel to patronize and he had certainly slaked his thirst.

He was introduced as 'a famous novelist of high repute' which overstated the case somewhat, but was rapturously received by the crowd. The words he mumbled to open the proceedings were, because of his semi-fuddled state, almost as incomprehensible as the books he wrote, but everyone was in the mood to be pleased, and pleased they were. He made them laugh, he made them sad, he made them thoughtful, then he wound up his speech with a joke at which they all laughed again. Then it was over. He was helped down the steps to mingle with the crowd, who immediately turned their backs and forgot all about him in their rush to buy whatever took their fancy before anyone else could lay their hands on it.

'Not the catastrophe I thought it might be,' Murray said.

'You sound disappointed,' Adrienne laughed.

'I am. I was looking forward to going back and telling my brother how one of his revered literary associates had made a complete fool of himself in front of hundreds of people.'

She snatched her hand away. 'You're cruel!'

'Yes, I am sometimes,' he agreed smoothly. 'So be warned.'

'I'd like my dog back,' she snapped, and tugged the lead from his hand. Then she bent down and picked Flick up, holding him in her arms and rubbing her cheek against his coat. She saw her mother, who having abandoned the cake stall to someone else, was also holding something in her arms.

Adrienne made her way through the crowd towards her and Murray followed. She found that her mother was nursing a baby. 'It's Joan Smithers' granddaughter,' Lorna said. 'Isn't she a pet? Six weeks old.' The two women cooed over the tiny figure, while Murray looked on.

Adrienne pushed Flick into Murray's arms, then held out her own. 'May I, Mother?'

'What, hold her, darling? Of course you may. Joan's daughter won't mind. In fact, I'm glad to hand over the little mite for a few minutes. I must see how the cake stall's going. I left young Blanche in charge.'

Reverently Adrienne took the sleeping bundle and gazed rapturously at the minute features. 'You're left holding the baby,' Murray commented dryly, 'while I'm left holding the dog.' He lowered Flick to the ground.

Adrienne showed the baby to him, pushing aside the shawl to reveal the baby's face. She gazed up at him, urging him to agree with her. 'Isn't she lovely, Murray?'

He didn't reply, but his lack of response did nothing to dilute her rapture. 'I wonder who she's like,' she murmured, 'her mother or her father?'

She glanced up at Murray again and caught the compassion in his face. There was pity there, too, and a kind of despair. 'What's the matter?' she asked, puzzled.

'My dear,' he said gently, 'if you love babies all that much . . .'

'Clifford will change his mind,' she said, her voice quivering.

'He *must*. I *know* he will.' She put her lips to the baby's forehead, and it was almost an act of defiance.

'Isn't it time,' Murray asked, his voice edged, 'you gave that child back to its mother?'

She sighed. 'I suppose so.' She searched the faces in the crowd and shielding the baby with her own body from the jostling and the pushing, made her way to the grandmother's side. 'One beautiful granddaughter safely returned, Mrs. Smithers.'

Joan Smithers laughed. 'Isn't she a love?' She caught the dazzle of diamonds on Adrienne's finger and glanced up at Murray, who was standing behind her. 'It won't be long, will it, Adrienne, before you've got one of your own?'

Adrienne coloured slightly. So Joan Smithers had assumed Murray was her fiancé. 'I don't know. I hope not,' she answered as they walked away.

Adrienne lingered at the jewellery stall, picking up a cameo pendant and holding it against her. 'Do you like it?' she asked Murray.

He considered the effect. 'Er – yes. It suits the personality of the girl holding it. Do you want it?' His hand went to his pocket.

She put it down immediately. 'It doesn't matter.' She turned away.

He picked it up, paid for it and gave it to her. 'It's yours.' He smiled. 'Afraid I can't present you with a baby, but I can at least give you this. Let me help you.' He slipped it over her head and adjusted it round her neck.

She thanked him and her hand covered the pendant as though it was the most precious thing in the world. 'I shall cherish it for ever.'

He saw the sincerity in her eyes and said seriously, 'I do believe you mean it.'

Augustus, who was mingling aimlessly with the crowd, spotted Adrienne and lurched up to her. He did not see Murray. He put his arm round her shoulders and greeted her with a knowing grin.

'Well, if it isn't the little secretary bird!' His lips found her cheek and she drew back as if he had savaged her.

'Hands off!' growled Murray.

Augustus started and a guilty smile spread across his face

like black coffee spilt over a clean table cloth. 'Sir Galahad himself,' he said, his voice thick. He lifted Adrienne's left hand. 'So he's made an honest woman of you at last. Con-con-gratulations, friend.' He raised a shaky hand. 'Sorry to intrude.' He lurched away.

'It's time we were going.' Murray sounded irritable. 'Where's your mother?'

They found her supervising the cake stall and told her they were leaving. She thanked Murray again for the cake, admired Adrienne's pendant and waved as they went on their way. Flick, off the lead at last, raced ahead.

Adrienne left Murray at the end of the lane. He thanked her for her company, said he would see her some time and walked away. As she watched him go she flagged. She looked at the ring on her finger, then at the pendant round her neck. She knew which of the two was the most precious to her.

Monday morning did not begin as well as it should have done. Lorna woke with one of her headaches and moaned all through breakfast. Flick was snappy and seemed to have caught the mood of the household. Adrienne herself felt a bit off colour, although she was convinced there was nothing physically wrong with her. She knew the cause of her 'ailment'. She also knew there was no cure for unreturned love.

When she arrived at Clifford's house, Murray was on the phone. As she passed him in the hall, he raised a hand to her, clicked his fingers at the dog and went on talking as though they did not exist.

He seemed to be discussing a report he was preparing. 'Look, Gretel, I'll have to see you some time. Is it possible for you to come and stay here for a few days? Clifford has some empty rooms. We could make up a bed for you. You could? That's fine. I'll look forward to it. I'll contact you again and we'll make definite arrangements.'

He was still talking when Adrienne went upstairs after leaving Flick in the kitchen. Clifford greeted her with a kiss – the touch of his lips on hers had become a ritual now – and told her he had a pile of notes for her to type.

'I've sat up half the night writing,' he said.

She wondered whether he would continue to do that after they were married. But if Murray was right and she and

94

Clifford had separate rooms, it wouldn't matter, would it?

She took the notes to the hut and got down to work. Flick curled up near the door. Mid-morning, Murray brought her coffee, and his own, too. He sat down as if prepared to stay for a while.

'I've got work to do,' she said pointedly.

'Are you telling me politely to get out?'

She nodded, smiling. 'I could always set the dog on you.'

He spoke to Flick and there was a touch of acid in his tone. 'Her wits this morning are as sharp as a scalpel. Watch out, boy, she's in a vicious mood. I can sense it.' Flick wagged his tail and nuzzled Murray's hand affectionately. 'But I've got a lot to say to her she won't like.'

She took a large mouthful of coffee and gulped it down. So she was in for another lecture, was she? That explained his presence. He hadn't come for the pleasure of seeing her. She laughed at herself for thinking that he had.

He drained his cup and replaced it with a clatter on the saucer. 'You know that once you're married, you'll have to give up Flick.'

She felt herself contracting physically, as if waiting for a raised hand to hit her. 'What do you mean?'

'Clifford won't have him in the house. You'll have to leave him with your mother, for good.'

'I can't do that!' She was outraged. 'I can't possibly part with him. Anyway, my mother would be hopeless with him. She hates dogs.'

He tossed back his head in disgust. 'That makes two of them. In that case, you'll either have to give him away – or have him destroyed.'

She felt sick. 'You delight in being brutal. You take sadistic pleasure in hurting people, especially me!'

'My dear Adrienne, I resent your accusations. I'm being neither brutal nor sadistic. I am speaking the truth.' The last phrase came slowly and clearly. 'And if what I'm saying is hurting you, then it's time you faced facts. I repeat, you'll have to give up the dog.'

There was a long silence. He watched her, his eyes narrow. 'You'll lose a lot of your illusions after you're married, Adrienne.'

She blurted out, 'Why are you talking to me like this?'

'Because, my dear, when I saw you with that baby on Saturday, I realized exactly to what frightening extent you were deluding yourself.' He softened his voice. 'How can I bring it home to you that Clifford won't have children?'

'Marriage will change him.'

'Why should he change? What particular powers do you possess that will make him alter his ways? He's no callow youth. He's reached the age of forty-three and for as long as I can remember, he's been what he is now. His life will be undisturbed by the acquisition of a wife, especially someone as self-effacing as you are. It's time you stopped living in your dream world. You realize, I suppose, that you'll continue doing his work after you're married? It would be too risky for him, with his craving for secrecy, to take on another secretary, a complete outsider. If he does, his secret about the authorship of the Damon Dane books will almost certainly get out. Have you discussed the subject with him?'

'No. I haven't even thought about it.'

'There seem to be a lot of things you haven't thought about. It's time you started.' His words hammered at her head, like someone forcing home a wedge.

'I wish you'd stop lecturing me,' she said miserably.

But he was remorseless in his pursuit of his objective. 'That pendant,' he nodded at the chain round her neck, 'have you told him I gave it to you?'

'No.'

'Why not?' he asked derisively. 'Afraid he'd put you across his knee for accepting presents from another man? My dear girl, my brother just isn't like that. He hasn't an ounce of masculinity in him. He has none, not one, of the primitive urges that make life worth living!'

'Your prejudices are showing,' she muttered sourly.

He grew angry. 'So you still don't take me seriously? You still think I'm talking out of pique, that I'm being petty as only a brother can?' He rose. 'My word, I'll have to do something drastic to get through to you.'

He went out, slamming the door and shutting in the dog who was hopefully preparing to follow him.

The day, having started badly, hadn't finished with Adrienne yet. She was taking dictation in the lounge that afternoon when Flick pushed the door open with his nose and ran up to Adrienne holding something soft and red in his mouth.

Clifford stared. 'He's got my slipper! Take it away from him at once and get the brute out of here! You know I can't stand dogs. How did he get it? He must have gone into my bedroom. I will *not* have him roaming round the house. I shall have to tell Mrs. Masters to tie him up.'

Adrienne experienced a surge of rage out of all proportion to the crime. In the shadows of her mind she acknowledged that the anger was really against Clifford for putting into words his hatred of the dog, thus proving Murray right once again. But since she could not expend her fury upon her fiancé, she turned it on the dog.

She did something she had never done before. She slapped him, hard. He stopped in his tracks and stared, eyes wide open. His tail drooped, his head sank, but his teeth remained obstinately closed round the object in his mouth.

'Put it down!' she commanded, her voice pitched high. 'Bad dog! Bad Flick!'

'For heaven's sake,' moaned Clifford, as if he were in pain, 'can't you *do* something? Haven't you got better control over the animal than that?'

She made a dive for the slipper, but knew at once that it had been the wrong thing to do. Flick assumed she had stopped being annoyed and was playing instead. He retreated, hoping to draw her after him. He bumped against Clifford's legs and Clifford jumped as though he had been shot, drawing his legs back and tucking them beneath him, at the same time brushing down his trousers distastefully.

Adrienne's hand stretched out and she managed to get a firm hold on the slipper. She pulled, but the dog pulled harder. Then, with her hand still on it, he began to shake and paw the unfortunate object until, terrified that he might tear the slipper to pieces, she let go. He raced joyfully out of the room, skated along the polished hall floor, swerved through the kitchen door and out into the garden.

Adrienne dropped her notebook and pencil and followed. Flick bounded down the garden, darting left and right, keeping just out of Adrienne's reach. He doubled back and chased past her. She stretched out her arm, half twisted sideways and made a dive for his collar. He eluded her yet again, but the impetus of her desperate movement carried her round with him. He was not where she expected and she fell.

There was a searing pain at the base of her spine and she sprawled on the ground, momentarily stunned. When she tried to straighten her twisted body and get up, she was racked with pain. She panicked and cried out. Flick had dropped the slipper at last and was watching her as if he sensed that something was wrong. He started barking and did not stop until Clifford appeared at the kitchen door, calling irritably, 'What's the matter with you, Adrienne?'

Did he think she was playing some sort of game? She gritted her teeth and answered, 'Can't move.'

'Can't *move*?' He did not seem to believe her. Without leaving the sanctuary of the kitchen, he raised his voice and called, 'Murray! *Murray*, Adrienne's hurt herself.'

She thought, petulant with pain and in her distress unable to keep the truth at bay, 'He's going to his brother for help again. Can't he *ever* stand on his own feet?'

She heard Murray shout 'Coming!' and felt a rush of thankfulness for his strength and dependability. He must have moved with the speed of light, because he was there at her side almost before his brother had finished speaking.

He bent over her. 'Trouble?' His hands were gentle as he tried to help her up.

She nodded, trying vainly to keep the tears in their place. 'It's my back. I seem,' she tried to move, 'to have done something awful to it.'

'All right, I'll give you a hand. Grit your teeth,' he said. 'I'm going to turn you into a more normal position.' Somehow he got her round. 'Now I'm going to lift you. Put your arm round my neck. I'll try to keep you as flat as possible. Tell me if I'm hurting.'

He did hurt, he couldn't help it because every movement jarred, but she did not tell him. Instead, she pressed her cheek against his shoulder and closed her eyes. 'I'm sorry,' she muttered, 'to give you all this trouble. I'm sorry, Murray.'

He did not respond. He carried her into the house. 'Which bedroom, Clifford?' he asked. 'Yours?'

There was a horrified 'Good heavens, no! Take her to Mrs. Masters' room.'

'I'll take her to mine,' Murray snapped. As he climbed the

98

stairs with her in his arms, he called down to his brother who remained in the hall, 'Good grief, man, you're going to marry the girl soon. Then you'll have to let her into your room. She'll have every right to be there, night and day, if she chooses.'

He lowered her with unbelievable gentleness on to his bed and removed her shoes. She was pale and almost sick with pain.

'It's my back, Murray,' she said again, her head falling sideways against the pillow. 'Every move I make is agony.' She ran a dry tongue over equally dry lips. 'What can I do, Murray?' Her voice rose as she appealed to him for help as Clifford had done.

He stood looking down at her, serious and thoughtful, and seemed to be seeking an answer to a question. Then he came to life. He had found the answer. He had made up his mind.

'Adrienne, would you let me examine your back? I want to try to establish the cause of the trouble. I think I know what you've done to yourself, but I want to be sure.'

She looked up at him bewildered and whispered, 'What good would that do? You wouldn't know—'

He interrupted gently, 'Adrienne, I'm a doctor.'

In the midst of her pain, she tried to take in what he said.

He went on, 'I'm not a scientist, as you seem to think I am. Neither am I a Ph.D. I'm an M.D., a doctor of medicine. If you don't believe me, ask my brother.'

She flushed that he could even think she doubted him. 'Of course I believe you. It was just a – a shock.'

'Now will you let me examine you? If you don't trust me on my own, you can have your mother here. Or Clifford, even.'

She flinched involuntarily at the mention of her fiancé and the action did not pass unnoticed. 'Of course I trust you, Murray. How could I do otherwise? I trust you absolutely.'

He nodded abruptly in acknowledgement of her words. He became entirely professional. 'Now tell me exactly what happened.'

When he had heard the story of how she had dived to catch Flick and had twisted and fallen, he thanked her briefly and asked her to turn on her side. It was agony complying with his request and he had to help her.

His fingers were gentle, probing and knowledgeable, and

after a few minutes he rolled her on to her back again. 'Did I hurt?'

'You didn't hurt, but moving did. The pain is shooting down my legs.' She was near to tears. 'It even hurts to lift my feet. How long will it last, Murray?' The question came in a whisper.

'It's hard to say. It may take days or even weeks to clear completely. As I thought, you've almost certainly torn a ligament at the base of your spine.' He sat beside her and took her hand and automatically his fingers felt for her pulse. 'I must warn you, Adrienne, it will be extremely painful at first. There's very little one can do. Only time will cure the trouble. I can give you some tablets to lessen the pain. Would you like me to call your own doctor?'

She began to shake her head, but stopped because even that was too painful a movement. 'No, thank you. I told you, I trust your judgment.'

He seemed to be only half listening. 'All the same, I'll give him a ring. It would be unethical for me to treat you in any way without telling him first.'

So she gave him her doctor's name and telephone number and he smiled down at her. 'Will you be all right if I leave you for a few minutes? Don't attempt to get up, will you?'

She smiled back weakly. 'I couldn't even if I tried.'

He abandoned his professional manner and whispered, 'At last I've got you where I want you.' He brought a tearful smile to her face. Then he left her.

He was soon back. 'I contacted him and he seemed quite pleased to hear from me and invited me round for a chat some time. Apparently he's read some of my research papers. I'm going to collect a prescription from him now for some tablets which should help you, but he confirmed my diagnosis and prognosis – that only time will heal it, plus rest in bed.'

'But, Murray,' she pleaded with him as if he could effect a magic cure, 'that's impossible. What about Clifford's work? What about my mother?'

His expression hardened. 'What about them? They'll just have to manage without you for a while, won't they?'

'But,' she wailed, 'Clifford can't do without me. There's all that typing to do . . .'

He became impatient. 'Look, Adrienne, just try lifting your legs and you'll have the answer in the result of your efforts.'

She did better – she tried to sit up, but with her head raised only a few inches from the pillow she bit her lip and sank back. 'It's no good. I can't move without pain.' She cried with weakness and frustration. 'M-my handkerchief,' she sobbed, 'I can't find it.'

He gave her his, then walked to the window, letting her cry but offering no comfort.

'I suppose,' she muttered quite unfairly, 'you're so used to seeing people ill you haven't got any feelings left. You've g-grown hard with the y-years . . .'

'Don't be an idiot,' he said, without turning round. 'What good would sympathy do?'

'A lot,' she whimpered, 'an awful l-lot.'

'My dear girl, you've got so much self-pity you can do without my sympathy. I've seen people much more "ill", as you call it, than you are, and with much more fortitude.'

'You're cruel,' she accused.

He didn't deny the accusation, but his astringent manner seemed to have some effect on her, and the sobs grew less. He turned and when he spoke he was detached and impersonal. 'If you've finished crying, I'll go and pick up the prescription. I'll send Clifford up to you. He'll give you the sympathy you crave.'

He went downstairs, calling to his brother. There seemed to be an argument, but Murray appeared to win, because footsteps, slow and unwilling, climbed the stairs. Clifford came in, but if she had hoped for sympathy from him, she was disappointed. Callousness, she told herself, seemed to run in the family.

He eyed her uncomfortably. 'How bad are you? Can't you sit up?'

'Of course I can't,' she snapped, her control momentarily slipping.

He looked put out and she relented at once. 'I'm sorry, Clifford, it's just that my back's so painful.'

'But what about my work?'

Stunned by his unkindness, she started to shake her head, but checked herself. The action jarred her back. 'I just don't know, Clifford. There isn't much I can do when I'm like this, is there?' He turned on an injured expression and she apologized.

'You'll just have to write it all in longhand, and when I'm better I'll have to work continuously until I catch up.'

Now he wandered to the window as his brother had done, turning his back on her. 'It seems,' she thought, 'that I've committed a terrible crime. They're all blaming me. They seem to forget I'm the one who's suffering.'

'It was that dog,' Clifford mused to the window pane. 'Why you can't keep him under better control, I do not know. You make too much fuss of the brute. You lavish such affection on him. You treat him as if he were human . . .'

Adrienne could not believe her ears. Was Clifford *jealous* of the dog?

'After we're married,' Clifford persisted, 'he'll have to be . . .'

He did not finish the sentence because Murray returned. Like a soldier being relieved at his post, Clifford went out.

'You look upset,' Murray commented sharply. 'What has my brother been saying?'

'He – he was talking about Flick. Just as you came in,' tears hovered in the background, 'I think he was going to tell me that after we're married, Flick will have to be – destroyed.' She whispered the word as though it hurt her lips to say it.

'As I've said till I'm sick of saying it,' Murray replied indifferently, 'it's on the cards.'

'But don't you understand,' she responded frantically, 'I *can't* let Flick go. He's mine. No one can take him away.'

'My dear girl,' still that maddening neutrality, 'you're wasting your breath in appealing to me. You'll have to plead with your future husband to spare your dog. ' He smiled derisively. 'When you're fit again, try going down on your knees. Clifford would love that. It would pander to his delusions of power which I'm sure he secretly cherishes.'

Torn apart by his deliberate insensibility to her problem, she told him he was callous, unfeeling and unkind. He saw the symptoms of extreme distress and softened his manner. He opened the bottle containing the tablets which her doctor had prescribed and shook two out on to his palm.

He smiled. 'Now that *is* something I've never come across before in all my years as a doctor. A girl having to choose two men, yes, but a girl having to choose between her dog and the man she – loves, definitely no.'

Adrienne did not smile with him. 'You simply don't care,' she muttered.

'You're quite right,' he answered levelly. 'I don't. It's your problem, your choice, not mine.' Her lips trembled and she began to cry again. 'Now I suppose you're going to intone as before that I'm cruel, I'm hard.' She covered her eyes with his handkerchief. 'You'll have to stop crying, Adrienne,' he said quietly, 'if only to take these tablets.'

His tone reproved her and it had the desired effect. He found a glass and gave her water to help the tablets down. His arm beneath her shoulders supported her while she swallowed the tablets. She thanked him and sank back on the pillows.

'Now,' he said briskly, 'your mother – she'll have to be told. As I see it, you'll have to stay here for a few days.' She began to object, but he cut her off. 'There are a number of spare bedrooms. Mrs. Masters will make up a bed for you. Whether Clifford likes it or not, he will have to take Flick back to your mother and collect your night clothes and anything else you need.'

She remonstrated with him, but it was useless. 'You wouldn't be able to stand being carried home, either in the car or in anyone's arms.' Her lip trembled ominously again and he sat on the bed. 'Look, my dear, you'll have to be braver than this. You'll have to accept it and have patience. That's all you need. You may not believe it now, but time will bring relief. Slowly, and I mean slowly, your back will heal. Then, when you're back to normal, you'll appreciate that normality all the more for having lost it, won't you?' She responded to the touch of sympathy in his tone and thanked him for his trouble.

He said, rising, 'I'll ask Mrs. Masters to make up a bed. Will you be all right while I'm gone?'

She couldn't tell him she wanted him to stay with her for ever. She smiled and turned her cheek to his pillow. It was damp.

'I'm sorry to have cried all over your pillow case.'

He smiled back. 'I'll survive it. I've had to put up with much worse things than that in the course of my career!'

In the end, it was Murray who took Flick back and told her mother what had happened. Before he left the house, she heard Murray's raised voice. 'Good heavens, she's your future wife, not mine. Can't you take *some* responsibility on your own shoulders?'

He slammed out of the front door and Flick barked with joy at going out for a walk with him. She began to wonder how her mother would take the news. What would she give Murray to bring back with him? She should have given him a list, but, doctor though he was, she had recoiled at the idea of talking to him about her personal requirements.

Murray returned and Lorna came with him. He stood in the background while she fussed over her daughter. Then, when she had decided she had fussed enough to make a good impression on him, her fussing turned to worrying – about herself, about being alone at night, and what would she do without Adrienne?

'You'll have Flick,' Adrienne pointed out.

Lorna barely suppressed a shudder. 'And that's another thing – I shall have to look after him, take him for walks—'

'I'll do that,' Murray said quietly.

Lorna swung round, effusive in her thanks. But Murray shrugged it off. 'I happen to like the animal.'

Lorna shuddered delicately again. 'I don't know how you can. After all, look at the trouble he's caused today.' She indicated her daughter's plight. 'If he hadn't been naughty and taken that slipper . . .'

'It wasn't naughtiness, Mother. It was normal high spirits. Only Clifford didn't see it that way. He got het up, so rather foolishly I tried to get the slipper away from Flick, whereas if I'd ignored him he would have dropped it at once.'

'Oh, I'm afraid I agree with your dear fiancé. I really must go and apologize to him. If I had my way, that dog—'

Murray came forward. 'I believe you have some things to give Adrienne, Lorna.'

She did not notice his terseness, and smiled up at him radiantly. 'You dear man, thank you for reminding me. Of course I have.' She opened a large bag and took out the clothes and other belongings. Murray walked tactfully to the window and stared out. When Lorna had finished, she said, 'Now, Adrienne, when can I expect you home?'

Murray answered. 'She'll have to stay here for anything up to a week, Lorna.'

'But,' she was bewildered, 'how do you know? Have you had the doctor to her?' Evidently he had not told Lorna about his own medical background.

'No, but I phoned him and he has prescribed some tablets and insisted on complete rest.' He smiled and said gently, 'If we took her home, you would have to look after her, wouldn't you?'

This astute remark had the effect he wanted. She put her hand to her cheek. 'Oh, but I couldn't possibly . . . I mean, with the headaches I get, I never know from one day's end to another whether I can get up myself.'

'Precisely.' Murray's voice was crisp and decisive. 'So, for your sake,' Adrienne wondered at his tact, 'we must keep her here, mustn't we?'

Lorna sighed, but it was not an expression of sorrow. 'Yes, well, I'd better go and see that dear man, Mr. Denning, although,' she paused for effect, 'now he's going to be my son-in-law, I'll have to call him Clifford, won't I?'

'You will indeed,' said Murray gravely, and showed her out.

He took her downstairs and left her with Clifford, then he returned to Adrienne. 'Mrs. Masters has made up a bed in the room next to mine. I'll take you in there and you must go to bed.'

She remonstrated with him. 'But it's only the middle of the afternoon.'

'You'll have to get right into bed, Adrienne. It's no use pretending everything is normal. Accept the situation, my dear, relax and reconcile yourself to it. It will help the cure.'

Defiantly she tried to lift her legs to the floor to prove to him that she was not as bad as he thought she was, but she flopped back, white-faced.

'Now will you believe me?'

'Yes,' she whispered.

He lifted her with great gentleness and she gritted her teeth. He carried her into the next room and lowered her on to the bed. 'Mrs. Masters will help you — unless you'd rather have your mother?'

Her horrified frown gave him his answer.

He left her and Mrs. Masters came in. Together they struggled with Adrienne's clothes and at last she was in her nightdress, lying fresh and relaxed in the brightly painted guest-room.

'Has my mother gone?' she asked the housekeeper.

'No, Miss Garron, she's still talking to Mr. Denning.'

'Is Murray, I mean Dr. Denning, with them?'

'No, I believe he's in his room. Did you want him?'

Adrienne shook her head. 'He's done so much, I don't want to disturb him.' She looked round. 'Is there anything for me to read, do you think?'

'I'll find some magazines, dear. You want something light to read when you're not up to the mark, don't you?'

She bustled away. Murray strolled in. He noted her slightly flushed cheeks, her hair combed and fluffed round her face, her too bright eyes, her frown of pain whenever she moved.

He asked, 'How do you feel?'

'A little better, thank you. Those tablets must be working. Perhaps it won't take so long for me to get better as you think.'

'Maybe you're right. Determination to get better is always half the battle. Whenever I see it in a patient, I know I've got that patient's co-operation – a very important ingredient in the recipe for recovery.'

'Murray, tell me about yourself.'

'Some time,' he answered briefly, and went out. His refusal was like closing a door in her face. She took the snub badly and to her dismay found herself near to tears again. He was a doctor and the fact seemed to put him more beyond her reach than ever. Doctors, she had heard, had their own small, exclusive clique. They were a fraternity, there was an understanding between them which seemed to operate even if they had never met before, as with Murray and her own doctor. They admitted few others into their social circle and then only the privileged ones.

Gretel was probably a doctor, too, so she was part of his world. When she had recovered from the loss of her husband, she would no doubt agree to marry Murray, and his faithfulness to her for so many years would be rewarded at last.

His being a doctor explained many other things – Clifford's reliance on his judgment and his opinions, his attentions during Clifford's recent illness, and his interest in her mother's psychological problems. It also explained – and she had to face the fact, painful though it was – his attempts to 'teach' her how to kiss so that she could pass her 'knowledge' on to her fiancé. The more she thought about the changed situation, changed by her new knowledge of Murray's professional status, the worse she felt about it.

Mrs. Masters came in with a pile of magazines. Mrs. Garron had gone, she said, and had sent her love. Murray did not appear again until tea time, when he helped Mrs. Masters to prop her up with cushions. Gentle though Murray was, she had to pull in her lips with pain as he lifted her. He stayed with her until she proved to him she could manage to eat her food without help, then he went down to have his meal with Clifford.

At bedtime Clifford came to say good night. Adrienne, worn out with pain, put out her hand towards him, perhaps in the vain hope that some of his ability to move at will might be passed on to her. She was also feeling sorry for herself and wanted sympathy and reassurance.

Hesitating a little, like someone who feared to touch a person not in full health in case he caught it, Clifford took her hand. At that moment she longed to be taken in his arms and loved as any engaged woman had the right to expect. She wanted him to whisper words of love, to tell her how much he missed her, how he looked forward to her recovery so that he could kiss her again without fear of hurting her.

She had never before wanted to be made love to so much as at that moment.

Clifford gazed down at her, a lost and helpless expression on his face. His fingers merely touched, they did not entwine with hers. His body was rigid, his eyes passionless and impersonal.

Her physical weakness made her bold and she whispered, 'Aren't you going to kiss me, Clifford?'

A look akin to shock passed across his characterless features and she felt humiliated, as though she had suggested something immoral, but he bent down and placed his lips on hers.

At that moment Murray walked in, apologized stiffly for intruding and went out. Clifford raised his head and stood up, embarrassed at having been caught by his own brother in the act of kissing his fiancée. He coloured slightly, said he hoped she slept well and left her.

The long night stretched before her, but she slept at last. It was in the early hours that she awoke and started worrying. How was her mother getting on? Had she settled Flick down for the night in his basket? What was going to happen about Clifford's work?

107

If she could have moved, she would have tossed and turned, but she was imprisoned by pain and could only fret and perspire and long for the dawn. She listened, but there was nothing to hear. If only there were a sound, even the rustle of a night animal outside would be a comfort. She stared but in the darkness there was nothing to see. The blackness beyond the window panes was like a solid ebony wall, a blackboard on which she wanted to scrawl in brilliant white chalk *'Help me!'*

If only she had a torch to light up the shadows. She remembered the bedside lamp and wondered if she could reach the switch. Her arm slid from the covers and groped sideways over the table next to her. The light had a rounded pottery base designed to appeal to the artistic sense rather than pander to the laws of gravity. It was more rotund at the top than the bottom and as her hand came up against it, its inherent instability made it topple and tip over. The clatter in the silence sounded like the explosion of a bomb. It had fallen quite beyond her limited reach so she was unable to stand it upright. Now she couldn't even turn on the light.

A door creaked open on the landing. There were soft footsteps on the carpet outside and someone came in. Murray's voice said,

'What's the matter, can't you sleep?'

'Oh, Murray,' she mumbled, stretching out her hand as she had done to Clifford. The light from the landing threw his shadow enormously against the wall and it moved with him as he approached, placing his hand in hers in a firm, reassuring grip. He sat on the bed.

'The lamp,' she said breathlessly, 'the lamp. I've knocked it over and I can't reach it to stand it up.'

He moved forward intending to right it, but her arms lifted and clasped his neck and she clung to him like a frightened child. For a few seconds he held himself away, then he placed his cheek against hers on the pillow.

Her feverishness took only a moment or two to burn his face and he tried to lift his head, but she would not let him go. He stayed perfectly still, giving her the comfort she desired, then resolutely, gently, he removed her arms from around his neck, righted the bedside lamp and switched it on.

His hand went to her forehead. 'My word, you're in a state! I shall have to give you something to settle you down.'

'I'm sorry,' she whispered, 'for holding on to you. I shouldn't have done it, but . . .'

'It's all right.' He closed the door. 'I realize I was only acting as a stand-in for my brother, compensating for his shortcomings as a lover.' He trod the carpet restlessly, hands in dressing-gown pockets. 'What I'd like to know is why you've worked yourself up to such a pitch. You're not ill, you know, you're only temporarily incapacitated.'

He hovered in the shadows out of the subdued circle of light cast by the table lamp and she felt she could talk to him without reserve. Her worries came tumbling from her – about her fiancé, her mother, her dog, the work she could not do, the trouble she was causing in the Denning household. He let her talk herself out, probably hoping that the mere act of telling would act as a safety valve.

He came back into the light and stood looking down at her. 'My dear girl,' his tone was light, 'most women would give a great deal to lie where you are, shelving their problems and letting others cope. But not you – you must lie there worrying as though the whole world depended solely on you and would stop turning if you were not there to help it go round!'

'I'm sorry,' she repeated, 'to be such a nuisance. I'm sorry too, to have disturbed you.'

He shrugged. 'I'm not unused to being disturbed. In my early years as a doctor, I grew accustomed to being on call night and day.'

'Were you,' she ventured, risking a second rebuff, 'once a practising doctor?'

'Yes, for two years I was a partner in general practice.' He sat on the bed and did not seem to mind her questions now. 'Then I had the urge to specialise and, having no wife or family to put before my studies, I worked for my M.D. It wasn't easy, but I succeeded.'

'And now—?'

'Now I'm Professor of Cardiology and head of the department of clinical cardiology at the university. I'm engaged in re-search, as I told you – research into the diseases of the heart, with special reference to the effects of diet on that very import-ant organ of the body.'

She felt very small. 'So that's why you kept trying to reassure me about the state of Clifford's heart?' And she hadn't believed him!

He nodded. 'I can assure you again, beyond doubt, that you have nothing to worry about on that score. At his request, I've examined him thoroughly on two or three occasions, and have told him there's nothing wrong with him.'

'But he won't believe you?'

'No. Whether it's because I'm his brother, or because it suits him better not to believe me, I don't know, but I suspect the latter.'

'Why doesn't he get a second opinion?'

He laughed. 'A good question, but my guess is that he would have to believe another doctor, whereas he doesn't have to believe me!' He stood up. 'I'll get that tablet.'

He was back in a few minutes. He gave it to her with some water, supporting her shoulders while she swallowed it. 'That should make you sleep – and stop you talking!'

'Murray, why did you—'

He held his head. 'Is there no end to her questions?' He smiled. 'Why did I what?'

'Keep it a secret that you're a doctor?'

He reached for her hand, entwining his fingers with hers as she had wanted Clifford to do. 'My sweet girl, I'm on holiday, so I wanted to remain, as it were, incognito. Once people know there's "a doctor in the house" they tend to pour out their troubles to him *ad nauseam*.'

She coloured deeply and tried to take her hand away, but he held it tightly. 'Trust you to take offence! I didn't mean you.'

'Then why didn't you tell me?'

'Because I couldn't risk its being passed on inadvertently by you to your mother, or via her to anyone else. Just think of what might have happened that evening I called at your cottage. Your mother wouldn't have let me rest until I'd diagnosed the cause of her headaches and all her other little aches and pains, would she? Now be honest!'

'You're quite right,' she agreed, in a small voice. 'But I promise faithfully not to breathe a word of your secret to her.' She yawned. 'That pill is taking effect already. What a nuisance! I want to keep on talking.'

He laughed. 'I've never known you so chatty. You should let down your barriers more often. Under sedation, you're a different girl. In the right circumstances, and a couple of those tablets, you might even have the courage to tell a man you loved him!'

She laughed with him. 'Talking of love,' she said, 'are you going to marry Gretel?'

'Now you're being cheeky,' he said. 'I'm not under any obligation to answer all your questions. You're not my sister-in-law yet, you know, so you have no right to interrogate me about my private life.'

Adrienne turned her head to one side and closed her eyes. She didn't ever want to be his sister-in-law. She wanted to be more, much more to him than that . . . She swept the thought out of the way like a man hitting a golf ball. What were those pills doing to her? She was drifting off into sleep and was dreaming. In her dream there was a man – she couldn't see his face because it was too dark – she felt his lips on hers with a touch so light it might not have happened.

The man was Clifford, of course. He must have been Clifford, because no one else would want to kiss her, not even in a dream. Whoever it was backed into the darkness and went away. She tried to run after him to see who it was, but her legs refused to move. Then she slept too deeply to dream at all.

CHAPTER EIGHT

SHE awoke next morning and wondered where she was, then it all came back. She thought optimistically, 'I'm better today' and tried to move her legs. She could move them, of course, but the pain she experienced in her back as a result of lifting them was unbearable.

So, overnight, nothing had changed. She was just as incapacitated as she had been yesterday. She stared up at the ceiling, despondent and fretful. Murray came in, dressed and overflowing with energy. She looked at him sourly.

'Sleep well?' he asked with a provocative smile. She didn't bother to answer. 'Did you dream you were climbing mountains or racing across the fields with Flick? Compensatory dreams where you could move about at will and your legs did as your brain told them? Then came the rude awakening, when you opened your eyes and found you were as stiff and immobilized as ever?'

'As a matter of fact,' she said acidly, 'I didn't dream at all – except,' she faltered, remembering, 'except at the start.'

'Was it a pleasant dream? Tell me about it.'

She shook her head and found it didn't hurt quite so much. 'Not worth it.' If she told him he would only laugh and say it was the effect of the pill.

'Oh.' He dropped his teasing manner and became professional. 'How are the aches and pains? Any more movement in those legs? Try them now.' She obeyed and winced. 'No improvement at all?'

'Perhaps, fractionally.'

'Well,' he said briskly, 'it's early days. Can't expect miracles.' His hand felt her brow. 'Not so het up as you were at three o'clock this morning.' He smiled down at her. 'My word, you were in a state!'

'You calmed me down.' She managed a smile. 'Thank you for what you did.'

He shrugged. 'It's my job.' She frowned. So he was classifying her as just another case.

Mrs. Masters bustled in. 'I'm bringing your breakfast, Miss

Garron. Would you like me to give you a quick wash?'

Murray laughed at Adrienne's horrified expression. 'But I can wash myself. I'm not an invalid!'

'Stop fussing,' said Murray, 'and we'll try an experiment. Let's see whether you can sit up. Mrs. Masters, adjust the pillows while I lift her.' His strong hands held her under her arms while the housekeeper piled the pillows high. With infinite care he raised Adrienne into a sitting position. Before he released her, he asked, 'Can you bear it?'

She gritted her teeth and nodded. 'Just about.'

'Good. We're making progress. Now Mrs. Masters will bring in a bowl of water and you can wash yourself, as you said.'

'But,' she wailed, 'I meant in the bathroom, not in the bed. I was hoping to get up today. I can't just lie here . . .'

'Look here, my girl, think yourself lucky you've got this far.' His tone was sharp. 'And you won't be able to stand that position for long. You'll want to slide down the bed again as soon as you've had your breakfast.'

Clifford came in. He hovered behind Murray and Adrienne stretched out her hand to encourage him to move nearer. With his usual reticence, he put his hand in hers.

'Go on, man, kiss her,' came his brother's irritable voice. 'Can't you see that's what she's asking for? Or,' his tone hardened, 'do you want me to show you how?'

Flushing deeply at his brother's calculated insult, Clifford bent down and put his lips to Adrienne's in a self-conscious, neutral kiss. He raised his head hurriedly, as if relieved that duty had been done, and had been seen to be done by his brother.

Clifford said to Murray. 'Now she can sit up, will she be able to take shorthand notes?'

Murray exploded. 'Good heavens, Clifford, are you quite unfeeling? Can you think of nothing but your work? Can't you put your fiancée's welfare first, for once?'

He strode out disgustedly, and it was not long before Clifford followed.

Breakfast over, Mrs. Masters removed the pillows and Adrienne slid down the bed again, as Murray had said she would. There was a hammering on the front door and a frenzied barking and she knew her mother had arrived. She heard Flick scrambling up the stairs and stiffened in advance of the onslaught when he discovered where she was, but Murray must have intercepted him on the landing.

She heard, 'Hallo, boy. No, you're not going in there. You're coming in here with me.' Much as Adrienne loved the dog, she wanted to thank Murray from the bottom of her heart.

Her mother's voice talking to her future son-in-law wafted up from downstairs and the stream of words was incessant like the flow of wine at a party. 'Clifford must be getting fed up with her chatter by now,' Adrienne thought, but her mother must have intoxicated him with her exuberance because his voice, when he answered, was remarkably free of irritation.

'May I come in, darling?' Lorna pushed her head round the door. 'My goodness, don't you look comfortable? Aren't you lucky, having such a lazy time? And here's poor me coping with everything at home!'

If that was calculated to give me a guilty conscience, Adrienne, thought, then she's succeeded. She coloured as if deserving her mother's politely phrased accusations. 'I'm sorry, Mother, I would get up if I could, but I wouldn't be much use . . .'

'Oh, but dear, I didn't *mean* it at all. You mustn't feel guilty, I *know* you can't help it. But Flick really is a handful . . .'

'Perhaps,' Adrienne said weakly, 'Mrs. Masters would take him over. Perhaps Clifford wouldn't mind if Flick slept downstairs in the kitchen while I'm here . . .'

'Oh, my dear, I simply *must* have the dog with me at night. I'm terrified of being alone! I hardly slept last night.'

'But, Mother, what can I do? Murray says it might take days,' she did not dare to add 'even weeks', 'before I'm back to normal.'

'Never you mind, darling. I'll manage. I've got to, haven't I? She clasped her hands like an excited infant. 'Do you know what your dear Clifford and I have arranged? Would you believe it – I'm going to help him with his work!' At her daughter's look of horor, she went on, a little hurt, 'Darling, I'm not helpless. I can take dictation on to the typewriter. I can type – with two fingers – you know I can. We've arranged it all between us. So there's no need for you to fret about your dear fiancé's work. I'm starting this morning. He jumped at the chance.'

'But, Mother,' Adrienne raised her head from the pillow, lowering it again swiftly because of a stab of pain in her spine, 'he can't stand the clatter of a typewriter. That's why I type in the hut.'

'Don't worry, dear. He says that in the special circumstances he'll steel himself to standing the noise. He said he'd put up with anything to get his work done – even me!' Her shrill laugh rang round the room. She bent down to kiss her daughter's forehead. 'I must go down to him. He's anxious to start.'

She went out, leaving her daughter flabbergasted. Murray came in. 'What was that all about?'

Adrienne explained, almost incoherent with astonishment. 'But, Murray, that means she'll learn his pen-name and his secret with it. She'll tell everyone . . .'

He wandered to the window. 'I doubt it. I think she'll be so flattered at being taken into his confidence, she'll hang on to his secret like gold dust. It will probably endow her with an inflated sense of her own importance.' He turned. 'Sorry to be so frank about your mother.'

'It's all right. I know her shortcomings. I've lived with her long enough.'

'Extraordinary,' Murray murmured, staring out of the window again, 'how you can see your mother's faults, but not your fiancé's. Ah, well,' he turned again, this time walking to the door, 'they say love is blind.'

The day passed, with frequent visits from Mrs. Masters, an occasional one from Murray and no sign at all of Clifford or Lorna. There was the persistent clatter of the typewriter which, even if it was rather slow and laboured, irritated Adrienne because it acted as a constant reminder that that was where she should be, down there working, not lying idle upstairs in bed. She fretted again that night, but took care not to waken Murray. Instead she lay there alone, worrying, chafing against the circumstances which had brought about her immobility.

In the morning, she decided, she would get up, whatever Murray said to the contrary.

But Murray had the last word again. 'Definitely not,' he told her when he called in before breakfast. 'How did you sleep?' She shrugged, not wishing to tell him the truth. He studied her face. 'From the look of you, not very well. Did you lie there worrying again? Why didn't you call me?'

She looked away. 'I didn't like to disturb you. It wouldn't

have been fair.'

'My word,' he smiled, 'if all patients were as considerate as you, doctors would have an unbelievably restful time!'

'You're not my doctor.'

'Agreed, but I could have given you something to help you sleep.'

She frowned. 'What does it matter if I don't sleep? I'm doing nothing all day except lying here staring at the ceiling—'

He strode across and seized a handful of her hair. 'If you don't stop pitying yourself, my girl, I'll use caveman tactics and pull this until you shout for mercy!'

She gave him a strained smile and he released her hair. 'All the same, I wish you'd let me try to get up.'

He pushed his hands into his pockets and studied her face again. 'I have to admit, I admire your incredible fighting spirit. It does you credit.' He lifted her hand from the quilt. 'You really want to try, despite the pain you'll undoubtedly suffer?' She nodded, her eyes hopeful. 'All right, later,' he promised, and left her.

He kept his word. She was half sitting, half lying in bed reading, after her afternoon cup of tea when he came in, removed her book and closed it with a snap.

'Now I've lost my place!'

'Too bad. You'll have plenty of time to find it again. You said you wanted to walk, and walk you shall. If it's painful, remember that it's really against doctor's orders and that you asked for it.' He looked at the bed. 'Before I pull back the covers, are you decent?' He smiled. 'You see, I'm being very considerate.'

She flushed and pulled down her nightdress under the blankets.

'There's no need to be so bashful with me. Come on.' His voice was brisk. He folded back the covers and with great care swung her legs round so that she was sitting on the side of the bed. 'Painful?' She nodded 'Want to go on?' She nodded again. 'Good girl!' She glowed at his praise. He put his hands under her armpits and slowly pulled her to her feet, putting his arm round her waist to support her. 'Now shall we go on?'

'Yes, please,' she whispered, gripping her lip between her teeth.

'I'm warning you,' he said, 'when you start to walk it will

hurt like hell. Don't say I didn't tell you. First, put your arm round my waist.'

She obeyed and asked, 'Where's Flick?'

'Shut in my room. He won't worry you.'

So they started towards the bathroom. Their progress was unbelievably slow, but Murray's patience seemed boundless. Each step she took was excruciatingly painful, but she would not give up. They paused for breath on the landing, and beads of perspiration stood out on her forehead. With his free hand he took out a handkerchief and dabbed at them. She smiled her thanks.

They reached their goal at last – the bathroom door. Before closing it on her he asked, 'Can you manage, or do you want Mrs. Masters to come up and help you?'

She said stoically, 'No, thanks. I'll manage.'

'Right. Call me when you're ready.'

Ten minutes later, he tapped on the door. 'Are you ready yet? I told you to call me. Don't you dare attempt that journey back alone!' She didn't answer. 'Unlock this door,' he ordered, then rattled the handle impatiently. 'Let me in, girl.' She mumbled something he could not catch. 'Look, I'm a doctor. I know all about the human body, female as well as male. There's no need to be shy with me!'

At last she turned the key. When he opened the door she was perched on the side of the bath, white-faced with pain and with fighting it. 'Good God, what a place to sit! If you fell from there you could undo all the good these few days of rest have done.' He lifted her gently into his arms. 'You're not walking back. You've done enough.'

She twisted her head from side to side, delighting in the fact that she could at least move that freely now. 'I want to walk. Put me down.'

He looked into her face, so near to his. 'If you don't keep quiet,' he threatened, 'back or no back, I'll spank you!'

She turned pink and hid her face against him. 'You can't speak to your future sister-in-law like that.'

'I can speak to her how I like!' he answered tersely.

Adrienne raised her head and looked into his face. He sounded annoyed. What had she said to upset him?

He carried her into the bedroom, lowered her gently on to the bed and pulled the bedclothes over her. Then he handed her the book. 'Now you can find your place again.'

She smiled up at him. 'Thank you, Murray, for all your help.' She added shyly, 'You really are a wonderful doctor.'

He frowned, seeming to refute her praise. 'Don't be stupid. Everything I did for you could easily have been done by your fiancé.' She looked crestfallen at his rebuff and he added a little more kindly, 'No doubt you're now feeling very pleased with yourself.'

She sighed and rested her head back against the pillows. 'Yes, but it hurt every bit as much as you said it would.'

He moved nearer. 'For such a slender, retiring young woman, you certainly have a surfeit of courage – not to mention tenacity. When you make up your mind to follow a certain course, you follow it to the bitter end, don't you? Nothing will deflect you from your ultimate goal.' He wandered round. 'It therefore follows that, no matter what I or anyone else may say to try to persuade you to the contrary, and point out to you the error of your ways, you will marry my brother, come what may. Even if,' he turned at the door, 'after an indefinable length of time you come to me and say, as you have just said, "Yes, but it – your marriage to Clifford – hurt every bit as much as you said it would".'

Lorna, who had been working for Clifford again, came up to see Adrienne before going home. Her eyes were brighter, her actions more vigorous and purposeful than Adrienne had seen them for years. She had a job to do, a reason for living at last. 'Therapy', Murray would have called it.

Lorna told her not to worry, Clifford's work was going well and she simply loved the books he wrote. 'He's lent me a lot of them, dear, and I'm passing the long evenings reading them. I'm not nearly as lonely as I thought I'd be, now I've got such lovely books to read.'

Adrienne reflected wryly, when Lorna had gone, that either her mother's taste in literature had deteriorated considerably in the last few days, or her reading of such books was coloured by a strong sense of newly discovered author-loyalty!

Clifford made one of his rare visits to her room. He, too, assured her that all was going well. Both he and Lorna seemed at pains to tell her, in an artless, roundabout way, that she was not as indispensable as she thought she was.

He was a little more affectionate than usual. He sat on a chair beside the bed and put his arms round her. He kissed her with less reserve and greater resolve than ever before. It seemed – the thought flitted in and out of her mind – almost as if he were practising. For a deeper relationship, she wondered, after they were married? She tried to help him by responding with as much warmth as she could muster, and as her injury would allow.

When he had gone, she lay back, wondering about his change of attitude towards her. How long would it last? Had Murray been talking to him? Had he 'programmed' him again, fed instructions into him on how to show his love for his fiancée?

Murray came in. 'You look flustered. Why?'

'Clifford's been in.'

'You don't mean to tell me he's been making love to you?' She didn't reply. She didn't need to, he could see the answer in her face.

'To be honest,' she said, 'I thought perhaps you had been talking to him again.'

He laughed unbelievingly. 'You mean giving him advice on courtship and lovemaking?'

She shrugged. 'It's just that every time you talk to him on the subject, he becomes a little more – well, loverlike.'

He laughed again. 'So you're astute enough to notice the fact? And you're not disillusioned that, at his age, he has to turn to his younger brother for such help? Will I have to hang around, I wonder, during the early part of your married life, in order to keep advising him on what to do next?' The half-truth in his words kept her silent. An eyebrow lifted quizzically. 'In what capacity do you think I'm advising him – as a doctor or as a man of experience?'

A look of pain passed across her face, which he noted with interest. 'As a doctor, of course,' she snapped.

'So you think I've led a blameless life? How do you know?'

She frowned and turned away. Of course she didn't know. She did not possess the knowledge which would enable her to come to any conclusions about his past. She only knew that she was disturbed by his nearness, by his strength and by his dominating personality, that she longed for him to make love to her as she knew her fiancé never would until the end of their days.

That night she was restless again, and each time she moved she felt a stab of pain in the lower part of her back. 'Call me,' Murray had said earlier, 'if you can't sleep.'

But she would not make herself a nuisance to him. She heard a noise on the landing and she watched her door come open slowly, her heart thumping.

Murray saw her eyes wide and staring. 'I thought so – lying there sleepless again, without saying a word.'

'Why did you come in? I didn't call you.'

He switched on the bedside lamp and smiled, despite her ill temper. 'It's the medical man in me coming out. Just checking up on a patient.'

'I'm not your patient.' She knew her tone was ungracious and that she should have been thanking him for his surveillance, but somehow she could not bring herself to do so.

'I didn't say "my" patient. I said "a" patient.' His tone was reasonable and mild and she felt ashamed of herself.

He held out a pill on a spoon and a glass of water. She shook her head. 'No, thank you. I'm not taking any sleeping pills.'

'Why not?'

'They make me dream—' She stopped, but he took her up on her statement.

'You said last time that you didn't dream after you had taken them.' He paused and smiled. 'Did you?'

She looked up at him wonderingly. In the dimness of the room, with his face half in shadow, he looked enigmatic and mysterious. Had it been a dream the other night – or had he really kissed her? As she looked at him now, tall, tantalizing, his eyes veiled, he looked capable of anything.

'Come on, take it. I'm not leaving you until the pill has gone safely down your throat.'

She swallowed it reluctantly and drank some water. He took the glass from her and put it down. Then he stood watching her, as if waiting for the pill to take effect.

She looked up at him, started to speak, hesitated, took courage from the fact that she could not see his face clearly and said, 'Murray?' He raised his eyebrows, inviting her to continue. 'May I ask you a question?'

'In what capacity? As a doctor, as a man – two different entities, you'll notice – or as your future brother-in-law?'

'As a – a doctor.' She sought his hand, but he drew it out of reach and pushed it into his pocket.

'Yes?' His tone became distant and neutral.

She whispered, because she was dreading a negative answer, 'Will I – will I ever be able to have babies?'

He did not reply immediately. Then he asked, 'What makes you doubt your ability to produce offspring?'

'My – my back.'

'Is that all?' She nodded. 'I can assure you that your back will heal in a comparatively short time, and if you're careful and sensible about lifting things, and don't do anything stupid like twisting to catch your dog – or anything else – you should have no more trouble with it in the future. It certainly shouldn't prevent you from bearing children. Does that satisfy you?'

'Yes, thank you.'

'Adrienne,' he dropped his professional manner, 'have you talked this over with Clifford?' She shook her head. Now he took her hand. 'You want children so much? My dear, how often do I have to repeat it – my brother will not have a family. I state categorically that his mind is made up and it's unalterable.'

'But, Murray,' she was pleading now, 'he'll change his mind, I'm sure he will.'

'As you've said before.' He threw down her hand. 'But he will not! Don't keep deluding yourself. Can't you see that I know what I'm talking about?'

She started to cry. 'You're prejudiced, you're biased.'

'And you're impossible stupid – wilfully so.'

'No, I'm not,' she sobbed. 'I want to go home. Tomorrow I want to go home.'

'Why?' he asked harshly. 'Running away from the truth again?' He seemed determined now, despite her condition, despite the tears, not to spare her. 'You shut your ears every time to what I'm trying to instil into that incredibly stupid brain of yours. All right, so you want kids – a perfectly natural wish for a young woman, especially an engaged one, to have. But—' his fingers spread out and gripped the top of her head, and he turned it towards him, 'are you listening? Let's be crude – that seems to be the only way left to me to break through your barriers, your mental block where Clifford is concerned – has it never occurred to you that your beloved fiancé might not be able to provide you with them? You're so innocent, so unworldly, you may not realize that sexual desire is not a constant, that the need for physical love varies from man to man, that some men may experience it *very rarely indeed*?'

She looked up at him, frightened now. 'Are you trying to tell me that Clifford—?'

'I know what you're thinking, but that's not what I mean at all. What I'm trying to say is this. Clifford needs a woman who pampers him, mothers him, runs around him waiting on him all the time. Not a warm-blooded girl as it's obvious you are underneath all that reserve, not a woman who makes demands on him either mentally or physically.'

He changed his tone and became more persuasive. 'Adrienne, you *must* listen to me. I'm speaking as a doctor, not as a "prejudiced" or "biased" brother, as you have the audacity to call me. You're the biased one, not I. I've been trained to look at things clinically, impartially, aseptically almost, as it were uncontaminated by the "germs of emotional involvement".'

She said desperately, 'How do you know that my need for physical love is not as small as Clifford's? How do you know I'm as "warm-blooded" as you say I am? How do you know I'll make demands on him of any sort?'

'My sweet girl,' he spoke softly, 'I remember a delightful evening not so long ago when I kissed you myself, when you admitted with your own lips that I had aroused you, when you responded to me with intense and unmistakable passion.' He sat on the bed, leaned over her and placed his hands on each side of her pillow, imprisoning her head. He whispered, 'Would you like me to repeat the performance, especially for your benefit, so that you can prove to yourself the extent of your desires?'

She had stopped crying now. The pill was working. She was tranquil, her eyes serene. If he had gathered her into his arms, she would not have had the power to resist him.

He lowered his head, his lips covered hers, but otherwise he did not touch her. When he raised his head, her eyes were closed.

'Sleeping beauty,' he whispered. She heard him, but felt too tired to wonder whether he was being sarcastic or sincere. She sighed and went to sleep.

He swept in next morning dressed in a formal suit. He asked, 'Do you still want to go home?'

'Yes, please,' she said timidly.

'And who's going to look after you when you get there? With your mother over here, you'll be on your own.'

'She'll give me my meals. That's all I want. And you promised to take Flick for his walks.'

'So you've got it all planned? All right, be it on your own head. You can go home – tomorrow.' He saw the disappointment. 'Sorry, can't be done today. I'm spending the day in town, meeting a colleague to discuss work. I shouldn't be back late, but all the same it will be too late to take you home. Since I appear to be the only strong man in the family, you'll just have to wait until I'm free to take you.' He went out.

'Murray!' She called him back, wanting to delay his departure if only by a few minutes. 'What about Flick?'

'He's with Mrs. Masters. She'll take care of him, don't worry. Anything else?' She shook her head. He strolled to the bed. 'Don't look so forlorn. I'm not forsaking you. I'm going out for the day, not out of your life – yet. Anyone would think you were all set to miss me. Even if you did, I wouldn't take it as a compliment. I'd know it was my help you were missing, not me.'

This time he did go and Adrienne didn't call him back. He swept out, taking his strength and his energy with him. She felt enervated, debilitated, her animation ebbing away like blood from a vital artery.

She had occasional visits from her mother and Clifford, but they did little to transfuse any life into her. Once they came together. Lorna looked at Clifford with an affected smile and told Adrienne how much she was enjoying herself doing her future son-in-law's work.

'Don't get better too quickly,' she urged her daughter, laughing. 'What will life be like when I've got nothing to do again?'

The day without Murray was drained of colour, like material faded by the sun. With Mrs. Masters' willing assistance, Adrienne went to the bathroom again, and even managed to walk round the room by using a walking stick. She rejoiced that at last she was making progress, and looked forward to being able to boast to Murray about it. Towards evening she found herself listening for his car, his footsteps, his voice. It grew dark, but still he didn't return.

Everyone went to bed. Adrienne slept fitfully. The key turning in the front door awoke her and she saw from her watch that it was two o'clock. Where had Murray been? Had his 'colleague' been a woman? She could not ask him because she had no right to pry. She slept again and awoke unrefreshed in the morning.

He breezed in straight after breakfast. He seemed in high spirits. 'Go on,' he taunted, 'ask me where I was last night. Put on the high-handed sister-in-law act and start interrogating me.'

She turned her head away. 'I'm not in the least interested in what you did last night.'

He laughed loudly. 'Curiosity is sticking out of you like prickles from a hedgehog's back! You're one big question mark.' He sat on the chair. 'All right, if you're not going to ask me, I'll volunteer the information. I met Désirée Charters in town, purely by accident.' Adrienne's head shot round. 'Yes,' he went on, 'I thought that would bring about a violent reaction. We teamed up – at her suggestion. We – er—' he inspected his nails, 'dined and danced.'

She turned her head away to hide the jealousy in her eyes, but she couldn't hide the slow revealing flush which crept up her cheeks. 'Did you enjoy yourself?' Her voice was flat.

Sadistically he leaned forward, caught her chin and turned her face to look into her eyes. 'Yes. I enjoyed the evening immensely.'

He saw the lost, disconsolate expression which betrayed her sense of utter inadequacy. A self-satisfied smile creased his face and he stood up. 'Right. You want to go home. Have you told your mother? No? Nor your fiancé?' He tutted. 'So you're leaving everything to me?'

She could only apologize. She couldn't tell him she had spent the whole time he was away thinking about him and watching the clock, and that everything else had gone out of her head.

She said proudly, 'I got up for a time yesterday. I walked round the room alone, with only a walking stick.'

'I'll bet it was painful.'

'Yes, but I put up with the pain. I can't go on lying in bed indefinitely.'

'She put up with the pain!' He imitated her voice. 'Stoic to the core, aren't you? Well, since you're so clever,' he handed her the walking stick which was hanging on the back of the chair, 'demonstrate how well you can walk.'

She pushed back the bedclothes, lifted her legs to the floor and with difficulty raised herself into a reasonably upright position. With slow painful steps, she moved a few paces. He watched her with a professional eye, his face impassive, his arms folded.

She walked round the bed to the window. She murmured, 'I feel like an old lady.'

'You look it,' was his unsympathetic comment. She turned slowly and faced him across the room. With an effort she smiled. 'Well, have I got your seal of approval?'

'You'll do,' he answered shortly. 'What you lack in agility you make up for in courage and determination. Yes, you can go home, if you insist.'

'It's not that I want to go home. It's just—'

'Just that you feel you ought to.'

'I appreciate everything you and Mrs. Masters have done—'

'But you're discharging yourself from my care.'

'Of course I'm not! When I'm at home, I want you to come and see me.'

'How very nice of you! Not presumably for my company, but for my medical skill.'

Adrienne didn't reply.

'Come on, get dressed and I'll take you over to your cottage in my car.'

'And Flick?'

'You'd better be sitting down before you're reunited with that boisterous hound. Otherwise you'll be back to square one and flat on your back again. I'll take you first and come back for him.'

'Murray,' she sat on the bed, 'will you tell Clifford and my mother?'

'Yes, I'll be your errand boy.'

She smiled apologetically. 'Sorry, Murray. I'd go myself but—' She indicated her helplessness with her hand.

She was waiting for him, fully dressed, when he returned. Without a word he scooped her into his arms. When she protested, he said.

'No stairs for you yet. It would take you an hour to accomplish the descent. Come on, don't be shy, hold on to me and get yourself comfortable.'

She put her arms round his neck and he smiled wickedly. 'I don't know about you, but I'm enjoying this!'

He carried her to his car and sat her on the back seat, lifting her legs until she was half lying on the seat. He folded a rug and put it under her head. She protested that she was only going a few hundred yards down the road.

'The slightest jolt,' he admonished her, 'could undo all the good these days of rest have done.'

He unlocked the front door of the cottage, returning to lift her from the car. Adrienne said agitatedly that she wanted to walk, and what would the neighbours think?

He said, 'That I'm carrying you over the threshold, and they would be right.'

'Doctors don't usually carry their patients over the threshold.' She smiled into his face. 'Unless they have evil intentions.'

'Stop being provocative, young woman. It's out of character and, although you don't know it, dangerous. You're not my patient – and I'm not your doctor. Remember that.' He whispered into her ear, 'so my intentions can be as evil as I like.'

He lowered her gently into an armchair in the sitting-room and she leaned back and sighed, looking round at the old familiar things she had missed without knowing it.

'It's good to be home again.'

'That,' Murray commented, perching on the arm of the chair, 'is an odd statement for an engaged woman to make. You'll be leaving home for good when you marry my brother.'

Hastily she changed the subject. She looked up at him. 'I feel as though I've been ill, but I haven't, have I?'

'It's probably the pain you've suffered. Don't think I don't know the agony you've been going through. A damaged back can be excruciatingly painful, both physically and, to a usually active person as you are, mentally, too.' He looked round. 'If you tell me where the kitchen is, I'll make a cup of tea.'

She asked, genuinely surprised, 'Do you know how?'

'That's an insult! Of course I know how. A doctor in my particular aspect of medicine is not waited on hand and foot by nurses as other doctors are.' He smiled. 'Unfortunately, I come into contact with them only too rarely.' He stood up. 'Now, where's that kitchen?'

She directed him and listened to the clatter of crockery and the hissing of the kettle as it came to the boil as though they were the most wonderful sounds in the world.

'I even found a tray,' he said, carrying it in, 'and some biscuits.'

As they drank the tea, he remarked, 'You're looking better than for some time.'

She could not tell him the reason for the glow in her cheeks. Nor could she tell him that as soon as he had gone, the glow would fade and give place to depression and gloom.

'There's an air of contentment about you. Don't you feel,' he put down his cup and glanced round, 'there's something – or rather, someone – missing?'

Adrienne was puzzled. 'No.' Her voice rose, making the word into a question.

He answered with a gleam in his eye, indicating that he had caught her out intentionally, 'Your fiancé? You don't miss him?'

She coloured and, because he had tricked her into admitting by implication that his presence was enough in itself to make her forget Clifford, she muttered irritably, 'Of course I do, except that he's never been here.'

He was scandalized. 'He's never been to his fiancée's home?'

'How could he, when even my mother didn't know of our engagement until recently? Clifford was insistent from the start that we should keep it a secret, but I had to tell my mother in the end because she thought—' she hesitated but had to continue because he would not be satisfied unless she did, 'she thought you were my "young man".'

He laughed. 'What was her reaction when you told her about your engagement?'

'Shock, because I'd done what she thought I would never do, become engaged. Then sorrow, at the thought of being left alone when I married.'

He whistled softly under his breath. 'In other words, she played the martyr?'

Adrienne nodded. 'Murray?' He looked at her. 'I was thinking of asking Clifford if he would allow my mother to come and live with us after we're married.'

He stood up. 'You're not serious?' She nodded. 'You mean you would be willing to burden yourself with *both* of them?' He could not restrain his anger. 'Your apathy, your unquestioning acceptance of your miserable lot in life drives me mad!' He clenched his fists and stuffed them into his pockets as if that was the only way he could stop himself from maltreating her. 'There are times when you're so dense, so stupid, I'd like to shake you until you cried out for mercy!' He went to the front door. 'I'll get Flick.' He slammed it behind him.

Adrienne sat rigid and fretting, attempted to stand and walk, but changed her mind. The restlessness inside her could not yet be translated into physical action. She clenched her fists as Murray had done and drummed rhythmically on the arm of the chair. She must not let even a shadow of doubt cloud the landscape of her future, the route she had charted for herself in her life with Clifford.

That her love for him was less than her love for Murray was a fact she could not dispute. But it was not as though she was devoid of feeling for her fiancé. She felt undoubted affection for him, she knew he needed her, that there was a place in his life which only she could fill.

He had told her he was not like other men in his need for love, and she had accepted it. Whatever Murray chose to say about her possession of all the normal passions and warmth of womanhood, she was convinced she could keep them in check, and that in time they would cease to matter. She turned her thoughts away from dreams of children as traffic is diverted from an obstruction in the road. If she could not have everything she wanted in life, then she would just have to become reconciled to doing without them.

The front door opened and a black and white bundle hurled itself through the sitting-room door, yelping with delight at having found his long-lost owner again. Flick leapt on to her lap and licked her face and the hands that had to hold him away.

She laughed at his boisterous welcome and when at last he was quiet on her lap, she hugged him. As long, she thought, as I'm not deprived of my dog, I can stand anything. She did not allow herself to remember how much Clifford hated dogs.

'My word,' Murray said, watching her, 'you show more affection to that animal than you do to the man in your life.' He went on, not sparing her, 'You know, of course, that it's a form of sublimation?'

She didn't answer. She could not deny the truth of the statement because deep down, she knew that once again he was right.

She raised grateful eyes to his. 'Thank you, Murray, for looking after Flick. I can't tell you how indebted I am to you.'

He shrugged away her thanks. 'You needn't think you can start taking him for walks yet. I'll come every evening and give him his daily trot across the fields.'

'Are you sure you don't mind?'

'Not at all. Exercise is something everyone needs, even heart specialists – like me. Even detective novelists – like Clifford. Tell that one to your future husband. If ever anyone needed exercise, it's Clifford.'

A car drew up outside and Murray went to the window. 'Good grief, royalty himself!' He turned to Adrienne. 'It's Clifford, bringing your mother home.' He went to the door. 'This is a state visit. Where are the trumpets, the red carpet?'

Lorna bustled in and raised her hands with delight. 'Fancy finding you here, Murray!' Flick jumped down from Adrienne's lap and, tail wagging, snuffled at Clifford's toes. He stepped back in disgust, moving one of his feet towards the dog in a prodding action which could have been interpreted as the beginnings of a kick.

Murray's voice cracked out '*Flick!*' like a shot from a gun and the dog ran to him for cover. Murray gave his brother a cutting look which should have incised Clifford like a surgeon's knife. But it didn't even begin to draw blood because Clifford replied with a pallid, anaemic stare as if he did not know what all the fuss was about.

The by-play between the brothers passed Adrienne by. The pleasure of returning to her home surroundings had temporarily blunted her sensibilities and she was too content to notice the tug-of-war tensions which plagued others.

'Clifford?' she murmured, with an inviting smile. Her arms reached upwards, and as he bent down she fastened them round his neck. It was the most positive demonstration of affection she had ever shown him and her mouth found his, not the reverse. Her kiss was an almost desperate attempt to draw from him some answering warmth, thus proving to Murray how wrong he was.

But her attempt failed miserably. Her arms fell away and when Clifford straightened, he had coloured with embarrassment like a young boy. With defiance Adrienne's eyes swung to Murray's. He had been watching, but his face was expressionless, his eyes blank, and she took comfort from that fact alone. At least he was not laughing at her.

Lorna had been watching, too, and she looked both a little puzzled and a little concerned. Adrienne began to have doubts as to whether she should have done it, but she argued that if she didn't make the first approach, there would be hardly any display of love between them at all.

All the same, she made up her mind never to make any demands on him again, not even for a kiss. If he did not come to her for love of his own accord, then she must learn to keep her emotions under strict control. If it did occur to her that the impossibility of the situation might one day get the better of her, then she passed the thought by like someone turning his head from an accident on the other side of the road.

Lorna started fussing round her daughter, bringing a stool to put her feet on, and plumping up the cushions behind her back. Adrienne submitted to her attentions more out of surprise than anything else. During her few days' absence, her mother seemed to have changed. Like an actress, she had altered her technique. She had abandoned her passive, minor role and taken over the part of the leading lady, exuberant, a driving force which could not be overlooked.

'Now,' Lorna clasped her hands in front of her chin in a theatrical gesture, 'who's for refreshments? Coffee?' Clifford began to shake his head. 'Savoury biscuits? Home-made cakes?' Clifford nodded, beaming.

Adrienne thought wryly that her mother had quickly learned Clifford's Achilles' heel. She sought Murray's eyes. He was smiling.

Adrienne said, 'Mother, Murray and I have just had a cup of tea. Murray made it.'

'How nice of him,' came the answer, 'but I'm sure you've both got room for a cup of my delicious coffee.'

Adrienne frowned. Since when had her mother made 'delicious' coffee? But the coffee Lorna produced was not delicious, it was barely drinkable. The savoury biscuits were mass-produced and the home-made cakes a little tough. But Clifford consumed his portion of the feast with unmistakable appreciation. His eyes glistened with something like emotion as he chewed his way through his future mother-in-law's offerings.

Murray, having declined all food, came to sit beside Adrienne and as the others talked, whispered, 'Your fiancé will be pathetically easy to please when you're married to him. The only appetite he will require to be appeased is that for food, nothing else. He'll require no orgies of love – only orgies of eating! Keep him well supplied with things to eat and he'll be happiest of men – and you the most frustrated woman on earth!'

He moved away before she could gather her wits and find a sufficiently crushing reply.

Before Murray left – his brother seemed disinclined to move – he said to Adrienne, 'You're by no means back to normal. I suppose you appreciate that? You'll have to use a walking stick for a while.'

'Oh, but,' said Lorna, 'you needn't think I'm allowing her to walk about. She's going straight up to bed. I absolutely insist.'

'But, Mother, I can walk now, with help.' Adrienne appealed to Murray. 'Surely I can start trying to get back to normal and not lie upstairs all day?'

'Of course, within limits – the limits imposed by the pain. If it becomes too great, you just stop moving about. It's as simple as that. Your back will get stronger every day.'

'Oh, but,' Lorna said again, 'she's not going back to work.' The statement shot out of her mouth like an escape of air from a balloon. It was almost as though it had come from her involuntarily, as if she had had no control over it. It betrayed her state of mind, her anxiety at the possibility of losing the job she had come to prize, and her feeling of possessiveness towards her temporary employer, not as a man but as a writer, a novelist of repute.

'When she's recovered completely,' Murray said quietly, 'I don't see why not.'

'Oh, but,' Lorna gushed, 'of *course*, when she's *ready*, but that won't be for some time, will it? I really think we should have had the doctor to her, don't you, Clifford? It's really not

131

too late to call him now . . .'

Adrienne looked at Murray, then at Clifford, who was look-ing at his brother. What would Clifford say? He was aware of Murray's wish to keep his profession a secret as much as he, Clifford, desired to keep his own pen-name a secret. He was surely not going to divulge Murray's true status now?

Adrienne rushed into the silence. 'Of course I don't need a doctor. He would only tell me my back was getting better, and that I must be careful in the future. I *am* getting better, Mother. See, I can move now.' With an effort she drew herself out of the chair and on to her feet, disguising with a smile the pain that still shot down her legs whenever she straightened up.

Murray, however, was not taken in by her bravery and he looked at her with compassion tinged with admiration. 'Well done! It won't be long now before you're away over the fields taking Flick for his evening walk.'

He said the words with a purposeful glint and watched Lorna's reaction with interest.

She flushed, grew agitated, fiddled with her brooch and con-tented herself with saying, 'Yes, well, she's not quite ready for that yet, is she?'

Before Murray left, he asked Adrienne, 'Are you staying downstairs or do you want to go up to bed?'

She answered, with a defiant stare at her mother, 'I'm staying down.'

'Right. This evening, when I come to take Flick for his walk, I'll carry you upstairs. Unless,' he looked maliciously at his brother, 'your fiancé would prefer to have the pleasure.'

Clifford coughed, cleared his throat and said, 'Well, if I were strong enough I certainly would, but as you know,' he was ad-dressing Lorna, not his brother, 'I'm not fully fit myself.' He patted his body where he estimated his heart was situated.

'You poor dear,' Lorna commiserated, 'there's you with that,' she nodded at his chest, 'and me with these,' she held her fore-head. 'We really do make a fine pair, don't we? But,' she ad-monished her daughter, 'don't think I haven't worked hard. We've achieved a great deal together, haven't we, Clifford?'

Clifford smiled his assent.

'I can see,' Murray said dryly, 'that after your daughter is married, Lorna, you'll be an ideal mother-in-law and your son-in-law won't be able to do without you.'

Lorna, missing the sarcasm, glowed.

Later, after tea, Murray collected Flick. Before he went out he carried Adrienne upstairs. He did not put her on the bed immediately. He looked into her radiant face, full of the pleasure she could not hide, whenever he was near. She expected him to speak, but he did not.

For something to say she commented, 'You seem to do nothing but carry me around these days.'

He smiled into her eyes. 'You're a terrible burden round my neck.' Still he didn't put her down. 'What will you do if you can't sleep at night? Without me nearby to dose you with pills—'

'I'll just have to put up with it, won't I?'

'Stoic, aren't you, as I've said before.' He lowered her gently to the bed. 'It's just as well. The sort of life you'll be leading with my brother, stoicism is a quality you're going to need in abundance.' He sat beside her and took her left hand in his, pulling at the engagement ring as if intending to remove it. 'Engagements can be broken, Adrienne. Do it now, before it's too late.'

She snatched her hand away and pushed the ring more securely on to her finger. 'Thanks for your advice,' she snapped, 'prejudiced though it is, but I'm not taking it. Clifford needs me.'

'Like hell he does!' was his acid comment as he went from the room.

CHAPTER NINE

DESPITE Lorna's pessimistic prophecy, Adrienne's back improved at an accelerating rate. But it was another fortnight before she was walking round the house with anything approaching normality and she still needed the walking stick occasionally for the stairs. She took Flick for short walks along the lane, rejoicing in her freedom from the four walls of the cottage. But to her mother's delight, she had not yet felt the urge to return to work.

One morning she decided to give Clifford a surprise. Taking Flick with her, she walked to Clifford's house. Murray opened the door, bending down to fondle Flick.

He looked up at Adrienne. 'What are you doing here?'

'Proving I'm fit enough to come back to work.'

He showed her into the lounge. 'Suppose it's against doctor's orders?'

They sat and Flick settled down at Murray's feet. Adrienne smiled. 'I've got a particularly obliging doctor. He's at my beck and call. He won't withhold his permission.'

Murray responded, surprisingly irritable, 'Don't tempt me, young woman. What are you aiming to do, provoke me? *Your* doctor! Beck and call, indeed! Your recent incapacity seems to have increased your impudence potential. In other words, stop being so cheeky!'

'Sorry,' she said, with a smile. He seemed mollified by her apology and she asked, more seriously, 'But it is all right, isn't it, if I tell Clifford I'm fit for work? I'd be sitting still all the time.'

He nodded. 'As long as you don't overdo it. How do you intend to break the news to your mother? You'll be depriving her of her pastime and plunging her right back into her psychological problems at one stroke. You could have your hands full coping with her moods in the next few weeks.'

'But, Murray,' she was anxious now, 'it's got to come some time. She's only been acting as a substitute. I can't give up my job just out of consideration for her mental wellbeing, can I?'

He frowned, bent down and played with Flick's ear, who

responded with a movement of his tail. 'No. Er – forgive me for asking, but presumably Clifford pays you a salary?' She nodded. 'After your marriage you will, I assume, continue doing his work. If so, what will happen to that salary he now pays you? Will it cease?' He saw her uncertainty. 'Don't tell me you haven't discussed it with him?'

'I hadn't even thought about it.'

He leaned back, smiling. 'I must say the idea intrigues me – a husband paying his wife to do his work.' He became serious. 'Isn't it time you thought about it? Isn't it time you thought about a lot of things?'

She stood up angrily and winced at the stab of pain in her back.

He said blandly, 'In your present condition, it doesn't do to get annoyed. Too much of a shock to your system.'

'How can I help being angry? At every opportunity you try either directly or in a roundabout way to make me change my mind about marrying Clifford. I know you only do it out of spite because you dislike him so much.'

Now he was angry. He stood and they faced each other. 'Choose your words better, my girl. If you want to know what I do it, it's my medical training coming out. It's concern for your future welfare as an individual, as an adult member of the society in which we live that motivates me, not because you're an acquaintance of mine.' She winced at his impersonal description of her place in his life. 'Nor is it because you're determined to make yourself my sister-in-law. I do it because I know just what's coming to you if you persist with this ridiculous engagement and subsequent marriage. Blame it, if you like, on my predilection for preventive medicine. I'm trying to protect you from the consequences of your own innocence, your naïvety, your total ignorance of the ways of the world.'

Her inability to answer him in terms as effective as those in which he was addressing her brought her to the verge of tears. While half of her knew he was talking sense, the other half was so prejudiced by her conviction that he was talking her out of her marriage merely to spite his brother that she shut her ears and her mind to his rational arguments.

She made for the stairs which she was still unable to climb without a slight twinge of pain. As she went up, Murray watched, holding Flick back by the collar. She received no welcome from her mother when she opened the door of Clifford's room. Lorna smiled, of course, but it was insincere. Clifford invited her in with a courtly gesture. He was, as usual, still in bed. She wondered if he would persist with the habit of delaying his rising until lunchtime after their marriage. The thought troubled her a little.

Lorna occupied the only available chair in the room, the portable typewriter on her lap, her two fingers poised, ready for the next words to be dictated. Adrienne sat on the bed. Her hand lay on the cover and for a few seconds Clifford's hand rested on hers. As a gesture of affection it was diminutive, but to Adrienne it was as demonstrative and meaningful as if he had taken her in his arms. It was also enough to bring a frown to her mother's face, but whether it was one of disapproval or apprehension, reminding her of her daughter's approaching departure from the parental home, Adrienne could not decide.

'Good to see you back to normal,' Clifford remarked. 'Are you fit for work yet, my dear?'

'Yes, I am,' was the reply, and there was decision and something of defiance in her voice.

'Clifford is so patient and understanding,' Lorna said, speaking deliberately in the present tense, as if staking her claim to the job she had taken over from her daughter and which her daughter was now threatening to take back. 'If I'm a little bit slow, he always waits for me to catch up.'

What else could he do? Adrienne wanted to ask, but knew the sarcasm would be wasted on her mother. 'I've done well, haven't I, Clifford?' Lorna was childlike in her desire for praise. 'Clifford says so. I'm quite willing, Adrienne,' she went on, making a desperate bid to keep her job, 'to go on working for Clifford as long as he likes. I mean, if you're *really* not feeling up to it ...' Her voice tailed off as she saw the determination in her daughter's face.

'I'm looking forward to starting again, Mother,' Adrienne said quietly, firmly suppressing a feeling of pity. 'I'm sure Clifford has appreciated all you've done—'

'More than appreciated it,' Clifford broke in. 'In fact, I don't know how I would have managed without her.' The smile which accompanied his words was unusually warm, and Lorna overflowed with pleasure.

Adrienne looked at Clifford sharply. He was not usually one

136

for dispensing flattery in any shape or form, and indeed, judging by his expression, his statement was genuine enough. It was heartening to know he got on so well with his future mother-in-law. It raised Adrienne's hopes that when eventually she asked him to allow her mother to live with them Clifford might be agreeable to the arrangement.

Next morning she took up her duties again. She set off for Clifford's house, Flick at her heels, her mother staring at her out of the window with unconcealed chagrin. Lorna had hardly spoken a word, except to say that she had a headache coming on.

Adrienne's heart sank as though it had weights attached to it. So she was returning to her old ways, was she? But there was nothing she could do about it. There was no doubt that Clifford could get on much faster with her help than with her mother's, in spite of Lorna's good intentions.

She did not catch a glimpse of Murray all day. When she went to collect Flick from the kitchen after work, Mrs. Masters told her that Dr. Denning was busy catching up on his work before his lady friend came to stay.

'You – you mean someone called Gretel Steel?'

'Dr. Steel, yes.' So Gretel was a doctor, after all. She was his colleague and his lady-friend, as Mrs. Masters had called her.

That evening, Adrienne went to bed early, feeling exhausted after her first day back at work. Lorna kept saying 'I told you so' in a voice so gloating Adrienne felt she would have to cover her ears to keep the words out.

She was in bed when Murray called for Flick and when he returned from the walk, she heard him ask her mother about her.

'She's gone back to work too soon, I'm sure she has,' Lorna explained. 'She's tired out. But she would do it. Nothing I said would make her change her mind.'

Murray laughed. 'Stubborn little puss, isn't she? I've discovered that for myself!'

They must have moved into the sitting-room, because their voices grew fainter. Then they returned to the hall.

'Do you want to see Adrienne?' Lorna asked.

Adrienne held her breath. 'Might as well,' was the answer. 'It's all right, I know which room is hers.'

He came in smiling. 'So you've overdone it.'

'No, I haven't. I'm just taking precautions by resting.'

'That,' he said, 'is a barefaced lie. If you ask me, my statement was more correct. I told you it would be some time before you were properly back to normal.' He looked down at her pale face, picked up her hand and slid his fingers over her wrist. Her face flamed, knowing he could feel her racing pulse. He raised an eyebrow and dropped her hand. He said, enigmatically, 'You can't pretend with me.

'So,' she commented with false casualness, 'your lady-friend is coming to stay.'

He frowned. 'My—?'

'Your lady-friend. Mrs. Masters said so. Dr. Gretel Steel.'

He laughed. 'Oh, Gretel. Yes,' he smiled wickedly, 'she is a lady, and she is my friend, so I suppose she could accurately be described as my lady-friend.'

There was a waiting silence, but he did not choose to fill it. Instead he said at last, walking to the window, 'Your mother told me at some length about the return of her headaches. Anyone would think,' he turned, accusation not far from his eyes, 'someone had told her I was a doctor.'

She replied, vehement in her disavowal of guilt, 'Well, *I* certainly haven't told her.'

'All right, all right. I believe you.'

'And I'm sure Clifford hasn't, either. After all, if he did, you could give away *his* secret to get your own back, couldn't you?'

He strolled to the bedside. 'Exactly how old do you think my brother and I are? Back in our childhood, when we spent half our time in petty squabbling and calling each other names? We've grown up a bit since then. At least,' he smiled provocatively, '*I* have.'

'That,' she countered irritably, 'was a subtle way of saying Clifford hasn't.'

'Yes, it was,' he answered, smiling disarmingly.

There was another silence, then she said, rallying, 'I don't suppose my mother's guessed. It's—' she looked up at him, 'it's your professional manner. It invites confidences. Somehow people feel you'll listen to them and they can trust you.'

'That's nice to know.' He spoke sincerely and his genuine modesty made her reach impulsively for his hand, as she had so often reached for his brother's. But, accustomed as he was to

Clifford's withdrawal on the impact of their fingers, Murray's positive response took her by surprise.

He reached out and took her other hand, too, bending over her. 'Do *you* trust me?' he whispered.

She looked at him unflinchingly. 'Absolutely.'

He removed his hands from hers, breaking off the contact and snapping the tension between them. 'You astonish me,' he drawled. 'After ignoring all my warnings about your future life with Clifford—'

'That's different,' she cried, dismayed by his reversion to cynicism at so intimate a moment.

'No, it isn't,' came the sharp reply. 'It's your obstinacy, your wilful deafness, your deep-seated prejudice because of my relationship to him.'

She drew in her lips. 'Another lecture.'

He said abruptly, 'Good night, Adrienne,' and was gone.

She did not see Murray again for some days. She supposed he was going all out to get through his work before Gretel arrived. She wondered when his guest was expected, but she didn't like to ask Clifford. He lived in his fictional clouds to such an extent that he probably wouldn't know.

Lorna had still not stopped sulking about being deprived of her job. She attended coffee mornings and committee meetings as before, but complained now about the 'bird brains' of the other women who 'sat about all day and didn't know what real work was.'

So cleverly did Lorna create in her daughter a feeling of guilt that Adrienne began to believe she had really deprived her mother of her 'right' to work for Clifford. As a form of compensation and almost of apology, she fussed around her mother more than ever, although, with the twinge of pain which still stabbed at her back now and then, it should have been the other way round.

She had asked Mrs. Masters to pass a message on to Dr. Denning, that she would be taking Flick for his evening walk in future. He had obviously taken the message to heart. He did not come to the cottage any more.

One sultry August evening she walked along the lane towards the road, Flick as usual hovering, nose to the ground, in the distance. The branches of the trees edging the path merged into an archway overhead and the heavy grey clouds formed a threatening shroud above the green leaves. Now and then, in the distance, there was a protracted roll of thunder, but the sun still broke through optimistically wherever it could find a gap.

In one of these sunlit moments, Adrienne saw a familiar figure standing at the end of the lane and her heart burned brilliantly like the sun at the sight of him. He seemed to be waiting for her.

'I thought I'd meet you,' he said. 'I felt like a walk, so I came. Been across the fields since you hurt your back? No? Then we'll go now. If it proves too much of a strain, I can always carry you!'

'It won't,' she said with dignity, and Murray laughed. They reached the path which took them across the fields, but Flick had walked straight on along the road, having become accustomed to doing so in the past few weeks. Murray whistled and the dog came charging back, tongue out, eyes bright, tail flicking and vibrating with joy at the prospect of seeing his old haunts again. Obediently he turned off the road and scampered along the path which led across the fields.

Murray took the dog's lead from Adrienne and stuffed it into his jacket pocket. Then he took her hand. 'In case you trip and do some more damage,' he explained, and she smiled up at him, her eyes dazzling like a burst of sunshine.

'Have you been busy?' she asked, after a while. 'I haven't seen you lately.'

'So you've missed me. I wondered if you would. Yes, I've been busy.'

His silence, his lack of explanation put her firmly on the other side of the fence, reminding her by implication that she possessed neither the intellect nor the education to understand even in layman's language the work he had been doing.

'Will you,' she asked, glancing at him obliquely, 'be working when Gretel comes to stay?'

'I doubt it. She'll be on holiday. Anyway,' his hand tightened as if her question irritated him, 'just what are you trying to get me to divulge?' He pulled on her arm and made her look at him. 'Inquisitive, as well as a stubborn little puss, aren't you? A brother-in-law doesn't have to tell his sister-in-law all his secrets.'

Now the tightening of her hand in his told him of the tension his words had created inside her. He looked at her curiously.

'I'm not married yet,' she snapped, and regretted the words as soon as they were out.

He made the most of them, as she knew he would. 'Well now, if that isn't the first chink in her armour! Have my tactics worn her obstinacy down? Have I made a break at last through the woolly blanket of her emotions, to the hard core of reason wrapped inside?'

'No, you haven't!' She tried in vain to pull her hand from his. 'I refuse to be intimidated by your bullying tactics. They've only succeeded in making me more obstinate.'

'At least,' he murmured mockingly, 'she admits to being obstinate. That's a breakthrough in itself.'

There was a roll of thunder, much nearer now, and the clouds had massed ominously and unnoticed over their heads. 'I think,' Murray said, looking round, 'we'd better find shelter. There seems to be an almighty storm brewing above us. If we don't want to be reduced to pulp by the rain in those clouds, we'd better move fast.' He whistled to Flick, who came scurrying back, unhappy about the rumbles in the sky.

They topped a piece of rising ground and saw some distance across a field an apology for a shelter. It appeared to have four walls and a roof, which was all they needed at that moment.

'Come on,' urged Murray, dipping his head as the first large drops of rain hurled themselves earthwards. 'You haven't got a coat. You'll get soaked in no time if we don't make that shed.'

They arrived at the opening – the door was missing – and dashed inside, Flick ahead, as the downpour began in earnest. The shelter was large enough to take three or four pieces of farm machinery, which had been stored there for protection from the weather. Straw was scattered over the concrete-hard earth which formed the floor, but there was nowhere to sit.

It was pelting now and the storm was coming nearer. Murray put his arm round her waist and looked down at her. 'Scared of thunder?'

She shook her head, her colour responding warmly to the odd tenderness in his voice. Flick roamed about, sniffing at the machinery and scraping and scuffling with his paws. There was a particularly brilliant flash of lightning, blinding against the storm-ridden darkness outside, and Adrienne winced in-

141

voluntarily. Murray's other arm came round her. She looked up into his face and he smiled down, trying to instil into her the confidence he felt.

With an impetuous gesture, she slipped her arms under his jacket and clasped his waist as he was clasping hers. She was hardly conscious of what she had done. She knew only that, driven by the circumstances into an impulsiveness quite alien to her nature, and affected by an unfamiliar uprising of desire which suddenly possessed her body, she wanted to get as close to him as she physically could.

They stood, locked together in an almost desperate embrace, and the tension between them was stretched to unbearable limits. His eyes, intensely serious, looked deeply into hers, up-turned, eager, questing. They forgot about the storm, they forgot about Clifford, about the engagement, about everything except that they were a man and a woman together, alone on a parched island in a cloudburst of rain.

His whisper came like a breeze stirring the tops of trees. 'What do you want of me, Adrienne?'

She shook her head because she didn't even know herself. She hid her face against him and could hear the drum-beat of his heart beneath her ear.

He shook her gently, seeking an answer. 'Adrienne?' the question came again, whisper-soft, urgent, insistent. She lifted her head and tried to speak, but words would not come.

She felt him pulling her down, impelling her backwards until her head touched the hard crust of earth beneath them. Straw thrust itself stiffly, abrasively through the flimsy material of her dress. There was a violent roll of thunder directly overhead, but she did not even hear it.

His lips closed over hers and exquisitely, relentlessly, pain-fully, his hands were robbing her of the power, the will to resist. Rain clattered and bounced on the corrugated iron roof, the straw beneath her shifted.

She heard him say, 'Relax, Adrienne, let yourself go slack. Yield to me, my sweet, don't shrink away,' almost as though he was teaching her, instructing her, telling her what to do.

She tried to obey and she climbed to the summit and there, deep in the valleys, through the mists, she came across oceans of feeling inside her, ebbing and flowing, rising and falling. She found herself giving and giving, and wanting in return. The

142

pounding of her heart filled her ears and became the centre of her being. With the primitive elements raging outside, it did not seem wrong to yield to the clamour of love, the primitive passions raging inside her.

It came to her through the storm clouds which fogged her brain that now was the moment of decision, the parting, like a cell dividing, between the old self and the new. It was for her, and her alone, to say 'yes' or 'no'.

His whisper came again, urgent against her lips. 'Shall I go on, my sweet? If I do, you'll be mine. There'll be no going back. Tell me, only tell me quickly.'

She heard the rhythmic panting of her dog, lying sleeping in a corner, and the decision she had to make between the past and the future assumed the clarity of a landscape before rain. All her upbringing, all her personal convictions, all her powers of reasoning, dulled even as they were by ecstasy, were violently against it. She could not let him take her like this, coldly, dispassionately, with deliberation, without one word of love.

The storm was receding now, the lightning flashes lighting up distant fields. Anger against him stirred inside her, anger, irrational though it was, which should have been directed against herself for having submitted so willingly to his advances. But it was the turning of the tide.

Reaction, bitter, sour, self-righteous, turned her emotions rancid. He had asked, 'Should he go on?' as though it was she who had desired it, had wanted it this way. 'What do you want of me?' he had asked, and she blushed at what the question had implied. Had he thought she was importuning him, and he had proved how willing he had been to oblige? She would have been 'his', he had said, taken away for ever from his brother, and that had been the driving force behind his actions, the only reason for what had happened between them.

He sensed her answer even before she gave it. His body grew hard against hers, his mouth brutal and his hands momentarily violent before he dragged himself away from her.

'Clifford,' she whispered pleading now, 'he needs me. He said so. I can't desert him. You *must* understand.' Her voice grew stronger, accusing. 'I know why you did it. Out of spite. You hate him so much you would even commit the final irreversible deprivation, you would even take me, his wife-to-be, away from him, so that I would never forget as long as I lived, no matter what might happen between Clifford and myself after we're married, that you were the first man ever to possess me. What a triumph for you,' she choked, 'what a mean, miserable triumph!'

He stood, towering over her as she sat, her head dropped forward to rest on her bent knees. 'So he's won,' he snarled, 'once again Clifford's won. He chose his girl right, didn't he? The loyal one, the dutiful one, the sacrificial type who glories in the sacrifice!' His words hit her like pebbles flung with the full force of a vicious hand. He looked down at her, contemptuous, derisive, and turned the tables on her. 'What, I wonder, were you trying to do? Take a lover even before the wedding ring was on your finger, a lover to compensate in advance for the sexual shortcomings of your future husband?'

'Will you stop insulting me, implying that I'm cheap . . .'

' "*Insult*?" "*Cheap*?" From whom did you acquire your peculiarly Victorian attitude to sex? That it's a sin, instead of something which draws lovers – true lovers – together and keeps them together, even for life?'

She did not answer his question, because he did not really require one. Instead, she accused him, in a voice she could hardly control, 'Ever since I've know you, you've set out to awaken me, deliberately and cruelly. *And I know why!* You did it to make sure, unquestionably sure, that, knowing your brother's distaste for such things, I become dissatisfied with him when he becomes my husband, to let me know by practical demonstration just what I shall be missing.'

'How perspicacious of you! Of course I set out to awaken you, as you put it. How else could I jolt you out of your innocence, your artless ingenuity, your incredible and pathetic ignorance of what a true marriage involves?'

So she had been right – he had no deep feelings for her, no feelings at all. It had been a calculated, almost clinical act to 'teach' her, instruct her in all the pleasures that lovemaking entails. And to tantalize her, torment her for the rest of her life with thoughts of what might have been, but which for her, as Clifford's wife, could never be.

He went on, brutal now, 'And I've never met a girl so ready, so eager to be awakened.' He smiled derisively at the fury which his words aroused in her. 'And you think,' he mocked, 'you can do without physical love? That you have *no need* for it? You, my sweet,' earlier he had used the word with infinite tenderness, now it had an ugly sound, 'are the most passionate woman I've come across in years, and my God, that's saying something. I am, after all, nearly thirty-seven. Tell me,' he sneered, 'what are you going to do with all that passion when you're married to my brother? I'll tell you. You'll push it underground, hide it away in a cellar of your mind, until one day it explodes like a devastating time bomb, and blows your neat, tight little closed-up world into an unrecognizable pile of rubble. But before that happens, and speaking purely as a doctor, I'll give you a prophetic glimpse of the future, your future, a résumé of what will happen to you after a year or so of living with my brother.'

She covered her ears, but he tore away her hands, fastened on to her wrists and jerked her up to face him. 'I'll make you listen. You'll become a neurotic. You'll grow like Clifford, like your husband. You'll take to illness as a means of escape. I've seen it all before in others. You'll never know true happiness. You'll suffer from withdrawal symptoms. Being what you are, you won't find relief from your misery, your frustration, by taking a lover. You'll try to pretend you're not like other women, and you'll go on pretending until the explosion comes.' He threw down her wrists and they hung limp and bruised at her sides. 'And when that happens, *I* won't be around to pick up the pieces!'

He stood in the opening and shut out what was left of the daylight. 'Don't expect me to attend your wedding. I shall do my level best not to come into close contact with you again for a very long time indeed.' He turned from her and looked out at the pouring rain.

'You can't go out in that,' she said, and her voice was high and unfamiliar. Then in a pleading whimper, 'You can't leave me here, alone . . .'

'Can't I?' He turned up the collar of his jacket, thrust his hands into his pockets and walked out into the downpour.

Flick started to go after him, but Adrienne, summoning her remaining energy, ran after the dog and seized his collar. He whimpered as Adrienne had done, then flopped down and lay still, his nose resting on his paws, blinking sadly at the empty doorway.

CHAPTER TEN

ADRIENNE never knew how she dragged herself home. She had waited until the downpour had turned into a sporadic drizzle. Daylight had turned into dusk and the barn she was sheltering in echoed with memories of Murray's whispered endearments as he had made love to her. The bright reds and yellows of the farm machinery looked pale now. All the same her eyes winced as they encountered them, like someone who had looked too long at the sun and was temporarily blinded.

Mystery lurked in the darkening corners and in the end she left the place as much to escape from the whispering shadows as to get back home. She trod the soaking path alongside the fields and clambered across the stile, now glistening wet. She wondered idly as she walked if the police had ever caught the unknown man who had been hanging round the village – the same man, she was sure, who had stared into the window of the hut a few weeks before.

She shivered and gazed around apprehensively. She hoped they had caught him, because it was almost dark now and Flick was some way ahead. She whistled and he came racing back. She caught him by the collar and remembered with a shock that Murray had taken the lead from her and put it in his pocket, where it probably still was. So she had to let the dog go again. But this time, perhaps sensing her fear, he stayed with her, trotting only a few paces ahead.

As she opened the door of the cottage, her mother gave her the welcome she had been expecting. She had been *frantic* with worry, she said. Where had she been? Sheltering from the storm, Adrienne said shortly, and went up to her room to change her clothes, her mother's complaints assaulting her all the way.

When she went to work the following morning, she told herself she would not have to see Murray. He would make sure of that. But as she left Clifford's room after taking the pages of dictation, Murray caught her on the landing.

Without a word he handed her Flick's lead. Her lips stiff, she thanked him, and he looked her over coolly, professionally, and asked in a toneless voice, 'You got home all right?'

'Yes, thank you.'

He nodded and returned to his room, snapping the door shut. She continued down the stairs, the pattern of the carpet merging and blurring dangerously as her feet rested on the stair treads. She went to the hut and sat at the typewriter, staring at the keys, her lips trembling. She must not let the tears overflow. Her mother would see that she had been crying and then the questions would start, and that she could not bear.

Next day Gretel arrived. Adrienne heard her voice before she saw her. It was low and gentle, her laugh was warm, like her personality probably, Adrienne thought, racked with jealousy. Later, they met by accident in the hall and Murray introduced them.

Gretel was brown-haired and attractive, her eyes frank and friendly, her manner full of unconscious charm. Murray had loved her once when she was young. He had not married, so he must love her still. Now she was free again, their eventual marriage would surely be a certainty.

Gretel looked at Adrienne, her eyes inquiring, and for a moment they flicked up to Murray's and he responded as though a question and answer had passed between them. They were in tune, Adrienne told herself in anguish, interpreting each other's thoughts like lovers.

'So I meet Clifford's fiancée at last,' Gretel said. 'When's the wedding?' She looked at Murray, smiling. 'Will we be invited, do you think?'

Adrienne rushed to cover the awkward pause. 'Not yet, Dr. Steel. In a – in a few months, I expect.'

'You don't know? I thought all brides-to-be counted not just the days, but the hours as well. I know I did.'

'You haven't met Clifford,' Murray muttered dryly, leading her away. 'That's a pleasure to come – when he can bear to get himself out of bed.'

Gretel laughed again and called over her shoulder, 'Please call me Gretel, my dear. I shall be calling you Adrienne!'

Adrienne smiled her thanks.

The days passed and August became September and the autumnal chill was upon them. Still Gretel stayed on. Adrienne and Murray rarely met, and when they did, Gretel was usually with him. Sometimes Adrienne would hear them laughing together in his room, and a surge of jealousy would rise into her throat and threaten to choke her. Why did they spend so long in there? Doubt and anxiety tore at her and her head would throb with misery.

One morning she met Murray on the landing. He was alone. She looked up at him, her eyes imploring him to speak to her as he used to do, to look at her with warmth instead of blankness amounting almost to non-recognition. He returned her gaze, remote, aloof, his eyes deathly cold, repelling in the depth of animosity they revealed. Her lip trembled so much she had to press the back of her hand against it to keep it still.

At the end of the day, when she was due to go home, Clifford showed Adrienne a letter. 'From my old friend Augustus Charles. An invitation to his literary evening. As you'll see, he particularly invited "my sweet little secretary".' Clifford smiled gently. 'You obviously made an impression on him, my dear.'

Adrienne thought wryly that that was probably an under-statement.

'There's a phrase in the letter I can't quite understand. He also invites your "boy-friend". Since he doesn't yet know about our engagement, to whom would he be referrring, do you think?'

Adrienne felt embarrassed. She explained that Augustus had met her at the village fête and seeing her with Murray, he must have assumed he was her fiancé.

Clifford frowned. 'And did Murray tell him he was wrong?'

Still embarrassed, she answered, 'Not exactly. I think Murray felt Augustus was too – well, drunk to be trusted with the truth. You see,' she fiddled with her handbag catch, 'our engagement hasn't really been announced officially, has it, Clifford? We didn't know at that time whether you wanted it known. I still don't.'

He reached for her hand. 'Adrienne, would you like us to announce it? If that's what you want, my dear . . . After all, you wear my ring.'

She nodded. There was nothing else she could do, she told herself desperately. Once it was common knowledge, it would build an even higher wall between herself and Murray, and that was what she wanted, wasn't it? Brick by solid brick, the wall would grow so that, in the end, she wouldn't be able to see him at all. Perhaps, with their engagement confirmed by an official announcement, she would even be able to forget Murray in time.

When Lorna heard about the invitation to the literary gathering, she said outright that she was livid with jealousy. 'Why can't I come with you? Ask Clifford, Adrienne,' her voice wheedled like a child trying to get round its mother, 'ask him if he could squeeze an invitation out of Augustus for me. Please, darling!'

But Adrienne was adamant. There were times when her firmness with her mother surprised even herself, and this was one of them. She knew the price of that firmness – a prolonged sulking session which might last for days, but this time she took the risk. She resolutely refused to mention the matter to Clifford. So her mother sulked, which meant a minimum of conversation between them, a complete withdrawal from household duties, attacks of countless prostrating headaches, drawn curtains and prolonged rests in bed.

Stoically Adrienne endured her mother's adult version of a childish tantrum. Steadily she refused to get her an invitation.

On the evening of the literary party, when Adrienne was dressing, her mother behaved so badly, she wondered whether it was wise to leave her. Lorna cried, sobbed, ranted, sat with her head in her hands and complained of pains all over. But when at last she was convinced she had finally lost, when she saw her daughter's unshakeable resolution to go without her, she dropped her play-acting as though the drama was over and the final curtain had come down. She was tired, she said, and would have an early night. She even brought herself to hope that Adrienne enjoyed herself, but was unable to resist adding, as a parting shot, 'And manage to forget your poor lonely mother lying unwanted in bed at home!'

When Adrienne arrived on Clifford's doorstep, Murray let her in. He was dressed as though he was ready to go out.

'Are you coming to Augustus Charles' party?' she asked, astonished, addressing her first complete sentence to him since the night of the storm.

Gretel, who was coming down the stairs, answered for him. 'Yes, we are. Clifford's invitation apparently included Murray, so Clifford wangled an invitation for me, too. Wasn't that kind of him?'

'That,' said Murray dryly, turning his back on Adrienne and his smile to Gretel, 'remains to be seen. You haven't yet seen the literary world at play, my dear Gretel. You have an evening of entertainment in front of you.'

She laughed and complimented Adrienne on how she looked. 'White,' Gretel sighed with envy, 'how I wish I were young enough to wear white with such simplicity, such grace.' She turned and went up the stairs. 'I've forgotten my gloves.'

Murray was blocking the way to the lounge. Adrienne stood in front of him and raised a pale face to his. 'Will you please let me pass?'

He leaned with his elbow against the wall. 'All in good time.' He looked her over in excruciating detail and said, his voice barbed with sarcasm, 'Purity personified. Untouched by man.'

From deathly paleness, her face was flooded with colour, and he watched her burning cheeks with an almost clinical interest. Slowly he moved to let her pass in front of him.

They were late arriving for the party. The ornately decorated room was crammed with people, and there did not at first seem to be a seat to spare. As Adrienne preceded Clifford into the lounge, the guests looked up as if glad of a diversion. Boredom had already settled like a cloud of dust on the faces of some of the old hands, with years of such gatherings to their credit.

But the eyes of others, newcomers to that form of literary socializing, were alert and expectant, as if they were still hopeful of something happening. That the 'something' might never materialize had still not occurred to them, nor had they realized that the source of enjoyment was contained within themselves and would have to emanate from them spontaneously, because the party spirit was something which could not be imposed from outside. It was either there, bubbling out of them regardless, or it was not. Somehow Adrienne felt it was not.

She searched nervously for their host. He was talking to a guest and appeared still to be in a reasonably sober state. Some people on the couch moved sideways to create a space into which she and Clifford were expected to squeeze. They fitted themselves in somehow and Clifford, instead of making things easier by putting his arm round her, kept his arm to himself and clasped his hands together between his knees, giving the impression that he was contracting himself into as small a size as possible. He looked slightly ridiculous, Adrienne thought, surprising herself by her sudden disloyalty.

Murray entered, following Gretel and his keen eyes found them quickly. He obviously interpreted his brother's cramped position as a desire to hold himself as far away from Adrienne as possible and his mocking smile made her colour rise indignantly.

Introductions were effected. Murray was described as 'Mr.' Denning, brother of 'our friend, the eminent and much-respected writer, Clifford Denning.' Gretel was announced as 'Mrs.' Steel. Obviously they had both opted for anonymity in such high-flown quixotic company. Gretel was offered an armchair which had been gallantly vacated by a male guest. She accepted with a gracious smile and Murray promptly sat on the arm.

The door opened and into the hopeful silence came Désirée Charters. The outfit she was wearing caused intakes of breath on the part of the women and an exhaling of appreciative whistles on the part of the men. The material was black with a cunningly-applied surface sheen and the dress was in two parts, the brief top and long, tight-fitting skirt being separated by a bare midriff.

Her large brown eyes swept round the assembled company, taking in the admiration of the men and the jealous hostility of the wives. Then her gaze picked out Murray and worked on him like a bird pecking at a crust of bread.

He bent down and whispered in Gretel's ear and she responded by laughing and whispering back. He put his arm across her shoulders and his smile held malicious anticipation as he watched Désirée move towards him, her body swaying enticingly for his benefit.

Adrienne could not hear the words of introduction, but judging by the frown which momentarily creased Désirée's brows, Murray must have introduced Gretel as his fiancée.

But it did not seem to be in Désirée's nature to crumple against opposition. She seemed instead to thrive on it. Undeterred by the fact that Murray's arm had now drawn Gretel as close as the furniture would allow, Désirée curled up on the floor at his feet, the better to gaze up at him with studied adulation.

Sickened by jealousy, Adrienne watched. Two women at his beck and call, both looking at him with love and adoration, because even Gretel was now contemplating his face with almost abject devotion. Murray, a smug smile turning up the corners of his mouth, seemed to be wallowing in their admiration.

For little more than a few seconds, he allowed his gaze to rest spitefully on Adrienne, then, having noted to his own satisfaction the extent of her jealousy, removed his eyes to let them dwell possessively first on one and then on the other of the two women who were paying him silent homage.

Adrienne tore her eyes away and turned them with ferocious interest on to the paintings on the walls. Of course he's enjoying it, she thought sourly. He wouldn't be human if he weren't. That, she vowed, was one thing she would never do – worship at Murray Denning's feet.

Augustus cut across her line of vision and obscured her view of the paintings she was studying with the eye of the connoisseur. He was holding out a drink. As she took it, thanking him, he looked pointedly at her ring, then with equal deliberation at Murray, opened his mouth to speak, but snapped it shut when Clifford, to Adrienne's astonishment, asked him 'for something stronger than sherry, old chap.'

With a low bow, and no astonishment – Augustus was obviously used to such requests from his associates – he moved away and returned almost at once with the request drink. Clifford swallowed it in one gulp and asked for another. Murray, who appeared to be watching, frowned.

Augustus downed his drink with a far greater expertise than Clifford, who had coughed as the second drink descended. Adrienne flinched from Augustus's alcohol-laden breath as he bent over her and said, his voice intimate, 'Enjoying yourself, girlie?' He plainly required no answer. 'Sorry I've forgotten your name, but never mind, to me you'll always be "the secretary bird".'

He winked meaningfully at her, grinned at Clifford and said to Adrienne, 'You like my paintings?' With his hand clamped to her shoulder, he propelled her off the couch towards the wall. 'Have a closer look, darling. Tell me what you think of them.'

She looked appealingly at Clifford, but she appealed in vain because he was frowning at her accusingly as if she was the one in the wrong. Her shoulder was urged further forward by a hand that was shaking just a little more each time another drink was imbibed. But a guest distracted Augustus's attention and he left Adrienne's side.

Having nothing better to do, she stood in front of one of the paintings and stared at it, uncomprehending. Someone came to stand beside her and touched her hand. She jumped, thinking it was Augustus. It was Murray. He, too, was studying the jumble of colours contained within an ornate gold frame, but his mind, like hers, was not on it.

'Clifford,' he murmured, 'is drinking more than is good for him. He's not used to it. You'd better warn him.'

She took umbrage at his dictatorial tone. 'It's not my responsibility if he drinks too much.'

He swung his eyes towards her. They were coldly accusing. 'Isn't it? You're going to be his wife. I should have thought that was a good enough reason for action on your part.'

'He wouldn't listen to me.'

His eyes narrowed. 'That's a poor start to a marriage, I must say. And in any case, I question the accuracy of your statement. I suspect it's more likely to be a shelving of responsibility on your part.'

'I can't understand why you're getting so worried. He's only had two.'

'Wrong again. He's had a third while you've been standing here with your back to him.' He smiled sardonically. 'You're wriggling, like live bait, aren't you? If it's any help, tell him it's bad for his heart. That should do the trick.'

'You,' she snapped under her breath, 'are the doctor. Tell him yourself!'

His look as he turned away made her want to crawl away and die. She watched him resume his seat beside Gretel.

An arm came round her neck and almost choked her. 'Have you,' Augustus's slightly slurred voice said close to her ear, 'had a quarrel with your boy-friend?'

She wondered if he had overheard the sour exchange with Murray. But apparently he was not referring to that.

'I mean,' he pointed, 'he's there, surrounded by females, and you're here, surrounded by me.' He gave a chesty laugh.

'But that ring is still on your finger. That can only mean one thing – you've quarrelled.' He tutted, shaking his head drunkenly. 'And he was going to make an honest woman of the little secretary bird!'

Indignant now, she said, off her guard, 'I'm not engaged to *him.*'

'Oh?' The glazed eyes drew away a few inches. 'Then who's the lucky man?'

Adrienne looked involuntarily at Clifford, giving the game away to the man whose wits, although dulled by drink, were sharp enough to interpret the reason for her look. 'Not *him?* Clifford Denning?' He roared with laughter, attracting the attention of the entire gathering.

Eyes all round them brightened. Was this, they were asking, the 'something' they had all been waiting for? The diverting release from boredom, the escape from the sameness of every similar literary evening?

'Listen, everybody.' Everybody was already listening, straining to hear. 'We've got a sly couple in our midst, a secret engagement. Our old and much-respected associate Clifford Denning's got a woman!' His words were running into each other like colours in a child's paintbox. He held Adrienne's arm high like a referee holding up the hand of a champion boxer. 'He's going to marry his little secretary bird. Our Clifford's engaged!'

His announcement was followed by applause to the accompaniment of a series of cultured, 'Bravo, old chap' and 'Congratulations, my dear fellow.' Clifford was scarlet with embarrassment and an unaccustomed quantity of drink. He shrank almost visibly under the barrage of good wishes, then stood, nervous and uncertain, his legs peculiarly unsteady.

'I was – I was going,' he seemed to be having some difficulty in gathering his thoughts together like a farm dog trying to muster stupid, disobedient sheep, 'I was going to announce it officially this evening, but my dear and valued friend Augustus seems to have pre-empted my prerogative to do so.' He smiled weakly.

So this, Adrienne thought, was the reason for his over-indulgence in alcohol – to strengthen his nerve for the great announcement. She glanced at Murray and immediately withdrew her eyes. He was grinning sadistically, and holding Gretel's hand as though his life depended on it. Désirée, Adrienne noticed in the second before she drew her eyes away, had her hand on his knee.

'Our revered host,' Clifford continued, staring about him with a hunted look like a man being held hostage by a gang of criminals, 'has very kindly done it for me.' He sank down, mopping his brow, as though he had delivered an hour-long speech. But Clifford's troubles were not over.

The arm round Adrienne's shoulders pushed her none too gently towards her fiancé. 'A kiss, I demand a kiss to seal the bond. Come on, old lad,' to Clifford, 'stand up and do your damnedest!'

But Clifford's retiring nature just could not rise to the demands made on it by the panting company, alert as a pack of hungry hounds, agog for his practical demonstration of love.

With a swift, clever movement, Augustus, determined to give his guests the entertainment they were demanding, pushed Adrienne on to Clifford's lap.

'Kiss him, girlie, if he won't kiss you.'

But she sat, stiff as a ventriloquist's dummy, petrified at what was to come.

'Go on, brother,' came Murray's jeering tones. 'Show 'em what you're made of. Show 'em you're a man!'

Recognizing the challenge and the biting mockery in his brother's voice, Clifford seized Adrienne and, emboldened by the drink he had deliberately imbibed, kissed her full on the mouth.

There were cheers all round them and voices urged, 'Keep it up, don't stop, old chap. That's the way! She's loving it!'

And Clifford did keep it up. Adrienne squirmed and then was still, enduring the kiss with growing disgust and loathing. His passions, which had lain dormant for so long, seemed at last to have been aroused, the passions she had tried so hard to find every time she had reached out her hand towards him – yet she felt nauseated and repelled beyond words.

Try as she might she could not respond. She could only endure the embrace and long for it to end. Her mind flashed back to Murray's kisses in the barn, kisses she had returned as passionately as they had been given. She cursed the treachery of her thoughts and told herself that if this kiss, this meaningless pressure on her mouth went on much longer, she would have to struggle violently to force him to stop.

The laughter grew louder and, to her overwrought nerves, became mocking. She could not stand it. She began to resist, to pull away. He let her go at last, his face flushed with effort and alcohol, his eyes triumphant as they sought his brother's. 'You see,' he seemed to be saying to him, 'I can kiss a woman, too.'

She drooped, drained of life, and the audience shouted, 'You've worn her out, old boy. You're a sly one!'

The laughter died down, the chatter resumed and she shifted from Clifford's lap to his side. Someone put on a record, someone else folded back the rugs.

'This is a celebration,' Augustus shouted, 'so let's dance!'

As the couples took to the floor, Adrienne dared at last to raise her head and face the other guests. Désirée was pulling Murray from the chair and leading him towards the other dancers. Gretel was smiling and did not seem to object.

Désirée pressed herself against Murray and his hand rested caressingly on her bare midriff. He seemed to have eyes for no one but the girl who was clinging to him as if she would never let him go. With compassion, Adrienne looked at Gretel. Had he no idea how a woman felt when she watched the man she loved holding another woman so intimately in his arms?

'The man she loved.' Sickened with jealousy, Adrienne tore her eyes away. She looked at her watch. Too early to go home. When would the evening end? The music stopped, started again, and Murray was leading Gretel on to the floor. He looked down at her with deep affection, listened with laughing indulgence as she talked. Did he treat all women as though they were the only ones in the world for him?

Like a voice speaking from another existence, his words on the night of the storm came back. 'If I go on,' he had whispered, 'there'll be no going back. You'll be mine.' And if she had allowed him to 'go on', would he afterwards have dropped her, cast her aside, as he seemed to have done to so many women in his life?

The evening stretched to just beyond midnight, then it was over. Murray and Gretel left first, Murray going without a single glance, as though he had forgotten her existence.

The September evening was mild, but Adrienne shivered and flung her coat round her shoulders like a cape. She sat in the front passenger seat of Clifford's car and closed her eyes. The party had been a fiasco, the announcement of their engagement a farce. Now that the effects of the strong drink had worn off, Clifford's manner had returned to normal. He was withdrawn and thoughtful and made no conversation.

The car was slowing down and she opened her eyes. 'Is something wrong? We're surely not home yet?'

'Someone in trouble,' Clifford muttered. 'He's waving us down. Must want a lift.'

Adrienne peered through the windscreen into the darkness. The headlights picked out the figure of a man directly ahead, facing them, his arms and legs spread out, forcing them to slow down.

Prickles of fear stung her body. 'Don't stop,' she shrieked. 'It's that man! Go *on*, Clifford, go on!'

'What man?' he asked mildly, coming to a standstill. 'My dear, he's in trouble, anyone can see that.' He braked, wound down his window and called out. 'Something wrong?'

'Drive on, Clifford,' she cried hoarsely, 'it's that man, the man who looked in the hut window.' She saw his puzzled frown and remembered that he had not been told of the incident. 'The man who's been hanging round the village for months, Clifford,' the words nearly choked her, 'he might kill us!'

'Don't be hysterical, my dear.' The man approached, making for the passenger's side. He was holding something in his hand. He lifted it up. It was a brick. He rattled the door handle.

'Open this door!' he shouted to Adrienne.

Clifford began to look concerned. 'The fellow's mad,' he muttered.

'I told you, Clifford,' she gasped. 'Why didn't you *listen* to me?'

'Open this door, or I'll smash this window!'

'*No!*' she screamed. 'Drive on, Clifford!' But Clifford was transfixed.

The window was smashed with a single blow and Adrienne was covered with splintered glass. A hand came through the gaping hole, sought for her wrist and found it. Her coat fell away from her shoulders and her bare arm was pulled through the broken window with such force that she screamed and tried to pull it back. As she did so, the edges of the shattered glass cut deeply into her flesh and she screamed again as an unbearable pain ran down her arm. She was covered with blood, but still the man was not satisfied. His hand returned, groped for the lock, found it and opened the door. He began to pull her through on to the road.

'Clifford!' Adrienne screamed, 'Clifford, help me! *Help me!*'

But Clifford did not move. 'I can't, my dear,' she heard him whisper, 'it's my heart. It might kill me.'

The man got her out on to the grass verge and pushed her over. His face came down and in the headlights of the car she saw how evil it was.

There was a screech of brakes, a shout, a series of blows on the man's back, a hand pulling his hair. A voice she did not know rang out, ordering the man to 'let the girl go'.

The attacker loosened his hold and dragged himself upright. He aimed a wild punch at the other's face and made off along the road, away from the village.

The man who had come to her aid helped her to her feet. He tutted. 'You need a doctor, miss. Your arm's in a bad way.' He helped her into the car and went round to Clifford's side. 'Sorry to have to say this, sir, but couldn't you see that girl needed help?'

'I know, I know,' whispered Clifford, 'but I'm ill. I couldn't do a thing. It's my heart, you see.'

The man looked dubious and rubbed the back of his neck. 'All the same, sir,' he was trying hard to be respectful, but burst out, 'he might have killed her!'

Clifford shook his head helplessly, his eyes staring, his hands trembling. Adrienne, white and shaken, her dress saturated with blood, tried inadequately with her handkerchief to staunch the flow from her wound. She wondered if Clifford was fit to drive the rest of the way home.

'Get her to hospital, sir,' the man urged, 'then phone the police. That man's dangerous.'

'The *police*?' If Clifford could have turned whiter, he would have done so. 'No, no, not the police. And not the hospital. I'll take her to my home. My brother's a doctor. He'll attend to her.'

He started the engine and prepared to drive on. Adrienne realized that they had not thanked the man for his assistance. She managed a few words of thanks, felt they were grossly inadequate in the light of all he had done and tried again, but the man waved them away.

'I didn't do anything, really, miss. But you get that nasty cut seen to quick.' With a wave he got into his car and drove away.

Clifford was silent, wrapped in his own thoughts. Adrienne closed her eyes and fought to prevent herself from reliving the incident, but the terror would keep returning. At last, to stop herself thinking, she asked:

'Why aren't you taking me to hospital, Clifford? I'd rather go there than bother Murray.'

'No, no, my dear. If I took you to the hospital, I should have to go in with you, and I couldn't stand the strain, the form-filling, the questions, the waiting ... You must remember my state of health.'

She fought her irritation, and said wearily, 'Well, at least you could phone the police, to protect other people, if nothing else.'

'The police? How could I? Think of the publicity – the truth about my pen-name would almost certainly leak out and – well, I simply couldn't allow that to happen. Think of the consequences ...'

What consequences? she wanted to ask. A lowering of his reputation in the eyes of his associates? And if so, would it matter so very much? Was his pride, his self-esteem so important that he even put them before an emergency such as this? His selfishness, his doctrine of self first, come what may, shocked her into an unbelieving silence.

He turned the car into the drive-way. 'Murray's home, thank goodness,' he muttered. He helped her out and into the house.

Gretel, who was in the hall, took one look at Adrienne and shouted for Murray. He caught the urgency in his colleague's tone and was down the stairs in a few seconds.

He went pale. 'My God, what happened?'

Clifford collapsed on to the hall chair, his head in his hands. There would be no explanation from him, Adrienne knew, so haltingly she told Murray about the incident.

Murray looked at her arm, raised his eyebrows at Gretel and murmured 'Stitches, I think?'

Gretel nodded. 'Hospital?' she asked, but Murray muttered, 'No time. She's lost too much blood already. I'll do it.'

He looked with something like disgust at his brother's apparent collapse. 'You look after him. I doubt if there's much wrong with him except shock, and you know how to deal with that.'

Gretel nodded and led Clifford into the lounge.

'Upstairs, Adrienne,' Murray said shortly.

She tried obediently to climb the stairs, but he swung her into his arms and carried her up. 'My dress,' she murmured, her head hanging back, 'you'll get blood on you.'

He did not reply. He carried her into his room and sat her on the bed. 'You'd better take your dress off.'

She looked at him, her eyes round and burning in her white face.

'My God, this isn't the time for coyness, girl. Take it off!'

With difficulty she did so, but winced as the material passed over her wound. He helped her pull it over her head and threw it outside the door. Her slip was stained. 'That too,' he said, but seeing the resolute shake of her head, he did not insist. He drew her behind him into the bathroom and with great gentleness cleansed the wound.

Back in the bedroom, she sat dazed on the bed, watching him open his medical bag. With difficulty, because her lips were stiff with fatigue and shock, she asked, 'Do you take that everywhere?'

'Yes. Being a doctor, I couldn't afford to be helpless in any emergency.' As he began to stitch the wound, he warned, 'This will hurt, Adrienne. I've no means of anaesthetizing you. Can you stand the pain?'

She nodded and gritted her teeth. But, coming on top of the night's experiences, the pain proved almost too much. She cried out and, reaching wildly for something to grip, fastened on to his jacket, but she told herself that he, of all people, would not want her to do such a thing, so she took her hand away.

He said gruffly, 'Hold on to me. I don't mind. You're being very brave.'

Encouraged by his kindly tone, she grasped his jacket again, bit her lip and lowered her head to rest on her good arm. At last, when she thought the pain would never end, he said he had finished. With skill he bandaged the wound and stood back, visibly relaxing as though it had been painful for him as well as for her.

'Tell me,' he said, putting his things away and closing his medical bag, 'what part did Clifford play in your rescue?'

She shook her head, hoping to put him off the scent and said weakly, 'There was no need. A man came along, a man in another car.'

But he seemed determined to get the truth out of her. 'You're not telling me, in a roundabout way, that my brother did nothing? That he sat there and watched you assaulted and, who knows, almost murdered?' She was silent. 'Tell me, Adrienne.'

'It was his heart,' she whispered, 'he said it would have killed him if he'd tried to stop the man.'

She winced at the unbelieving curse he uttered. 'And you mean to tell me,' he ground out, 'that you still intend to marry him? A man who's as cowardly, as yellow, as craven as that?'

She did not answer.

'Then,' he snarled, 'you deserve everything you're asking for, every single, miserable thing you're going to get!'

They stared at each other, he pale, drawn and angry, she white, shocked and overwrought. She appealed to him with her eyes, pleading with him to soften towards her, to offer her comfort, but his face remained hard and cold.

Tears welled up and she could not control them. 'Murray,' she whispered, holding out her arms, 'please, Murray . . .' He didn't move.

She stood, and walked unsteadily towards him, sobbing. Not entirely in control of her own movements, she slipped her arms under his jacket and clasped him round the waist as she had done in the barn on the night of the storm. She pressed her cheek against him, as if trying to coax some kindness out of him, and draw some of his strength into her own shaking body. She sobbed his name over and over again.

He stood stiffly for a few moments, tolerating her hold, then, as if he could not stand it any longer, put his hands behind him, unclasped hers and replaced her with a mixture of professional gentleness and masculine roughness on the bed.

He seemed to be shaking, too, but it was not with emotion, it was with anger, blazing anger. 'There are times,' he ground out, 'when you bring out the man instead of the doctor in me, and *this is one of them*! I refuse,' he said though his teeth, 'to be used any more by you as a substitute lover in place of my brother, as a compensatory factor for all that he is not. If you want affection, if you want comfort, if you want love, get them from him, not me.'

Their eyes clashed and held, his in anger, hers in torment. As a last desperate gesture of appeal, she turned her palms upwards on her knees. Receiving not a flicker of response, she collapsed in a storm of tears on to his pillow.

She was racked with crying, with pain, with misery. Sometimes the sobs caught in her throat and she almost choked. His only response was to move away. Then, as if her display of emotionalism was driving him mad, he went out of the room and left her alone.

CHAPTER ELEVEN

BESIDE herself with desolation, Adrienne whispered his name between sobs, soaking his pillow. There had been no need, she told herself, for him to have 'made her his' that night in the barn. She was his for life without the physical act to complete it. She knew now that she had grown up. She had gone so far beyond Clifford that she could not even contemplate marriage to him now.

Whether Murray wanted her or not – and he did not – she was his for life. No other man could ever mean as much to her as he did. The realization, oddly, seemed to calm her. The crying died down, the sobs ceased and she lay spent on his bed.

She had cried away her tension, she had cried out the shock that had been locked inside her. Now she was tranquil, sedated not by medicine, but by natural means. When he returned, she was still lying there. He must have thought she was asleep, because he moved quietly to go out again, but she stirred and sat up.

'I'm sorry,' she murmured, pushing her hair away from her face, 'but your pillow's soaked.'

'I can stand it. I've coped before now with pillows saturated with things far worse than tears.'

It was a statement intended to comfort, but it increased her misery. It hinted at a world about which she knew nothing, a side of him, remote and mysterious which, in her brief acquaintance with him had remained hidden – the professor, the accomplished doctor, the man in charge of other doctors, he was all of these things standing in front of her. Yet all she knew about him was his kindness, his desire to heal, his kisses and his lovemaking. His hardness, his coldness and his cruelty.

There was no kindness in his eyes now as he looked down at her. 'Have you got a coat?' His voice was dead.

'In Clifford's car.'

'I'll get it. You'll have to wear something over that,' he indicated her bloodstained slip, 'on the way home.'

'What about my dress?'

'Mrs. Masters is coping.' He went out to get her coat.

Adrienne winced as he helped her on with it. 'Does your arm hurt?' he asked.

'Yes. It's throbbing terribly.'

'It will, for a few days at least. You'll just have to put up with it, put to the test those powers of endurance you're going to need so much after your marriage.'

Tears threatened, but she checked them. Where was his sympathy, his kindness now, when she needed them so much?

On the way downstairs, she asked, 'Clifford?'

'It's all right, your gallant fiancé is being looked after well enough by my colleague. Gretel knows her stuff. She won't let him die.' He underlined his sarcasm with a derisive smile.

She was glad of the darkness on the short drive home. She turned her head away from him and rested her cheek against the upholstery.

'You'd better spend the next day or so in bed.' His peremptory advice came out of the darkness. 'It seems to have shattered you in more ways than one. Perhaps you've now learned what an unscrupulous character my brother is.'

'It's not that.' Her lip trembled at his harshness and it showed in her voice. 'You don't understand what it was like. You weren't there. That man was a maniac. I thought – I really thought,' her voice dwindled to a whisper, 'I was going to die.'

'All right,' his voice was gruff and his hand covered hers briefly. 'I understand a great deal more than you think I do.'

Her head swung round and she asked passionately, 'Then, Murray, why—?' Why, she was going to ask, are you treating me like this? But how could she ask such a question? She saw the hardness of his profile as if it had been sculptured out of stone. He had humiliated her enough for one night. She wouldn't give him another chance. He would only put her from him again, as he had done in the bedroom.

He remained impassive even as her question broke off. 'Can you cope with your mother alone?'

Her mother! She had forgotten the explanations, the fuss, the complaints which would greet her on the doorstep, the shock her appearance would cause.

'Yes, thank you.' She didn't want Murray, of all people, to witness her mother's reaction. All the same, he followed her into the house.

There was the shock she had expected, the tutting and the moans. Then came the questions and she had to do her best to protect Clifford from the criticism she was sure would come his way if she told the truth.

But Murray cut right across her halting efforts to gloss over Clifford's negative part in her rescue. He told the truth, the stark unsparing truth, relating in excruciating detail how his brother had not lifted a finger to help Adrienne in her distress, and that it had been left to a complete stranger to go to her aid. And if it hadn't been for him . . .

'Oh,' cried Lorna, 'poor Clifford, the poor man! In his state of health, of *course* he couldn't do a thing. Tell him I *quite* understand and forgive him from the bottom of my heart.'

Murray looked shocked beyond words. 'But, Lorna,' he said, 'it's *your daughter* we're talking about. If that man hadn't come along, she might have been raped or, let's face it, even murdered. Doesn't that mean anything to you?'

'Oh, but,' answered Lorna, shutting her mind in her well-practised way to the unpalatable facts, 'I don't suppose anything so horrid would really have happened.' She glanced at Adrienne. 'And she *is* all right, isn't she, except for being rather messy and having a nasty graze on her arm.'

'*Graze*, Mother? The wound went so deep I had to have stitches in it. Don't you understand?' Adrienne was appalled at the exhibition her mother was making of herself. She looked at Murray, but he was leaning forward in his chair, his head resting against his hands as if he had given up all hope of instilling any sense of responsibility into the selfish woman who, through her daughter's coming marriage, was one day to become a member of his family.

'I expect,' Lorna went on comfortingly, 'Clifford told the police, so when they track the man down, we'll all be able to sleep more safely in our beds.'

'No, Mother,' Adrienne said quietly, 'he did not inform the police.'

Lorna paled. 'Oh, but my dear, then I shall have to do it. I shall be terrified out of my wits until they catch that man, that – that madman.'

She almost ran to the telephone in the hall. Adrienne rose to follow, but Murray put out a restraining hand. 'Let her do it. Someone has to.'

'Murray?' He lifted his eyes which were trained and lifeless. 'Please believe me when I say I'm sorry to have subjected you to this.'

He shrugged. 'What of it? All the same, the more I see of your mother, the more I realize how you've become conditioned to tolerating my brother's arrant selfishness.'

It was comment enough. Now she knew exactly what he thought of her mother.

They heard Lorna's garbled account of the assault in the darkness of a country lane, heard her surprised, 'Oh, did he? I'm so glad. Now perhaps you'll be able to find this horrible man and make us all safe again. Yes, tomorrow. I'll tell her. Goodnight.'

She fussed into the room. 'The man who saved you had already reported it,' she said. 'But they were glad I phoned as they now know who was involved. Adrienne dear, they're coming to see you some time tomorrow for a statement. You'll be at home, won't you, darling? You won't be able to work with that nasty aching arm, so I shall go over to Clifford's and do his work.' She was overjoyed at the prospect and did not bother to hide it.

Adrienne writhed with embarrassment. That she should be going on like this in front of Murray ...

'There's some typing I must finish, Mother. I *must* go in.'

'Adrienne,' Murray's voice was warning her, 'a day or two in bed, I said—'

She answered, determination giving her the courage to meet his look of steel, 'I'm going to finish that typing if it kills me.'

He drew in his lips, said under his breath, 'If you aren't the most stubborn, obstinate little devil I've ever come across ...'

'Thanks for your concern,' Adrienne replied with dignity, 'but, pain or no pain, I've quite made up my mind.'

'By heaven,' he growled, 'does nothing make you deviate from your set course once you've started on it? Are you impervious to *all* arguments, no matter how rational, how balanced, how fundamentally correct they may be?'

'Tell you what,' Lorna offered brightly, 'you finish your typing, dear, while I take dictation from Clifford. I can use the portable typewriter on my knee as I did before.'

Adrienne capitulated. 'If you must, Mother.'

Murray heard her weariness. 'Bed and a hot drink, Adrienne,' he told her quietly.

Lorna bustled out, murmuring, 'I'll run a bath for her. Oh, dear, all that blood . . .' She was play-acting again, Adrienne thought, enjoying herself, not quite the leading lady, but near enough to it to take the centre of the stage now and then.

Murray had risen and was standing in front of her, hands in pockets. 'All right, so you do that typing and probably make your arm worse as a result. But afterwards, *you go to bed*. And if you refuse to take my advice,' he put his hand on the top of her head and pressed it backwards so that she was forced to look up at him, 'if you dare to defy my orders – doctor's orders – again, I'll carry you upstairs, undress you myself and put you into bed. Have you got the message?'

She coloured deeply, nodded, and he let her go. 'All the same,' she stood unsteadily, still prepared to face his anger, 'I'm going to finish that typing, even if it takes me all day.' His eyes blazed. 'Then,' her tone was placatory now, 'I'll come back home and rest.'

He seemed appeased and willing to accept the compromise. He went to the door.

'Murray?' He turned. 'Thank you for all you've done this evening. I'm sorry,' she could not meet his eyes, 'about the way I behaved in your bedroom.'

If he accepted her apology, he gave no indication of it. 'Those stitches,' he nodded at her arm, 'you'll have to get your own doctor to take them out. I won't be here to do it. I'm leaving in a few days.'

Clifford was quite amenable to having Lorna back as his assistant. So, next day, she duly installed herself in his bedroom and took dictation, while Adrienne finished her typing in the hut.

She sat for a while staring out of the window, Flick at her feet. She hadn't slept well. She had kept herself awake – it wasn't difficult with the pain in her arm – because she had been terrified of reliving the assault through her dreams. As she had lain there in the darkness, she had tried to work out how to tell Clifford of her decision not to marry him. There was no going back on that decision now.

But she realized that in returning his ring, she would have to resign from her employment. And her job was their livelihood. She and her mother could not do without the money. In such a small village, there would be no other suitable work and the nearest town was six miles away. With no car, and a poor bus service, how would she get there?

There was nothing for it but to continue as his fiancée for a while, until she had thought of a way round the problem. At least he was not the sort of man to make demands on her, whose lovemaking she would have to tolerate whether she liked it or not.

Flick's ears moved. He growled softly and went to the door, hearing footsteps. Murray? Adrienne's heart pounded. It must be, it surely couldn't be anyone else. But Flick was not behaving as though it was Murray. It was a stranger who appeared in the open doorway.

Might he come in? he asked politely, and in he walked without an invitation. Half-way down the path, Mrs. Masters appeared, a little agitated, but she turned and went back as if she had done her best.

'I'm from the local paper.' He produced his card. 'Parker, from the *Morning Review*.' He sat on the spare chair. 'You are—' he consulted his notes, 'Miss Garron, Miss Adrienne Garron?'

'I am, yes, but I'm very sorry, I don't wish to make a statement to the press.' He could see her agitation and scented a story.

'I'm not wanting a statement, you know. A few details will do, Miss Garron.' He was being cleverly diplomatic and she could see by his manner that he would not go until he had got what he wanted. 'This man who attacked you has been a menace to the villagers here for some time now, and they all want a few titbits of gossip about him to chew over with their bacon and eggs.' He laughed loudly, probably intending to put her at her ease. He saw her bandaged arm. 'He did that?'

So, in as few words as possible, Adrienne told him what had happened. 'A stranger in a car came along, luckily, and got rid of the man for me.'

The reporter, in the act of taking notes, asked with studied casualness, 'You were not alone in your car? You had a man with you? Someone called – er – Denning, Clifford Denning?'

'Yes,' she fell into the trap, 'my fiancé—' She snapped her mouth shut.

'And he—?' The reporter's eyes were ingenuous. 'He fought the attacker off, of course?'

'Well, he—' She moistened her lips. 'There was no need. I told you, the stranger came along ...' She realized she was making a mess of things. 'My fiancé's heart – it's not all it should be, so ...'

'I see.' The reporter's eyes narrowed thoughtfully, betraying that he had stumbled on the truth, the astounding truth she had been tricked into telling him, that her fiancé had done nothing at all to help, but left it to a stranger, in fact ... And she was blundering on trying to defend his inaction. She could almost hear the reporter thinking, 'His heart, indeed. I'll bet it was. My word, this is a story!'

He stood, slipping his notebook into his pocket. He thanked her, his eyes lifting momentarily to the bookshelves above her head.

'Ah, Damon Dane stories. Good stuff, I'm a fan of his.' His eye, trained to take in details, dropped to the typewriter, read a few words. That was enough. His notebook came out again. 'You don't mean to tel me that – er—' he consulted his notes again, 'Clifford Denning *is* Damon Dane?'

'Please,' she implored, 'he wants to keep it a secret. It must *not* be publicized. Promise you won't ...'

'The press, Miss Garron, the freedom of the press.' He waved his notebook in front of her. 'The truth will out, you know. Whether I use it in my story or not, it would come out some other way.' He raised his hand, his eyes shining. He had a story in his pocket which would assure him of a whole page, plus his name at the top of it. It might even bring him promotion. He left her, running between the trees and out of the side gate in his eagerness to commit his story to paper.

Adrienne's fingers operated the typewriter mechanically. She had to get the typing finished first, then she must think. Should she tell Clifford, warn him about the reporter's visit, or await events and hope against hope the young man had taken pity on her and suppressed Clifford's pen-name? Although she preferred the latter, she knew in her heart she would have to tell him. After all, Mrs. Masters knew the man had come because she had let him into the house.

She finished her typing and found Mrs. Masters in the kitchen. 'I tried my best to send him away, dear,' the housekeeper said, 'but he would come in. I told him Mr. Denning was busy and couldn't see him. Hadn't he got a secretary? he asked. I said yes, but she was busy typing down the garden. And he was away to the hut before I could stop him.'

'But he knew my name, Mrs. Masters.'

'Got it from the police, dear. He told me they phone the police every day for any stories that might be going. And the hospital and the fire station. Got their noses into everything, those reporters!'

So Clifford was told. He took it badly. He shook with anger, blaming her for the indiscretions of her tongue as though she had told the reporter voluntarily. He refused to believe that the young man had been astute enough to discover the truth for himself.

Adrienne returned home, thankful to escape from his sullen accusations, and pleased to leave her mother there to calm him down.

The story broke on an astonished village. 'Famous Author Watches While Fiancée Assaulted,' the headlines shrieked at them. 'Damon Dane, writer of daring detective novels with intrepid heroes, sat back and watched the near-rape of his secretary-fiancée, leaving it to a stranger to drive the attacker off. Ironic, you may say,' the reporter had gloated, 'but it's true. Clifford Denning,' the inhabitants were informed, 'lives in isolated splendour in a lavishly appointed house, hiding his famous pen-name because he dreads publicity. It's a secret, said his fiancée, promise you won't publish it. But I made no such promise,' the reporter thundered on and on . . .

'Darling,' said Lorna, 'did you have to tell that horrible journalist so much? I don't know *what* Clifford will say!'

'Mother, I *didn't* tell him. He found it out for himself.'

The phone rang. Was it Clifford? Adrienne dived to answer it. It was Murray. 'Did you, I wonder,' came his weary voice, 'aim to give your fiancé the heart attack he's convinced he will one day suffer? Did you have to tell the whole darned story, let the secret out with such abandon? I suppose you know you've ruined his image for good, and that he'll sulk about it for the whole of your married life? Listen to this.' He quoted,

' "Famous writer of detective novels sits back and lets criminal assault the girl he loves." '

'Murray,' she pleaded, 'you *must* believe me! I did *not* tell the man. He's a reporter, he's trained to ferret out secrets, you must know that!'

'All right,' he sounded resigned, 'but even if I believe you, others won't. I've had to put up with my dear brother's tirade ever since he opened the damned newspaper first thing this morning.'

'I must come and see him straight away and explain,' Adrienne said agitatedly. 'I'm sorry you've had to put up with so much . . .'

'I should think you are!' She started to protest. 'All right, you didn't mean to do it. But I can tell you this, *he* won't believe you. Thank heaven Gretel and I are getting out of this madhouse soon!' The receiver crashed down.

Clifford refused to see her. Adrienne was dumbfounded. This she had not expected. Mrs. Masters tried persuasive tactics, but it was all of no avail. He would not see Miss Garron, she said, and that was that.

'I'm ever so sorry, dear. It was my fault really. I shouldn't have let that reporter in.'

'But you couldn't help it any more than I could,' Adrienne assured her. 'The man took matters into his own hands.'

Murray came out and saw her standing forlornly outside Clifford's bedroom door. Mrs. Masters discreetly left them. When Murray heard what was going on, he threw back his head and laughed. 'So he's shut you out! Imagine the headlines, "Famous author sulks, refuses to see girl he loves!" What's he going to do after you're married to him, and you displease him? Lock you out of the house? My word, you've got a happy life in front of you!' He slammed his bedroom door.

Two brothers, she thought dismally both with one thought in common – to shut her out of their lives. On the no man's land of the landing, she drooped helplessly. Nothing for it but to go home and tell her mother. Perhaps she, with her own peculiarly maddening brand of persuasiveness, would succeed in securing an audience for her with the 'famous author', and talking some sense into him.

Lorna was delighted to oblige. 'I'll coax him into seeing you, darling. I'll tell him you're heartbroken, shall I?'

She dashed off without waiting for an answer. This, Adrienne told herself, was the beginning of the end. There was no problem now about breaking off the engagement. She couldn't go on working for a man who could behave so childishly, let alone remain engaged to him. Somehow she would have to find another job, even if it meant buying a bicycle and cycling into the town every morning.

But how could she return his ring if he wouldn't see her? There was nothing for it – she would have to go over to the house, turn the handle of his bedroom door and walk in, without waiting for an invitation.

She would give him the rest of the day to simmer down, and tomorrow morning she would confront him and tell him of her decision. The day seemed endless, its monotony disturbed only by the arrival of her mother, who ate a quick lunch and dashed back as soon as she had swallowed the food, saying Clifford was anxious to get on.

'No,' she told Adrienne, 'he says he won't see you yet, dear. He's so angry with you he says you need teaching a lesson.'

If Adrienne had not been so miserable, she would have laughed as Murray had laughed. *She* was the injured party, *she* had been the victim of a vicious assault, yet Clifford was behaving as though she was to blame. Couldn't she be nasty back if she liked, because of his callous indifference to her plight when it had happened? If it hadn't been for that stranger . . . She shut her mind to what the consequences might have been.

Next morning she raced out of the house in front of her mother, left Flick with Mrs. Masters and flew up the stairs. Before her courage failed her she turned the handle of Clifford's bedroom door – and found it locked. She couldn't believe it.

He called out petulantly, 'Who is it?'

But she didn't answer. If he knew who it was she would never gain an entry. She looked across at Murray's door. It, too, was closed. If she asked him, if she told him why she wanted to see Clifford, would he help her? He would crow, of course, because he had won. She was doing what he had been urging her to do for weeks – end her engagement. She crept over the soft carpet and tapped on Murray's door. No answer. She tried again. Good heavens, was he sulking too? Was it something else that ran in the family?

Softly she called his name. Mrs. Masters heard and stood at the foot of the stairs. 'Dr. Denning's gone, Miss Garron. He left last night.'

Adrienne was stunned. He had gone, and without saying goodbye?

'And – and Gretel?'

'Mrs. Steel went with him, dear. There's only Mr. Clifford now.'

She had to find some words with which to answer the housekeeper, something, anything to send her away. 'I see. Well, it doesn't matter.' The housekeeper went back to the kitchen.

So he had gone. Now she would never see him again. How could she, once she had ceased to be Clifford's fiancée, and had left her job?

She collected Flick from the kitchen. 'Mrs. Masters?' The housekeeper looked up from her work at the sink. 'Did – did Dr. Denning leave his address?' Mrs. Masters looked puzzled, so Adrienne hastily improvised an explanation for her impulsive question. 'It's my arm. You know he stitched it? I wanted to ask him something about it.'

Mrs. Masters dried her hands. 'Yes, here's his address.' She took a piece of paper from behind some tins marked 'sugar' and 'flour'. 'And look, there's his phone number. Why don't you give him a ring? He won't mind, dear, if it's that important.'

Adrienne found a scrap of paper in her pocket. 'I'll write it down, then you can have this back.'

Adrienne thanked her, put Flick on the lead and arrived at the front door just as her mother rang the bell. To avoid her mother's questions, she pretended that Flick was pulling on his leash too hard for her to stop.

She took Flick for a walk. There was nothing else to do. When she arrived home she gazed longingly at the telephone. With Murray's number in her pocket, she had only to lift the receiver, dial, and he would be there, talking to her – but what reason would she give for calling him and what would they talk about? Her broken engagement? Would he be smug and say 'I told you so?' Would be he pleased? Or would he not care a damn?

She sighed. She knew she would never bring herself to phone him, so she would never know, would she? He had gone, and he hadn't even said goodbye.

CHAPTER TWELVE

ADRIENNE attended her own doctor for the necessary treatment to her arm. At last, after what seemed an interminable length of time, it had healed enough for the stitches to be removed. She had still not seen Clifford. She had given up trying. Lorna was happy doing his work while Adrienne acted as housekeeper at home and carried out all the household duties.

Perhaps, she thought wryly, this was the solution – her mother working, earning the money, while she, Adrienne, stayed at home growing more and more bored as her mother had done. It was ironic how they had changed places. She could see herself going on with this terrible, cabbage-like existence, into the distant future, growing old with boredom, crazy with boredom . . . She looked at Clifford's ring which she still wore on her finger. Its dazzle, its sparkle mocked her now. She tore it off, found an envelope, put the ring into it, sealed it and addressed it. Her mother would have to be the messenger, the engagement would be over, the ring returned, and she need never see him again.

'Yes, I'll take it to him,' Lorna said cheerfully, when she came home for lunch. She was not in the least put out by her daughter's decision. 'I always said he was too old for you. Murray would suit you much better.'

Adrienne shook her head. Would her mother never learn? 'Murray will marry Gretel, Mother. He loved her years ago.'

Her mother was momentarily disconcerted. 'Who told you that?'

'Clifford. And Murray admitted it.'

'But,' Lorna returned, 'it doesn't mean he loves her now.'

Adrienne frowned, hope flaring for an instant like a struck match. Then, the light extinguished, reality dimmed her eyes. 'But, Mother, when he left he didn't even say goodbye to me, so . . .' Her voice tailed off.

'Oh,' said Lorna complacently, 'he'll be back. I feel it in my bones.' And with that inspiriting if unscientific prophecy, Lorna took Adrienne's envelope and left the house.

All the afternoon Adrienne waited for the frenzied phone

call from Clifford, demanding that she take the ring back, persuading her to change her mind, saying he was frantic with sorrow. But it didn't come. Nor did her mother. Teatime came and went. Adrienne grew so anxious she decided to phone Clifford's house.

Mrs. Masters answered. 'Yes, your mother's still here, Miss Garron, shut up with Mr. Denning. They're working, I think. Don't worry, dear, she'll be back soon. Just keep her tea hot.'

When the food had been kept so long it was almost inedible, Lorna returned. She was radiant. She held out her left hand. There, on her engagement finger, was Adrienne's – Clifford's – ring.

'Darling, congratulate me. I'm going to be married – to Clifford!'

'Mother,' Adrienne shrieked, 'you're *not*!'

'But, darling, I am.' She looked quite hurt. 'After all, I'm only three years older than he is.'

'But, Mother,' her daughter cried, 'you don't mean Clifford actually *proposed*?'

'Well, not in so many words.' She sat down and admired her hand. 'You know,' she digressed, gloating, 'I always did fancy this ring. It's beautiful.'

Her mother's coolness, her disarming honesty, left her gasping. She felt like a swimmer about to go down for the third time. It couldn't be true that Clifford had switched his affections easily, so obligingly, so accommodatingly from daughter to mother!

And had her mother all these months been *jealous*?

Lorna smiled up at her with childlike frankness. 'I suggested it. I told him we were ideally suited. I could look after him as he needed looking after. I told him our temperaments were perfectly matched.'

She's right, Adrienne thought, astonished at her mother's astuteness. Was she not so naïve, after all?

'In the end,' Lorna went on, still admiring the diamonds which sparkled on her finger, 'he agreed that it would be an excellent arrangement.'

But what about me? Adrienne wanted to cry, as her mother had cried when told of her own engagement to Clifford.

As if she had read her daughter's thoughts, Lorna said, 'After we're married, I shall of course live with him. And you, darling, can live here. You won't mind being on your own, will you? You'll have Flick, after all.'

Adrienne looked at her closely. Was there a wicked glint in her eye, a sort of exultant triumph at the turning of the tables? If there had been, it had lasted no more than a fraction of a second.

'Clifford sent a message. He said he's sure you'll understand. He would like to see you. I think he wants to make amends now he's going to become your stepfather.'

After lunch next day, when Adrienne had recovered from the shock of her mother's engagement, she took Flick for a walk. She had to get away to the peace and freedom of the green fields. She needed space in which to think, to breathe, to contemplate the changed pattern of events, to work out in which direction her own future lay.

Her footsteps were, of their own volition, taking her towards the barn in which she and Murray had sheltered during the storm. She felt somehow that there, and only there, would she find the answer. It was a feeling that had nothing at all to do with reason, and it would not be ignored.

As she walked, a fantasy was enacted in her mind in which she found him waiting, his arms outstretched. She would run into them and be wrapped around by his strength and his love.

So strong was the effect of this daydream that she experienced a terrible sense of deprivation and disappointment when she found that the barn was empty. The farm machinery was there, of course, in different positions, having been used for the harvesting and returned. The colours had faded, the machines looked well used and here and there spots of rust were showing.

Where they had lain and made love a farm tractor stood, with almost sacrilegious disrespect. The scattered straw moved in the breeze which blew in through the open doorway and she heard again his whispered words as he had asked her, 'Shall I go on? There'll be no going back. You'll be mine.'

Now, when it was an irretrievable part of the past, she recognized his consideration, his restraint, his thoughtfulness in asking her, where other men would have blundered on in blind and selfish disregard of her wishes.

She sank down on the hard rutted earth and cried. Flick came up to her and she hugged him, rubbing her wet cheek against the rough hairiness of his head. He panted and licked her face as if doing his best to cheer her up. Nothing, his tail said, licking madly, is ever as bad as it seems.

She stopped crying at last and dried her eyes and the dog raced away into the farthest corners of the barn, seeking new scents, new excitements.

She looked up and for a passing second saw the outline of Murrays' figure in the open doorway. He was not there, of course, because the picture was in her mind, but she felt his presence so strongly it was almost tangible. It was the moment of decision. She rose purposefully and went out into the October sunshine, urging Flick to follow. She hurried past the fields, ploughed up now and ready for next spring's sowing. Flick overtook her and sped on.

Adrienne had made up her mind. As soon as she got home, she would phone Murray. She would say, 'I've broken off my engagement to Clifford. My mother's marrying him instead. I just thought you'd like to know.' Then she would ring off.

Nothing would come of it. It wouldn't really interest him now, because he would soon be marrying Gretel, but at least she would have had the satisfaction of telling him, the reassurance of his knowing what she had done.

She flung her coat on to the stairs and before her resolution crumbled away, dialled his number, waiting with throbbing heart for her call to be answered. The buzz in her ear went on and on, until she realized that it was mid-afternoon and that he wouldn't be there because he would be away at his place of work. Ignoring her reason which told her to ring off, she held on, still willing the miracle to happen, reproaching herself at the same time for being a fool.

But the miracle did happen – the call was answered. A woman's voice said, 'Professor Denning's residence. Can I help you?'

Adrienne recognized the voice. It was Gretel's, and she seemed to be breathing hard as though she had been running. This was a situation Adrienne had not anticipated and she stuttered over her reply.

'N-no, thank you. It – it doesn't matter.'

'Who is that?' Gretel persisted. 'Professor Denning is out. Dr. Steel here. Can I take a message?'

Adrienne knew she would have to give her name. She could

not ring off in silence because Murray, being a doctor, would not rest until he had discovered the caller's identity in case it was an emergency.

'Adrienne Garron here. It doesn't matter, Dr. Steel. Thank you all the same.' Then she did ring off.

Disappointment weighed down her limbs as though they were encased in plaster. She dragged herself to an armchair and sank her head into her hands. So Gretel was at his flat. What else had she expected? She was going to marry the man, wasn't she? Of course she would treat his home as hers.

She made herself a cup of tea, but it didn't help at all. Her mother came in, her exuberance repugnant, thrusting Adrienne even farther into the abyss of depression into which she had fallen like a victim floundering in the waters at the bottom of a well.

Lorna announced that she was returning to Clifford immediately after tea. 'Do come with me, darling. He wants to see you. He's longing to hear you say you forgive him and that you're pleased about us.'

'No, thank you, Mother.' She did not care if she never saw Clifford again. 'Tell him I understand and am pleased for both of you.'

So Lorna set off, saying cheerfully she didn't know when she would be back. 'But you've got Flick, haven't you, darling, so you won't be lonely.'

If Adrienne had thought her mother capable of irony, she would have suspected it then, but her mother's face was blandly innocent and she decided in the end that it was a typically quixotic 'Lorna' remark.

She stared out at the early dusk, wondering what to do for the rest of the evening. Then the ring of the telephone wrecked the silence, playing havoc with her nervous system and paralysing her momentarily with the crazy thought that it might be Murray ringing back.

Only the conviction that it was her mother phoning to urge her to come across and make her peace with her future stepfather made her lift the receiver and announce herself.

Murray's cool, even tones greeted her with, 'I understand from Gretel that you phoned me this afternoon.'

It was a stranger talking. It wasn't Murray, he wouldn't speak to her as coldly as that. Confused by his frigid tones, she answered irritably.

'I told Dr. Steel it didn't matter, so you needn't have bothered.'

'Well,' he sounded equally irritable, 'I have bothered, so now I've been good enough to take the trouble, you might at least tell me why you wanted me.'

The inevitable tears filtered through. She said thickly, 'I only wanted to say,' she swallowed, 'that I'm no longer engaged to Clifford. My mother's marrying him instead. I just thought you'd like to know.' Then she replaced the receiver.

She gave in to the tears. It was easier than fighting them. She had longed for the sound of his voice, and now she had heard it, heard the harshness of it grating like sandpaper rubbed over a roughened surface, she bitterly regretted the impulse that had made her contact him in the first place.

The phone rang again. She covered her ears, raced upstairs and threw herself on the bed. *She would not answer!* Even if he rang until midnight, she wouldn't answer. But the ringing went on and on until it nearly drove her mad. She would go down and take the receiver off the cradle, but once she had heard the caller's name, and had confirmed it was Murray, she wouldn't speak into it, she would leave it off.

She raised the receiver to her ear. 'Adrienne! *Adrienne!* Will you answer me?' She just listened. 'Adrienne, are you there? If you don't reply, or if you put that phone down again, I swear I'll ring the police and get them to go round to your cottage and find out what's wrong. *Now* do you hear me?'

'Yes,' she whispered.

'Right. Now I've got your attention, answer the following three questions. First, is it true that you've broken off your engagement to my brother?'

She told him, barely audibly, yes, it was true.

'Second, did I hear correctly when you said your *mother* was going to marry him?'

'Yes,' she whispered again.

'Now the last question, and after that you can go, if you still want to.' He took a breath. 'Will you marry me?'

She opened her mouth, started to speak, but nothing happened. '*Adrienne!*'

He was growing impatient. She would have to say something, anything would do. 'But – but why?'

'Why?' he almost shouted. 'Why does any man ask a woman to marry him? Because he loves her, because he wants her more than he wants any other woman in the world. *Now* will you answer the question?'

'But, Murray—' She sounded stupid even to herself, but there seemed to be nothing she could do about it.

'For pity's sake,' his voice came through hoarsely, 'answer me. Look,' he seemed to be trying to keep his patience, 'do you love me?'

'Of course,' she said clearly and with no hesitation whatsoever.

' "Of course," she says,' he mimicked her, now beside himself with impatience, '*then why won't you answer my question?*'

'Of course I'll marry you, Murray. I've never really wanted to marry anyone else.'

'All right,' he seemed to be panting like a man at the end of an obstacle race, 'you've given me the answer I wanted. The rest will keep.' There was a short pause and she grew afraid of the silence, the distance between them which was keeping them apart as surely as if they were on opposite sides of the world. She wanted to touch him, to have the reassurance of his kisses, to look into his face and try to guess what he was thinking.

'*Murray!*' He must have sensed her distress, because he answered immediately.

'It's all right, my darling, I haven't gone away. I was trying to work things out. Will you come to me? If I could I would drive down and collect you, but unfortunately I'm tied up tomorrow until lunchtime, but I'll arrange things so that I have the afternoon free.'

'Tomorrow, Murray? But how can I—?'

'Yes, tomorrow, Adrienne, do you hear? Get out of it, my sweet, leave the two of them to fend for themselves, to find their own feet. You've made it easy for them long enough. In any case, I'm your first concern now. And you're mine. I'm not letting you stay there as an unpaid servant one moment longer than necessary.' He told her the times of the trains. 'Get a taxi into the town – I'll pay all your fares. Catch the train – the journey takes nearly three hours – and I'll meet you this end at the station. Adrienne—' he stopped abruptly, then, 'Oh, God, this is a hell of a way to talk to the girl you've just proposed to.

I can't even touch you—' He broke off again. 'Adrienne, promise me you'll come tomorrow.'

'I promise,' she whispered. Then she remembered. 'Murray,
what about Flick?'

'Flick? Bring him with you, of course. He's part of the
family. He introduced us, remember!'

Adrienne was in the train, on her way to Murray. Her eyes were
closed and she was swaying with the gentle movement of the
carriage. Flick was asleep at her feet. There were one or two
other passengers in the compartment, but she was hardly aware
of them. The rest of the world had ceased to matter since
Murray had asked her to marry him.

She had easily ridden the storm of her mother's tearful pro-
tests the night before on her return from Clifford's house.

'You can't leave me just like that. What am I going to do
without you?'

All so familiar, Adrienne thought, but this time she hadn't
felt an ounce of remorse. It was only a matter of time before her
mother moved in to take command of Clifford's house – and
Clifford's life. Her own departure might even hasten the marriage, which would be a good thing for them both.

'I'm going, Mother,' she had said firmly, and Lorna had had
to accept the fact.

When at last she had become reconciled to the idea and had
recognized that her daughter could not be dissuaded, Lorna
changed her tune and had begun to enthuse about Adrienne's
coming marriage.

'Of course,' Lorna had said, crowing, 'Murray's not as
talented as Clifford, but—'

'Mother,' Adrienne had returned quietly, 'I think you should
know that Murray's a doctor.'

'No, dear, not a *real* doctor. A Ph.D. You told me.'

'Mother, he's a medical doctor, so you see, he *is* a "real"
doctor, as you call it.'

Lorna was stunned. She held her throat and croaked, 'So
you're marrying a doctor?' She had flung her arms round her
daughter's neck. 'My goodness, that's wonderful! Of course you
must join him tomorrow. How delightfully useful to have a
doctor in the family!'

Now Adrienne smiled to herself. 'Give me good notice of the

181

wedding,' Lorna had said when she saw her off in the taxi that morning. 'Then I can buy something to wear that's really worthy of the occasion.' She had assured her mother that she would.

A journey had never seemed so unending as the one Adrienne was making to meet the man she loved. She did not notice the changing pattern of the countryside, the hills in the distance, the build-up of industry as they passed through large towns and cities, the residential areas being developed on every available piece of land.

Her head was resting against the upholstery, her ears attuned to the urgent repetitive message of the wheels, her eyes rejecting the landscape that passed before them and looking inwards instead. She was dwelling on the meeting at the end of the journey, the message of love which would pass between their eyes as well as their lips.

The pace of the train was slowing, imperceptibly at first, then there was no doubt about it. They were entering the terminus, the great echoing station with its high vaulted roof, its noise and its hustle.

Adrienne quietened Flick, who was growing restless, sensing a change in the air through the slowing rhythm of the wheels and finally the jerk of the brakes. Now they were standing at the station and the carriage door was flung open by another passenger. Then Adrienne and Flick were the only ones left. As she reached overhead to pull down her cases, Flick started to bark. 'Hurry,' he was saying, 'everyone's gone.'

'Adrienne?' Murray was in the doorway and Flick was going mad. Murray fondled him and played with him for a moment, telling him, 'I followed your noise, dog. Thanks for directing me.'

Adrienne turned and their eyes met. They smiled, but there was not a spark between them. Nothing happened. She felt cold inside, and for the first time, uncertain. What had she done? Run away from home – yes, that was what it amounted to – to meet a man, a familiar stranger, but a stranger nonetheless.

He frowned, took her cases in each hand and led the way out of the carriage. 'Can you manage the dog?' he asked, tonelessly.

'Yes, thank you.'

They walked side by side along the platform. 'Sorry it's so far,' he said, clearly trying to make conversation, 'but you were a long way up the platform.'

Well, she would help him out. 'Have you got your car?'

'Yes, but I had to put it in a side street.'

'Oh, I'm sorry to give you all this trouble.'

He moved his shoulders as if it didn't matter. She produced her ticket and they passed through the barrier. He put the cases down.

'Have you had lunch?'

'No, but I'm not hungry.'

'You must eat. We'll find somewhere before we go to my place.'

'No, thank you. I couldn't eat a thing.'

He heard the waver under the firmness of the words and must have decided not to press the point. 'All right, we'll go straight home.'

'Home'? Where was home? It was his home, not hers. He put her cases in the boot of his car and drove out of the town.

Adrienne closed her eyes and relived the meeting of her dreams, the flying down the platform into his arms, the abandoned kiss, the barking of the dog, the laughing indulgent eyes of the passers-by as they gazed at each other, unable to tear themselves apart.

Why, a demon laughed inside her, he's hardly looked at you, let alone touched you. He had proposed last night on the phone, hadn't he? She hadn't dreamed that, too? Why had he done it?. *Out of pity?*

He must have glanced at her. 'Tired?'

She opened her eyes. 'No, just thinking.'

'What are you thinking, Adrienne?'

'Nothing important. Not worth repeating.' Suppose she had told him, 'I was thinking you don't love me. You haven't told me so. You're sorry for me, that's all.' She glanced at his profile and he was frowning again.

'Having second thoughts?'

She looked at him sharply. 'No.'

'What's the matter? Still hankering after my brother?'

On the verge of tears she said, 'Oh, let's get to your place.'

'Home,' he corrected her.

'Your place.'

He drew in his lips.

His flat was spacious and well furnished. There was a large

183

comfortable living-room and two bedrooms. The kitchen was a housewife's dream. Had it, the demon inside her asked, been planned with Gretel in mind?

'Come and sit down, Adrienne. I'll give you a drink.'

'I don't want a drink, thank you.'

He said quietly, 'You'll have a drink, Adrienne, even if I have to force it down your throat.' His voice held a warning she had to heed.

'But,' she said, capitulating and taking the glass, 'I haven't eaten for hours.'

'I'll find some biscuits.' He tipped a packet on to a dish and she took one. 'Take two.' She took another.

He gave Flick a drink of water. 'Hey, Flick,' she heard him say from the kitchen, 'this is yours. Can you read? It says, "Dog, d – o – g." I brought it just for you. And some dog biscuits.'

A lump came into her throat. So he had been out to buy some things for Flick, almost as if he welcomed him into the household.

'He's made more fuss of Flick than he has of you,' the demon whispered. It didn't occur to her that the dog had reciprocated Murray's advances in good measure.

Murray threw himself into a chair opposite her, picked up his glass and asked, 'Was the journey tiring?'

'Not really.' Should she tell him, I was so excited about coming to you, I hardly noticed where I was? 'Flick was good.'

'And were you?' He was smiling.

She was on the defensive at once. 'I always am.'

'Are you?' came softly, reminiscently.

Now he was referring to the night of the storm and she thought he was mocking her. She coloured and stiffened. 'Where's Gretel?' she asked, her lips taut.

He shrugged. 'Working.'

'But when I phoned and you were out, she was here.'

He watched her thoughtfully. 'So that's what's eating you?' he murmured. 'Believe me or not, she came here to collect some important papers I'd inadvertently left behind. As she was climbing the stairs, she heard the phone ring and got to it just in time before the caller – you – rang off.'

Adrienne remembered she had sounded as though she had

184

been running. Murray drew himself out of the chair and wandered across to her. He took her hand and Adrienne's heart hammered against her ribs. But he only wanted to look at the wound he had stitched.

'Just admiring my handiwork,' he said, smiling. 'I see it healed well.' He lowered her arm, but retained her hand.

'Yes, thank you.' She moistened her lips. 'Murray,' she whispered, 'why did you ask me to marry you? Out of pity?'

The moment it was out she regretted it. He flung down her hand and her heart fell with it. 'Why did you agree to marry *me* – because I was better than nothing?'

She stared at him. Were they really quarrelling? Or was he as unsure of her as she was of him? He pulled her out of the chair to stand in front of him. He was still frowning.

'Adrienne, last night on the phone you said you loved me. You've given me no proof whatsoever of the truth of that statement since the moment we met at the station today, no sign, nothing.'

'But, Murray, how can you say that? I—' 'Go on, say it,' the demon said wickedly, 'tell him you love him more than anyone else in the whole world.' She shook her head. In her dream she could have said it, but not now, not in cold reality.

His hand came out, palm upwards, as if inviting her to place hers in it. So he was making it easy for her, was he? She stared at his hand, but didn't touch it. Instead she did what instinct prompted to do, what she had done twice before – on the evening of the storm, and that night in his bedroom.

She slipped her arms inside his open jacket and clung to him, pressing her face against him and hiding the tears that would keep threatening to flood her eyes, like a rising river reaching danger level. She felt the strength and the hardness of him and for a moment he stood motionless, as he had done before.

Then he put his hands behind him and tugged apart her clasped hands. With a convulsive movement he jerked her into his arms and he was kissing her as if his life depended on it and she was responding with his passion, and it was as if they had never been apart.

Later, he held her away and looked into her shining eyes. He shook her. 'You kept me guessing, you little minx. What got into you? You were like a stranger—'

'But so were you. You were so cool I began to wonder if I'd

185

dreamed it all.'

He drew a piece of paper from his pocket. 'Look at this and then tell me you dreamed it. It's a special licence. We buy the ring this afternoon and you're marrying me tomorrow.'

She was aghast. 'But, Murray, my mother wants to come to the wedding. It can't be tomorrow. She wouldn't have time—'

He pulled her on to the couch and into his arms again, as if he could not bear to have her out of them. He was smiling broadly. 'Let's have our first quarrel. Flick can be the referee.' He whistled and Flick came bounding in. He sat on his haunches in front of them. 'You see, he's waiting to adjudicate. I wonder who's side he's on? Now, my darling wife-to-be,' he caught her chin, 'I state here and now that I'm not going to have my future mother-in-law at our wedding. Nor am I going to have my brother.' His hand went to his head 'Good grief, what an odd relationship – he's also going to be my father-in-law! The sooner I forget that, the better. Well, Miss Garron, are you going to argue with me and tell me you insist on having your mother there? otherwise it's all off!'

She smiled up at him, her eyes sparkling. She sighed and cuddled up to him, whispering, 'No, doctor. I'll do anything you say, doctor.'

He tipped up her face and murmured against her lips, 'That, my sweet, in the circumstances is dangerous provocation. However, by summoning all my self-control, I can restrain myself for another twenty-four hours.'

'Murray,' she looked into his eyes, 'you haven't told me once that you love me. You made me tell you, but—'

Swiftly, and to her complete satisfaction, he rectified the omission. When they came down to earth again he said, 'Now I suppose you want to know when it all began?'

'Yes, please.'

'Well, that day in the café in the park, I was, as you know, peacefully drinking my cup of tea and brooding about my work, when I saw a slim, shapely – being a man, that was the first thing I noticed! – attractive young woman come in with a dog and it down at a table at the other side of the room. I was very taken with this young woman and was wondering how on earth I could manage to speak to her when her dog cleverly manoeuvred the introduction!'

'When I told you my name, did you know who I was?'

'Of course I did, and it was then that I realized I'd arrived on the scene too late, because you were engaged to my brother. Clifford had written to tell me about you, so, having a vacation approaching, I decided to go and stay with him for a day or so for the purpose of vetting his new fiancée. I couldn't understand how any girl on the level could dream of marrying my brother! I was convinced she must be after his money – he's not exactly poor – so I though I'd take a quick look at her and go abroad for a long holiday and leave her to the fate she deserved.'

'But you didn't.'

'No, because when I saw the girl in question, I knew I had to take action. Dearest, you were so innocent, so straightforward, so disarmingly honest I decided you had to be protected from your own foolishness, whatever the cost. I must admit I was not entirely altruistic in my actions – I happened to have fallen in love with you myself.'

'So,' she wriggled in his arms, 'that was why you spent hours trying to persuade me to break off the engagement?'

His arms tightened. 'Stop wriggling, sweetie, you're distracting me!' He answered her question. 'Not entirely. Leave me with some honour! Being a doctor and knowing my brother's nature and character inside out, I could see the consequences of your marriage to Clifford being, in the medical sense, disastrous. I knew that if you married him, you would suffer both physical and mental agonies. I had to try to talk you out of it. Quite apart from the fact that I wanted you for myself, it was my duty as a doctor to warn you. But talking to you on that particular subject was like trying to persuade a river to flow the other way. I nearly gave up.'

He rested his cheek against her hair. 'You remember when I left you to go to meet Gretel? I was at my lowest ebb that night. I was convinced I'd lost and that Clifford had finally won.' She lifted her hand and stroked his hair. He caught it and put it to his lips. 'You remember I stayed away longer than I intended?'

'Yes. I thought I'd never see you again.'

'You weren't far from the truth. I nearly didn't come back.'

'But why not?' she whispered, her voice unsteady.

187

'Because I couldn't bear to see the girl I loved throwing her life away on a man who didn't really love her but who only needed her for his own selfish reasons. Then I decided I couldn't sit back and let you go without a fight. Even if I couldn't make you love me, I could at least make yet another attempt to stop you ruining your life by marrying Clifford.' He paused and lost his seriousness. 'But when I discovered what an obstinate little minx you were, and that no matter what I said, I couldn't produce a single crack in your armour—'

'You did in the end.'

'When was that – after Augustus's party?'

She nodded. 'That was the last straw, but it was a gradual process. All the time you thought you were getting nowhere, you were slowly persuading me and wearing away my resistance. Anyway, I loved you more every time I saw you, so you were bound to win in the end!'

'That night,' he asked softly, 'after I stitched you up, was that when you tried to tell me, in your own way, that you loved me?'

She nodded and said, her cheek against his, 'You rejected me.'

'Sweetheart, what could I do? If you knew how near I came that night to throwing aside my resolve not to tell you I loved you, and taking you in my arms ... Seeing you lying there crying yet being unable to comfort you after all you'd been through was sheer hell.'

'But, Murray, why didn't you?' Even now there was anguish in her voice.

'Because, my darling, I was convinced that if I'd told you I loved you, you wouldn't have believed me. I was sure that with your customary impudence you would only have accused me once again of saying it to spite my brother, of "stealing you away from him" simply for the sake of it.'

She said defensively, 'But I was convinced you loved Gretel.'

'I did, many years ago, so many in fact I can hardly remember it now. I doubt if she'll marry again, and even if she does, it won't be to someone like me.'

'But at Augustus's party—'

He broke in, 'She collaborated with me in keeping Désirée at bay.' He grinned. 'Very effectively, too.'

She said plaintively, 'I'm sure you were enjoying yourself.'

'Of course I was. What man wouldn't, with two "adoring" women gazing up at him, especially when the one he really wanted was turning him to ice with her freezing eyes?'

Some time later he said, 'Now to discuss more important matters. I've booked you a room for one night at a small hotel near here. We'll take your cases there this evening. But now we'll eat. Afterwards, we'll buy the ring. And in—' he consulted his watch, 'a little less than twenty-four hours from now, my home will be your home and you will be my wife. Then,' his eyes glinted, 'I shall have some very important unfinished business to attend to.'

'Yes, doctor,' she whispered, gazing up at him, 'anything you say, doctor.'

'Flick,' he addressed the dog who was still sitting on his haunches watching them, 'she's at it again. I do believe she's egging me on, despite my warning.' He caught her face between his hands and looked into her shining eyes. 'Are you?'

She smiled, but it was answer enough.

'I'm warning you, my girl,' there was a dangerous note in his voice, 'you're playing with fire. Are you aware of that?'

She nodded.

'Right, my darling,' he said, 'this is where you get your fingers burnt.' He pulled her towards him roughly and his mouth claimed hers.

With infinite tact, Flick rose, stretched lazily, wandered into the kitchen and curled up contentedly in a corner.

Harlequin

the unique monthly magazine packed
with good things for Harlequin readers!

A Complete Harlequin Novel

You'll get hours of reading
enjoyment from Harlequin
fiction. Along with a variety
of specially selected short
stories, every issue of the
magazine contains a
complete romantic novel.

Readers' Page

A lively forum for exchanging
news and views from Harlequin
readers. If you would like to
share your thoughts, we'd love to
hear from you.

Arts and Crafts

Unusual handicraft articles are a
fascinating feature of Harlequin
magazine. You'll enjoy making your own gifts and
indulging your creativity when you use these always
clear and easy-to-follow instructions.

Author's Own Story . . .

Now, meet the very real people who create the romantic world of Harlequin! In these unusual author profiles a well-known author tells you her own personal story.

Harlequin Cookery

Temptingly delicious dishes, plain and fancy, from all over the world. Recreate these dishes from tested, detailed recipes, for your family and friends.

Faraway Places . . .

Whether it's to remind you of places you've enjoyed visiting, or to learn about places you're still hoping to see — you'll find the travel articles informative and interesting. And just perfect for armchair travelling.

An annual subscription to the magazine — 12 issues — costs just $9.00.
Look for the order form on the next page.

Don't miss your copy of North America's most exciting and enchanting magazine!

Subscribe now to the Harlequin Romance Readers' Own Magazine . . . Harlequin available only through Harlequin Reader Service
12 exciting editions for only $9.00
